BY MAURICE CARLOS RUFFIN

We Cast a Shadow
The Ones Who Don't Say They Love You
The American Daughters

THE AMERICAN DAUGHTERS

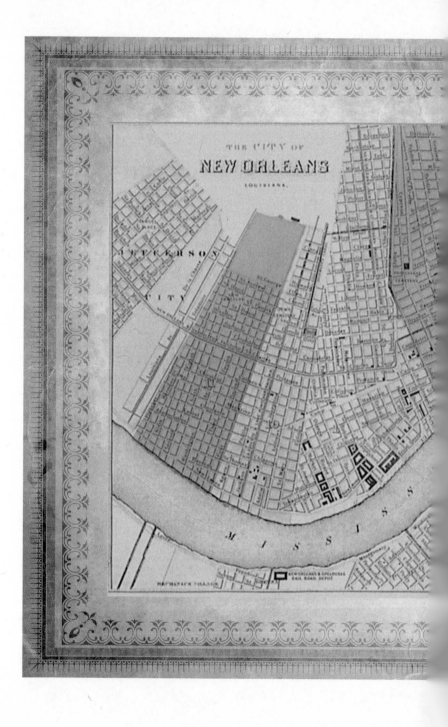

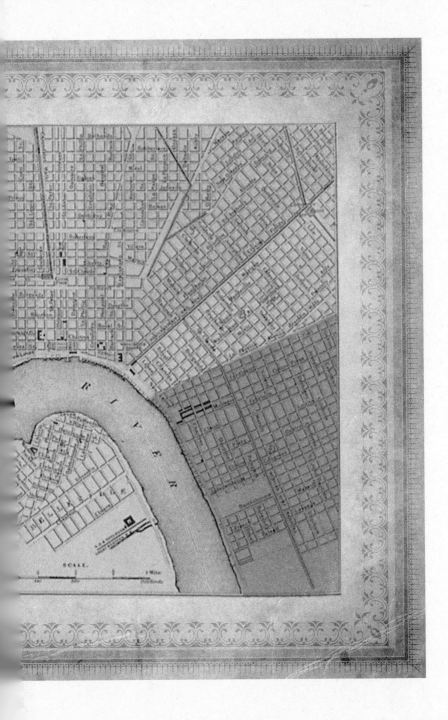

SCALE.

— The — AMERICAN DAUGHTERS

A NOVEL

Maurice Carlos Ruffin

ONE WORLD
NEW YORK

Copyright © 2024 by Maurice Carlos Ruffin

Published in the United States by One World, an imprint of Random House, a division of Penguin Random House LLC, New York.

ONE WORLD and colophon are registered trademarks of Penguin Random House LLC.

LIBRARY OF CONGRESS CATALOGING-IN-PUBLICATION DATA
Names: Ruffin, Maurice Carlos, author.
Title: The American daughters : a novel / Maurice Carlos Ruffin.
Description: First edition. | New York : One World, 2024.
Identifiers: LCCN 2023025013 (print) | LCCN 2023025014 (ebook) |
ISBN 9780593729397 (Hardback) | ISBN 9780593729403 (ebook)
Subjects: LCSH: Enslaved women—Fiction. | Women—Fiction. |
Slavery—Fiction. | United States—History—1815–1861—Fiction. |
Historical fiction. lcgft | LCGFT: Novels.
Classification: LCC PS3618.U4338 A84 2024 (print) | LCC PS3618.U4338
(ebook) | DDC 813/.6—dc23/eng/20230605
LC record available at https://lccn.loc.gov/2023025013
LC ebook record available at https://lccn.loc.gov/2023025014

PRINTED IN THE UNITED STATES OF AMERICA ON ACID-FREE PAPER

oneworldlit.com
randomhousebooks.com

2 4 6 8 9 7 5 3 1

First Edition

Map © G.W. Colton/Mary Evans Picture Library
Old paper background and frame art by eleonora_77/Adobe Stock
Ornament and typewriter paper background by Vector Tradition/Adobe Stock
Black paper background by Dmytro Verovkin/Adobe Stock

For our mothers . . .

we are each other's
magnitude and bond.

—GWENDOLYN BROOKS

Love is contraband in Hell, cause love is an acid
that eats away bars.

—ASSATA SHAKUR

Once you really know yourself, can't nobody tell
you nothing about you.

—MEGAN THEE STALLION

THE AMERICAN DAUGHTERS

PROLOGUE

. . . in grasping my pen and putting my hand to page, I felt as though I existed for the first time. I was the property of no one save myself. Therefore, I could freely give of myself to those I loved, no? As my mother promised, I had once and for all time found a place for myself in the world. A place of complete freedom, the freedom of birds, flower petals, and the stars above . . .

. . . see people kept asking me if Ady's was a true story. I never lied, now. I admitted the work I did to fill in the gaps and complete the narrative. By this time, the book had been reprinted twice. I played down my involvement because I never wanted the hoopla to be about *me*. It was *her* story, you feel me? That couldn't last. I see that now. Try as I might to stay out of the way, I was involved in ways I didn't understand. See, *they* were trying to tell me the story was just fiction from back in the day, but I knew in my heart Ady was real. Have you read *Confession?* Yes. I'm talking about Ady's diary. No? That's your loss. You ever do read it, you'll see she practically glows from the page. Next thing I know, someone showed up saying they had some of her hair and wanted to test mine. I let them. It was a match! Now, ain't that something? That changed everything. Everything!

—Jackson Milia-Signalman (1975–2019),
March 26, 2017, at Petry House (Connecticut)

1.

OF ALL THE tiresome habits of men, what drove Ady, known here as Antoinette Marianne du Marche, to her wit's end was their impulse to expand the pettiest of their lives' moments to epic proportions. Such men exalted minor disagreements to the level of legend, delivering a coup de grâce to the jaw of a Yankee three times their size. Of course, none of these meager men had a good trade. They were all captains of industry, each of them, but the barons of Holland and New York would soon eclipse their fortunes. Such men never encountered a bird pecking for sustenance, no; the creature was always a wolf at the door, its teeth eager to rip the tendons from a man's throat.

Of course, this was the basement into which Ady's life had fallen. In the high-ceilinged dining room of her self-proclaimed father John du Marche's Vieux Carré townhouse, she imagined how recollections of the night might be transformed in the retelling, if any of them survived. It was early still, but the men were already several sheets to the wind. A spittoon lay rolling on its side. There was a scattering of empty brown bottles, and a filthy apron was draped on the kitchen doorknob. Hers or Lenore's or another's, Ady wasn't sure.

In this pulsing night, the men were occupied sharing drunken jokes about their exploits and their half-despised cronies, and so, of course, the bodies of the women present could become the only source material of the Massacre of March 1862. All the better to distract them.

The banner, procured by Lenore, hung beneath the crown molding and proclaimed QUADROON BALL. Ady stood below the cursed thing, wrestling in the mud of these men's desires. Ady's dark thin shoulders shone glorious—like blackberries in moonlight—above the peach fabric of her dress. "Quadroon Ball" evoked visions of grandeur, of wealthy, powerful, re-fined men engaging in light scandal out of view of their pale, dismissive wives back on their slave labor camps also called plantations. This was no ballroom, though it might counte-nance a schottische or Viennese waltz. She imagined that these facts wouldn't matter; that there would be a false version of her in the retelling. By this reliance on mythology and nostal-gia, she imagined, the men desired to burnish their self-regard.

After they won the war, this night was meant to become a part of their origin, proof of their mastery of the world. But now, these men—round-bellied, wall-eyed, and gasping—were too distraught for the fiction to hold true.

The redness of du Marche's face stood out even at twenty paces. He wanted something, wine or bread and cheese, or her. She removed the wooden box from the sleeve of fabric at her waist. She ran her finger along the engraved ivory top—a cameo of Napoleon at battle. She opened it, pinched snuff into the plane between her thumb and forefinger, and inhaled the material into her nose. She watched on as du Marche con-torted his face at her.

She, to most observers, was not down amongst the dregs of society. She was comely and tall with her thick hair wrapped in a tignon in the style of her mother. In public, she wore fine silk over crinoline and that night with the boy-men finer silk still, for it was required. Her governess, God rest her, Mrs. Orsone, had taught her penmanship and the appropriate placement of weighty silver utensils, the most grandiloquent French, the deepest curtsy. Ady had played Chopin blindfolded in that very parlor.

New Orleans was at that time at war with itself, as always. It was the core of the South: wealthiest, worldliest, and most in love with its own beauty. A wealth and beauty carried, of course, upon the haunches of people like Ady.

Du Marche glared at her. She withheld the disgust she felt from reaching her face and looked up at the grandfather clock, thinking, one more tick tock of the clock on the last night of her life. Soon she would join her mother.

Ten years earlier, she had been riding in the back of a long cart, lying against her mother's breast. There were other people, too, whom she had never fully forgotten. A boy with large eyes who played with his toes and poked his tongue out at her. It had been a long trip, days from a place called Constancia that she would never fully remember. The woman next to her mother with skin like riverbank clay craned her head to look past others. Her neck had scars like vines.

"It won't be long now," Ady's mother, Sanite, said.

"Woman, how you know?" a man said. "Not like you from here." The women and children were tied to each other. But the men's hands were tied together so tight that the flesh of the downside of the man's palms was purple.

"Ain't no stream wide as that," she said. "I been here before. The last time someone sold me down the river. Before I escaped."

"You ran away?" the man asked, his eyes wide.

"Can't nobody hole me less I let 'em."

He went from disbelief to smiling.

One of the white men on the seat at the front of the cart cracked his whip over their heads.

"You jigs better shut up," he said. "I hear any plotting, and I'll tie a stone to yer neck and turf you in."

"For our mothers," Sanite said.

"What's that again?" he said.

"I say, 'Yes, mister driver.'"

Lenore squeezed Ady's hand roughly and smiled that awkward smile—her unguarded smile—she had worked so hard to own. Ady knew Lenore was trying to soften her mood, knew that Ady was swimming through a swamp lake of emotions. Around Lenore she often felt like a rabbit in a warren, waiting out the farmer above. But the present circumstances made her that much more anxious. Appropriately so.

Lenore cupped Ady's hand and kissed the knuckles. Ady was disposed to turn and walk away, but as she stepped forward, Lenore spoke, their fingers still grazing.

"Let us do what we've come to do."

Ady nodded. "Let us do it through and through."

In the dining room, Ady approached her father, who sat at the long table with half a dozen men. After he gave them gifts of cigars, she performed a rendition of Mozart's "Requiem" that the men politely clapped at. She could tell her father was displeased—she'd spent most of the evening down in the kitchen where Mrs. Beryl refused to allow her to assist instead of up there entertaining, as she was meant to do. *You'll get giblet gravy all over your fancy lace and then Master du Marche will hold it against me, no thank you very much.* The men's table was larded with grapes, soft cheeses, and sauces. She thought Mrs. Beryl had prepared something worthy of Dionysus, although the half-eaten dish of rarebit before her father played against the effect. She could see his teeth marks along the bread crust, the saliva that dotted his lips' corners. Bile rose in the back of her throat.

"I'd like to make sure that you're acquainted with my Antoinette," he said.

"Is this the one?" said a man to their right. He was clean-shaven with the meticulously tailored clothes of a Virginian. Lenore had come around the table and was now sitting on his lap; the bows at the knees of his stockings grazed Lenore's leg.

"Your own?" said another man, chewing on hazelnuts, a dish of shells at his wrist. Ady couldn't see John du Marche's face from behind, but she knew he was smiling.

"She's a cherry, that one," a man said from the far end of the table, slamming his wine goblet down. "A dark cherry if ever I saw one."

John du Marche placed his hand against her lower back. It wasn't an uncommon gesture from him.

"Enchantée," she said with a curtsy and exited, closing the parlor door behind her. Ady felt coldness in her head and movement in her stomach. She turned, continued out onto the balcony, and vomited over the railing. A white child, likely a street urchin, was passing by. He stared at her for a moment and ran away, dropping his cap in a puddle.

John du Marche had purchased Ady's mother and herself at the auction near the foot of Conti Street. Their seller had a servant, a Negro like them, scrub their faces, ears, and teeth with a rag. He then shoved them into a large room where they watched a naked man step off a block and join the four others he was sold with. A man in a white wig pointed at Ady, had the same Negro servant tear her apart from Sanite, who was forced to wait by a column.

Ady had never stood before so many people. Ringed around her were more than two dozen white men. Off to the side stood the unsold, as still others, recently purchased, were either being held near the walls or led away in chains by their buyers.

"As you can see, a likely girl," the man in the wig said. "A babe. Aged about seven years, wouldn't you say? Make for a right good scullery maid, don't you think? And down the line, you get all the little piglets she produces." Many of the buyers chuckled. Ady was older than five, but small at that time. Her mother would often place her on her shoulders and tell her that one day she would be tall and free. Though she was afraid, she never let her eyes fall from Sanite's.

"Come on, gentlemen, bids up, let's move it along. We've got another shipment just docked at Barracks. Cooper, I wager you need a little one, eh? She can fetch pails of water to your boys on the shore muck."

"No thanks," said a short man. "The last squink I bought only lasted a week. Turns out the alligators in Des Allemands are partial to chicks." Laughter rose around him. "Quiet down, you rowdies. I spent a barrel of half dimes on that one!" The wigged man shook his head.

"I shall take her."

"Representative du Marche, I hadn't seen you in a moon. You're a good sight."

"Not so fast," said du Marche. He wore a top hat and blue velvet morning coat. "I'll take her at ten percent below your asking price."

"Now, wait a minute. What's this? You tryin' to run me out?"

"Calm your passions, Birks. You know very well you robbed me on the five my man just purchased for my fields. I could easily cancel that sale and go down to Congo Square. Their stock doesn't look like it spent a month at the bottom of a hold."

Birks sputtered. "Fine," he said, clearing his throat. "Because you're an upstanding citizen and habitual buyer, but don't the rest of you pirates start dreaming of fairy queens and markdowns." The other men laughed again.

"And Birks," du Marche said.

"Sir!"

"I'll take that one over there at market price, if she is indeed the mother."

Birks turned to Ady's mother. "You spawned this one?" Sanite nodded.

On the balcony, Ady clutched the ornate cross at her neck, hard enough to break the skin of her palm. Lenore had given her the pewter cross. She did not see the speck of blood appear.

"Don't you bother about her," Mrs. Beryl's voice said from the portal to the kitchen. "She just had too much sherry. And they say we Irish toss 'em back."

Before Ady and her mother were sold to du Marche, they had been made to walk barefoot for days. Once her blindfold was removed at the city limits, she saw her small feet were blistered, swollen. It didn't matter that most of their path had been along dirt and mud; both Ady's and Sanite's feet were ripped and blood-crusted.

Ady felt a cold lick from the night wind. She pushed the edge of her foot through the gap between the wrought-iron bars on the balcony. Had she and her mother really walked a hundred miles barefoot? How was that possible? How allowed? Ady felt a hand on her shoulder. It was Lenore. Ady wasn't sure, but beneath the makeup she thought she saw the pink of upset on Lenore's taupe skin.

"I don't . . ." Ady said.

"What?" Lenore asked.

"I don't want you to do this with me," Ady said. Lenore lowered her face and smiled.

"What are you thinking?"

Lenore took Ady's hand. "If this is to be your last night on earth, then it's to be mine as well."

After the sale, John du Marche moved Ady and her mother into the city townhouse far from the rural plantations. The journey from the prior owner's plantation was long, endlessly so, and neither mother nor child had shoes. They were only allowed in the cart for short stints before the driver put them on leashes behind. He had a special pique for Sanite, who refused to be quiet at his insistence. She must have known she was too valuable to his profit margin to drown.

As they entered the courtyard, Ady felt the cold of the rounded cobblestones against the curves of her almost numb feet. Sanite, whose name was an aspect only of itself, had whispered to Ady to throw her last name away. Ady, an aspect of her given name, Adebimpe—didn't have a last name, Sanite said; the plantation owner's name was supposedly attached to them both.

Sanite moved her hand toward the bayou. Ady followed her hand's path but saw nothing. Then she heard a plop in the water but understood it to be the sounds of free animals, frogs, snakes, or possibly a stray wolf.

When John du Marche collected them to begin their journey to his home in New Orleans, he seemed more animated, buoyant even, his voice more country. Stopping at a statue of a muse in his courtyard, he pointed and talked, as though they were guests on holiday, giddy, tripping over his words. A long knife hung in a scabbard at his waist.

"This is one of the oldest buildings in town, two score and five years ago they constructed it. When I left my father's home, it was one of the first townhouses I saw, right between that old dress shop and the paper seller, knew that one day it would be mine, knew that I would bring servants here into my employ. I had a small pied-à-terre before this until last year, but God grants his blessings to those who are patient." He stopped at the staircase, several emotions crossing his face, bemusement, curiosity.

"Do you speak?"

Sanite nodded. Ady knew that her mother wasn't afraid of any man on earth. Some might have said, indeed some of the other enslaved people at the plantation did say, within and out of earshot, that they had never seen a woman so fearless or so foolish. Ady knew that it was Sanite's fearlessness that led to their being sold off. Sanite had hexed the owner of the slave labor camp—also called a plantation. That owner didn't believe in such spells until he did, and he decided to enact his revenge on her. But even after such revenges, Ady saw his eyes quiver—the way a man's eyes quiver when he believes he is about to be struck from behind—as the cart left with her mother and her trailing behind, both bound by the neck with leashes to it.

Ady saw the back of Sanite's neck there in the courtyard. Purple-red bruises sat on both sides from friction. John du Marche neared Sanite. He eyed her neck, then he sniffed it.

"I understand out there in the fields certain standards of conduct prevail. But here in the city, no such rules obtain. Well, my rule obtains, and I shall have you speak when spoken to."

"What if I ain't got nothing to say to the likes of you?" Sanite said.

"That's better," his face more serious. "And this one. Birks said that she was seven, but he's wrong about most things." He stooped down. "Tell me, little one. Your true age."

The girl had been told by her mother never to reveal to a white person that she understood numbers and certainly not that she could read or that she had any understanding about any fact that wasn't stated immediately before by an owner or overseer. At Constancia, the slave labor camp, also called a plantation, that they had been exiled from, Sanite left Ady in the shack of an old woman who cared for the children of enslaved people, the children who were not yet able to carry a bucket or fetch the lady of the house's mother-of-pearl hair comb. The old woman taught the children in secret. Sanite wanted her daughter to know how to count and read, and perhaps even one day write.

"I'm ten," she said, knowing if she did not answer, or was caught lying, there would be consequences.

"Ah," he said. "I reckoned as much. You will eat better here. Might even grow to be tall like your mammy." Addressing Sanite: "What's this scar on her arm?"

Ady knew he was referring to the score mark a few inches above her wrist. It was a slash of raised skin that Ady couldn't remember how she got. The score had just always been there.

"She fell against one of them soil tillers," Sanite said.

"Hmmf. Well." He reached into his pocket and produced a wrapper, which he opened, blossoming a tile of chocolate. "I wager you'll like this. Imported from Holland, at great expense."

The girl leaned into Sanite's leg. She didn't want to take anything from this man. The other man had ignored her and her mother. But this man paid an attention to them both that made Ady keep her distance even if she was drawn to the chocolate, for she was hungry, and it was food.

"What's my work, mister?" Sanite asked.

"My, you're all business." He tossed the chocolate on the ground. "You're on the lighter side, unlike your offspring, so I imagine they had you in the house. But you look worn, too, and not just from the journey. I'm guessing eventually they planted you in the patches, had you picking what? Cotton? Sugar cane?" Sanite nodded. "Speak, dammit!"

"Yeah. I spent a few seasons in the house. Then a few in the field working mostly cane. Then one more inside again." Sanite kept her eyes cast toward his neck, not his feet, as most others would have. Ady thought her mother wanted to grab his neck.

He turned around, scanning the courtyard slowly, and then

looked back at Sanite. "You are to do everything. I have my plantation up near St. Francisville, where I live and spend the Sabbath. Occasionally, my wife and children visit here." Ady twisted into Sanite at the mention of his family. At Constancia, the overseer's children, poor whites who lived at the edge of the property, had their fun at her expense: throwing rocks, pulling her hair, kicking her legs. Sanite had instructed her to never hit back or she would get herself killed. Du Marche stuck a hand in the gap created by his unbuttoned shirt.

"I'm an important man, if I haven't made that clear. I sit in the wheelhouse of government alongside Governor Mouton. And I have business connections who visit from here to the District of Columbia." He coughed.

"But usually I will be alone, for I run my trade from up there." He gestured to the second story of the townhouse. "When I am not present, you are to clean, purchase goods, take deliveries, manage repairs, and tend to all affairs of this estate short of my central business. It does not matter that your kind cannot read or write. My vendors know my preferences and my man handles the menial business."

"And when you present?"

"What's that?"

"What's my work when you here."

"Every matter I just spoke on. Also, cook. Launder and mend my apparel. And other personal duties." Du Marche walked over to a set of green stairs and climbed. When he reached the second-floor entrance, with his hand on the door to the townhouse, he stopped.

"Why are you two standing there like a pair of goats?"

"Where you want us?" Sanite asked.

"I suppose you do need somewhere to lie." He pointed.

"Those quarters. Second level at the back. The other quarters and the privy are for visitors." He nodded at Ady. "I'm sure whatever her name is, it won't do in my house. The wife thinks nigger names are heathen blasphemy. Call her Antoinette."

Their quarters was a single room with a pallet and a chamber pot, nothing else. The pallet, which was a ragged pile of straw, took up most of the room. They'd had a cast-iron stove at the slave labor camp also called a plantation, and even a small plank table, and although Ady did not wish to return there, fearing for Sanite's safety, she had questions, such as how they would feed themselves. Sanite was a good cook and could do more with a tin pot and a handful of grain than seemed possible. Still, that wasn't what vexed her; she was unsure what to call herself even in the privacy of her own mind.

"I don't want another name, Mama."

"You a child and you ain't really got no wants, but you right," Sanite said. "I ain't studying about him." Sanite wrapped her arms around her daughter and stroked her hair. "Yeah. He'll call you that. But I never will. Never let that name take a spot inside you. One day, you'll be free, and you can't be forgetting who you really is."

He stayed for over a week that first time. Each morning, du Marche tested Ady or Antoinette by calling her by her new name, waiting to see if she'd slip up and not respond. She never once did. On some days, she was instructed to enter the townhouse and sweep the floors or empty his spittoon, which was heavy brass and awkward as a sack of grain, difficult for her small arms to wrap around. One evening, Sanite stood in the kitchen pounding meat on the counter. She glanced at Ady, who sang a quiet melody.

"I guess you can help here," Sanite said. "Bring over that pan. The big one." Ady laughed, but Sanite shook her head.

They prepared for him a meal of shank cooked just so, gruel, bread lightly toasted (and if too burnt, fed to the dogs), and two flagons of ale. He was particular in his demands. He gave them each two moth-eaten dresses and had them stand on opposite sides of the large dining room table while he ate.

When he finished, he dragged a cloth across his mouth and asked why their noses were always running. Ady had been sniffling since moving into their new quarters. "Don't tell me that I shall have to sell you two off already. Just like Birks to market a pair of frails."

His bringing forth the possibility of their sale pushed past Ady or Antoinette's natural resistance to speak in his presence.

"It's the sheets, mister," Ady or Antoinette said.

"The sheets? What the devil are you talking about?" du Marche said. Sanite shot Ady or Antoinette a stern look, meant to still the flow of words from her mouth, but he insisted. "Go on. Say what you mean, Antoinette." Ady looked from Sanite to du Marche but knew she had no choice but to answer.

"It's right cold in them quarters."

"How absent-minded of me," he said. Du Marche smiled as if he were truly happy. It was the first time Ady or Antoinette had witnessed this act. He was missing several teeth on the left side of his mouth. "I have just the item." He went outside onto the balcony and into one of the other quarters and reappeared with a thin sheet. "Little Antoinette, clean up the kitchen. I want it spotless. We will see to it that this is the proper sheet for your grand quarters."

The kitchen was on the second floor, just off the balcony above the privy. From the kitchen, one could see straight across the courtyard and into their quarters. Ady or Antoinette went about clearing the table and mucking out the pots, and as she was folding the tablecloth for the wash, she heard noises. Across the courtyard, she saw du Marche on top of her mother, whose head was turned to face the wall, her palms flat on the pallet.

Later that night, Ady or Antoinette sat on the floor by the door watching Sanite on the pallet, her legs flat before her, stare at the bare wall. They had been sitting in their positions for some time.

"You should work roots on him, Mama," Ady or Antoinette said in a loud whisper.

Sanite snorted.

"Turn him into a frog!" Ady or Antoinette said.

"Hush, girl, I ain't no witch."

"But I seen you do magic like what you did to old marse."

"Pfft, you don't know nothing," Sanite said.

Ady or Antoinette looked from her mother to the green door slats where she looked over at the quarters across the courtyard, the moon's glow descending on their faces. She imagined another them, a different them in those fine quarters feasting on yams and bread. Of drinking fresh milk. Of swallowing heaping spoonfuls of cake. Her stomach was sour, she turned back to her mother.

"I see you, daughter," Sanite said. She patted the pallet next to her own leg, and Ady crawled next to her. Some of the pallet's hay was drying out and it scratched her thighs as she settled next to her mother. Sanite brought Ady close to her body. "You don't need to worry on me. I'll guard you. That's my work."

.   .   .

On the next night, Sanite did not move when she was called from the townhouse. He called again, but Sanite squatted on the floor. She held in her right hand the cleaver that she had used to chop and mince a large, tough flank earlier that day.

"Mama," Ady or Antoinette said. She heard du Marche set a booted foot onto the stiff wood outside of the second-story townhouse door, heard him trundle the woodway toward the corner of the balcony where a plank always squeaked unhappily on its nails. She heard his footfalls passing the two adjacent quarters. He would be there momentarily.

"Mama," she said again.

"I hear you," Sanite said. "I need you to be quiet, daughter."

It was then that his steps stopped, his shadow visible in the night.

"I fought in Florida for the government," he said. His voice was low and slow, the flourish he used gone from it. "I don't suppose you're familiar with those wars? Against the Seminoles? No? I didn't think so." He spat. "Those tribes lived on those lands for a long time, a very long time. They were stubborn. I gather I would have been stubborn too if that were my birthright. Every time settlers moved into the area there would be a brief period of peace. Then the Seminoles would come in with a raiding party of fifteen or twenty on horseback. Fierce warriors against limp older chaps and schoolmarms in bonnets." He stepped away from the doors. Ady caught a glimpse of the upper half of his face flickering in the light of flame. He was leaning against the balcony railing, which mildly creaked with his weight.

"We fought them for years, pint-sized skirmishes here and there until eventually most of them were gone or retreated into the swamplands that no white man would want. But I fought with an old treasure hunter who fought in earlier battles, perhaps fifteen years before, back when the Seminoles far outnumbered the settlers and men like myself who would bring the land to heel. He said that was a far more enjoyable war, bloodier too. Back then, they would gather a large force of strapping men—no sticks or axes among them; every man had a rifle—a true well-maintained militia, one might say. And they'd wait for the warriors to make their move. If the Seminoles were in a standard raiding party, that made them easier to hunt. They would just follow them back to their land. Even the best twenty warriors of a village are nothing against a battalion, you understand? Two or three hundred men might as well be a prairie fire. That was the old-timer's job and that's the method he taught to me. To draw out the flesh so that they might seal their own fate."

"Mama," Ady or Antoinette said, under her breath. Sanite slowly shook her head and placed a finger over her own lip.

"Not now, my daughter," she said through clenched teeth.

The green-slatted door swung open, and he stepped into their quarters. He held a heavy silver chamberstick in one hand. The glow from the candle flickered on the walls. In his other hand, he held a gun.

"Which me would you rather encounter tonight? The hired gun or the battalion?"

Sanite, who was seated at the edge of the pallet, had slipped the knife into the hay. She stood up and left the room with him.

Over the next days, the pattern repeated. Not the prelude,

no more speeches were made, but the conclusion was the same. He hollered, and Sanite heeded. Until the fifth day, when Ady or Antoinette followed her mother to their door and grabbed her hand and squeezed.

"Stay out, my child." Sanite gently disentangled their hands. Ady or Antoinette returned to their quarters, but as soon as she heard the door close, she ran across the balcony and banged on the door, the wood rattling under her fist.

"Mama!"

He opened the door. The stench of brandy flowed around him. "What is the meaning of this?"

Ady or Antoinette lowered her head. "Let my mama out or I'll call something down on you."

He cocked his head to the side, and a low burp escaped his lips. "Let my mama out." He laughed as he leaned against the doorjamb. Suddenly he shot an arm out to push Ady or Antoinette back. His hand didn't connect as roughly as Ady or Antoinette thought it would, but he closed the door as she fought for balance. She cursed herself for not anticipating his shove. She stood with her shoulders against the railing, breathing heavily. She stood and waited until the door again opened and Sanite stepped out. When Sanite saw her daughter, Sanite gaped in disbelief. She brought Ady before her body and walked her back to their quarters.

On the balcony of the townhouse, Lenore had gone back inside. Ady pressed her stomach against the cool balcony rail to relieve the ache. It didn't help. Behind her, someone had started playing a fiddle in the parlor. A bit of vomit stained the front of her dress.

LISTING ON A SLAVE AUCTION BILLBOARD: NEW ORLEANS

February 10, 1851

The Owner of the following named and valuable Slaves being on the eve of departure for Europe, will cause the same to be offered for sale on Saturday February 12, at Twelve o'Clock

1.   COURTLAND, a mulatto, aged 45 years, a first rate cook and driver for a carriage is strictly honest, temperate, and a first rate subject.

2.   SANITE, a mulatress, aged 24 years, a good cook and accustomed to housework in general, is an excellent and faithful nurse for sick persons, and in every respect a first rate character.

3.   ADEBIMPE, her child, a creole aged 7 years, speaks French and English, is smart, active, and intelligent.

4.   DANDRIDGE, a mulatto, aged 33 years, a first rate dining room servant, has but few equals for honesty and sobriety.

5.   NARY, his wife, aged about 31 years, a confidential house servant.

6.   MARY ANN, her daughter, a mulatress, aged 14 years, speaks French and English, is a superior hairdresser.

3.

SOON AFTER DU MARCHE brought Sanite and Ady to the townhouse, he left. In the months that followed, he would leave for days at a time, occasionally for a full week. His primary residence was his slave labor camp called a plantation, a half day's ride out of town. That distance provided some silence, the succor of distance, a lamb's peace as the lion sleeps. It was during these breaks that when Ady's chin fell, Sanite could lift it.

Occasionally, du Marche leased them out to work for residents in nearby homes. Those residents in one form or another seemed like variations of du Marche. Ady had the feeling of moving from one room in the townhouse to a room in some other man of industry's house without ever departing the original premises.

They worked a clerical office once where three attorneys scribbled on paper, snacking on cakes as the eldest nipped from a flask. "Hurry it along, you two," the inebriated attorney had said. "I'm paying your master for thoroughness and speed. You are passing the bar of the former but not the latter."

"What's that face you making?" Sanite asked as they arrived back at the townhouse.

"He gets money off of us?" Ady asked.

"For each movement of our hands."

"That don't seem fair."

"I don't vision it is."

At the corner of Good Children and Bienville there was a five-story home that Sanite and Ady spent three whole days cleaning. It had been the residence of a foreign minister, but he had died, and his government had bequeathed the mini-palace to the City of New Orleans as a gift, someone said. The French Quarter was full of such grand houses, which sat hip to hip along the cobblestone arteries of the neighborhood. The world Ady had come from was now infinitely multiplied. And du Marche's townhouse was not the grandest amongst them.

Sometimes Ady accompanied Sanite around town on er-rands of procurement. This was the only time she could really see the quarter. They bought house supplies from the dry gro-cer and the coffee carts. All of these activities, working in other townhouses and visiting sellers, was astonishing to Ady. She had grown up mostly in the house at Constancia, a very big house with a half dozen other enslaved Negroes pressed into service, not to mention those being tortured in the fields. Al-though Sanite had explained to her, without much detail, that there was a whole world beyond the low dipping fields and the river that bordered the land, Ady, through the processes of staying within those walls or in Ascension Parish with its trees and slave labor camps called plantations that stretched into the horizon, came to subconsciously believe the Constancia big house was, for better or worse, the better part of the world.

She wasn't blind. She saw how the field-working Negroes were kept and treated. So while she clearly understood that there was a difference between her life in the house and the lives of the children of the owner of that plantation, the ones whose peach and crêpe skins echoed the flesh beneath an apple peel, she also understood that there was something about the townhouse that elevated all within it. Even her.

Yet as she took in the scalloped trims and pastel-colored houses, it wasn't, she realized, the grandeur of these residences that captured her attention, it was the people who lived and worked in them. Each house was maintained by a person or group of people—butlers, maids, valets, and footmen might well have been blood. But Ady heard murmurings about these enslaved workers. Not all of the Negroes of New Orleans were enslaved.

New Orleans was a town of streets laid out on a grid that corresponded to the directions of a compass but skewed. No street ran true north or true west, but rather all was diagonal. They walked and walked, and Sanite made sure they took their time about it. She would gently touch the uppermost part of Ady's arm and Ady, noting that Sanite's feet were skidding across the pavement, would ease her stride. Often, Ady had no idea where they were even going and on what account. They roamed with no money; Sanite didn't handle his money, or she only rarely did, and even then, just coins. Most of the purchases she made on his behalf were done on credit. Ady looked over as they passed a shoemaker standing at the door of his shop. He stepped inside, and through the window, she saw people handing over coins and bills, knew that anything could be exchanged for the correct quantity, even her very self. If Ady had dollars in the proper amount, she would purchase shoes. He had given them plain boots, previously worn. Ady's were too big, so she stuffed them with hay from their pallet to secure the fit.

The Mississippi churned by, a rippling walnut-brown sheet,

as Ady sang. She knew only a few songs but knew them well. They were songs she only barely remembered learning before they came to the city. The songs sat in the deepest part of her chest and emerged easily from her mouth. Sanite sometimes told Ady to stop talking, but she rarely bade her to stop singing. To the contrary, within a note or two, Sanite would grab Ady's hand, and they would walk in rhythm, hand in hand, for the length of a song. It was during those certain moments, as Ady held a note that shook her body, that Sanite's eyes pointed toward someplace beyond the sky.

Ady saw in her mother's face a kind of obsession for this walking. She did not walk fast, but she only stopped when she had to—at a wall of people or when an omnibus blocked their path. *All this air to roam where we please. This is just the start.* It had never occurred to Ady that freedom meant precisely this: the ability to use one's legs to carry oneself where one chose.

Sanite was required to carry a pass—a folded sheet of paper that she herself could not read. The pass allowed the enslaved Negroes of the city to travel within the limits without their masters. Failure to produce a pass most likely meant capture, confinement, and resale. Ady saw slavers and policemen and men in top hats demanding the production of these passes from others like herself and her mother.

There were other Negroes who when asked to produce a pass revealed a slip of paper that was not a pass, but something else altogether. Sanite, who was generally unbothered by the affairs of others, stopped to gaze upon them. The unbinding of a leather pouch carried at the hip. Or perhaps a hand dipped into a coat pocket. The deliberate—never hurried— unfolding of the slip. The handing of the paper over to the authority, who themselves though white of skin often clearly could not read, furrowing their brow and turning the slip this way and that. The return of the slip. And then that Negro man or woman, light-skinned or medium-skinned or dark-skinned, held their ground until the shaken authority figure huffed off. These Free Negroes came in more types than Ady could hope to classify. But one thing they held in common: Their chin never touched their neck.

"Free papers." Sanite expressed awe and envy at those Free Negroes, often in the same breath as reverence. "Those Creoles think they everything under the sun. They might just be."

The only thing that dazzled the innermost reaches of Ady's (and for that matter Sanite's) heart more than watching the Free Negroes act audaciously Free were the ships at port. Lined up right next to the open market, docked along the piers or skimming by on the wide, brown, churning waters of the Mississippi were skiffs, rafts, steamers, paddle-wheelers, pirogues, three-masters, and, once—Ady saw it, Sanite's eyes couldn't make it out at the distance—a pirate ship identified by its skull and bones on black fabric. Ady would not know for many years what a pirate ship was, but she saw a Negro woman in a red scarf wrapped tightly against her crown, the tail of the fabric whipping in the waters' wake-breeze. She stood in the bow as the ship serenely floated away from the city and toward the unencumbered waters of the Gulf of Mexico, the promise of a whole Earth beyond.

That pirate spirit was also in the Free Colored women in their tignons and wide-waisted summer-colored dresses. Ady watched how they walked the streets, in groups, going about their affairs with their noses up and their chatty voices unencumbered. She never saw anyone ask them for their passes. It was as though their very nature was their pass.

And there was still one other thing that dazzled the spirit of both mother and daughter. Du Marche didn't allow them to partake when he was present, indeed, he had forbidden them to walk to Congo Square under any circumstances on Sundays. Sanite ignored him, and on Sunday mornings, if he was away, she ensured that their plain gray dresses were clean. They wrapped white scarves around their hair, powdered their bodies with baking soda. Congo Square was in the back of town, beyond the northern border of the French Quarter but not past the cemetery. It was a short walk, and halfway to gathering they heard the rising of voices and the beating of drums and gourds.

Many people gathered in the open square, which included a market that rivaled the ones by the river and in the Second Municipality. Sanite and Ady would make their way through the crush of bodies so that Ady could see the men squatting behind their djembe, their hands patting a formidable beat, while others paced the edge of the circle with shekere, ekwe, ogene, tambourines, marimbas, bugles, and banjos. Dust rose from the ground in waves. Crows dipped into the trees. A woman burned sage. Ady most loved the dancers, the women who occasionally paired off in the sweltering sun, and the men who did the same. Ady wasn't afraid to step into the circle herself while Sanite clapped from the sideline. Sanite was surprised that first time, seemed ready to forbid Ady's participation, a handkerchief falling from her hand. But Sanite nodded at Ady, and Ady continued. The girl possessed the spirit of freedom. She threw her head back and added her voice to the swell of voices as her feet moved so quickly beneath her, it was as if she might fly.

4.

A LONG PARCEL NEARLY as tall as Ady arrived and Sanite took it into the parlor of the townhouse that overlooked Chartres Street. Sanite undid the twine that bound the parcel and removed the brown paper. There lay du Marche's latest purchase, a dark wooden statue of a woman, undoubtedly, to be added to his cabinet of mini-statues and trinkets from across the globe. The carved planes of the wooden woman's body suggested to Ady the body of her mother, of the women at the slave labor camp also called a plantation, of possibly her future self.

"I shouldna opened this," Sanite said, for she was not allowed to investigate items John du Marche bought for his own pleasure. Not that there was any way for her to know which items fell into which category. Sanite rewrapped the statue, tied it back up. At the bedroom window, Ady watched Negro children toss a sack back and forth in the street. One of them was a chubby boy.

After their first weeks in their new home, Sanite had allowed Ady to venture out of sight of the townhouse and into the open-air prison that was the city. Ady took delivery of meats from the butcher, of candles and burning oils from the chandler, of fresh quills from the stationer. She was usually gone for no more than a quarter hour. Each of these places had storefronts for eligible customers, but Ady was obliged to find the rear entrances for service. On one particular day, as soon as she rounded the back corner while enthusiastically singing, she heard a rustle off to the right by a bin used for refuse. A ball of fur or fabric or fuzz moved in the morning haze. She froze. No, it was a plump boy—younger than Ady— digging in the garbage.

"Why you looking at me that way?" he said.

Ady stood in shock at the boy whose face was as open as her own, regarding her with large dark brown eyes. He wasn't like the other orphans who roamed the streets. He wore old cord pantaloons and a burlap half cape. Though his clothing was rough-hewn and smudged, there was something in the way he carried his body.

"I—I ain't mean to."

"You act like you've never seen somebody before." His voice was decidedly higher in pitch than Ady had originally thought.

"You're a girl."

"And?"

The girl straightened and turned toward Ady until they were a stone's throw apart. She was alone, not with an adult. She was dirty like the white urchins who ran about the same way stray dogs did. She even wore pants, too long for her legs, rolled up to the calves like some of the urchins did. That's what Ady had never seen. A girl urchin. Certainly, not a Colored girl. The confusion had Ady's heart beating into the upper chambers of her lungs.

"I guess I ain't expect you."

"That was a quite nice song you was singing just now." Ady realized the disconnect was between the girl's ragged appearance and her manner of speaking. The girl sounded like one of the Free Negroes who had some schooling. But the inflection of her voice reminded Ady of the time du Marche imitated her at the townhouse.

"What's your name?" Ady said.

"I cain't really sing myself," the girl said, ignoring the question. She shook Ady's hand, and Ady was surprised at how soft the girl's hand was. "Sakes." The girl stared at Ady's palm. "Calluses. You must work awfully hard." Ady pulled her hand away and hid it behind her body.

The door of the establishment swung open and a white man appeared in a bloodied apron.

"Heh, what's this—a congregation in my lot?"

Ady had received items from the man before. He wasn't the cruelest, but he wasn't kind either. The girl didn't seem to care that he was addressing them, hardly seemed to notice him at all. She was still watching Ady as Ady began to back away.

"Where you going?" the girl said.

Ady stared at her own hand, noting the nicks and rough patches.

"I—" she said, and then ran as fast as her legs would carry her. Ady did not stop her sprint until she arrived at the townhouse courtyard. After entering the gate, she glanced back as if she believed she had been followed and realized, almost subconsciously, that she was disappointed she hadn't been.

"Did you get what you went for?"

Sanite was hanging his white bedsheets on the courtyard lines, clothespins between her lips. Ady didn't respond.

"Adebimpe!" Sanite said.

"Ma?" Ady rubbed her hands together. She felt as if she were holding stolen things.

"You all right? Them people was bothering you? Tell your

mama, and I'll have them running for the swamps." Ady inter-
twined the fingers of her two hands out of the sight of Sanite.

"Mama?"

"Uh-huh?"

"Are our hands hard?"

Sanite looked down to her own palm. "Yes, I vision they
is."

Sometimes Sanite and Ady would take walks to the out-of-
doors market by the river for cabbage or beans. It was crowded
from dawn until dusk, a great mass of humans in constant
pursuit of consumption. Sanite held Ady especially close to
her during those trips. Ady always objected. She enjoyed holding her mother's hand, but in the market proper Sanite often
brought Ady's hand up to the area between her breasts and
kept it there as they moved. Ady felt Sanite's heart like a language, but Ady sometimes got tired of her arm being pulled
overhead, so she would yank her hand free. Sanite would chas-
tise her for it. The slavers couldn't just take anyone they saw
because of the pass system. But the system was flawed, Sanite
had explained.

"When I have the pass they can only do so much. But if I
got the pass, you don't. They do anything they want with you
then." To be undocumented in such a manner may have meant
real danger, but Ady couldn't quite embrace the fear, believing
against all reason that as long as she was so close to her mother,
there could be no separation.

The pass allowed for either Sanite or Ady to sojourn the
city for a week at a time; the pass only allowed for one person

to be excused at a time. Once expired, it was a risk for either of them to leave the townhouse and courtyard; any man on the street could claim them.

"One of these days, heart, we going," Sanite said.

"Where?" Ady asked, but her mother didn't respond. Sanite never answered when Ady asked "when," either, but it was clear to Ady that Sanite did not intend for them to stay under du Marche forever.

Some weeks after Ady first encountered the girl behind the shop, Ady saw her again. In the shadows beside St. Louis Cathedral. She wore what she had before, a rough shirt with pantaloons and a burlap half cape. The girl's skin was a lighter brown than Ady's. Her lips and eyes were delicate and centered by a broad nose. Her face seemed cut from a kind of precious stone.

"You again," the girl said. "That way you ran off. You . . . are rude."

"I didn't mean to be."

The girl was quiet for a moment before answering, "That's good enough for me."

"Why are you wearing boys' clothes?"

The girl smiled. "They're my brother's."

"But why?"

"Because I can."

"Oh."

"Want to play?"

"What's that mean?"

The girl scrunched her face. "Were you raised by goats or green lizards?"

Ady laughed.

"Why are you chuckling?"

"You're different."

"I'm not the one who never played."

Ady lowered her head. The girl smacked her lips. She threw something against the gray stone of the church. It bounced back to her hand.

"Catch, Ady," she said.

"Oh, no. Don't do that," Ady said. But the girl threw the object at Ady, who didn't react quickly enough. The object hit her in the forehead. The girl laughed. "Now you're playing."

Ady rubbed her own forehead and laughed. She picked up the object. She didn't understand what she was holding. It looked like a bunch of flattened worms. But it couldn't have been.

"Those are rubber bands. They fell from a cart. I don't know what they're for, but they're good like that in a ball shape."

Ady agreed.

"How you know my name?"

"The old man who works for the shopkeeper you ran from said you go there all the time." The girl fell forward onto her hands and flipped forward without stopping, back onto her feet.

"What's your name?"

"Call me . . . Ares." She bent down and collected the ball.

"Huh?"

"I'm the God of War. Look alive!" Ares threw the ball at Ady so hard that she hardly registered the motion. But that time she caught it.

They spent the better part of an hour tossing the rubber

band ball at the church and between each other. Ady realized that the sky was dark blue. She had forgotten to pick up the box of cleaning supplies like Sanite asked.

"I have to go home," Ady said. They were walking up the muddy street, dodging puddles.

"You live in that one next to the dress shop and the stationer?" When Ady nodded, Ares continued, "I heard that place was haunted. That the old owner used to do bad things to people."

"Well, where do you live?"

"Out here." The girl raised her hands and spun around. "On the streets. Under overhangs. And in the heavens amongst the other gods. I am the most awesome and feared of all."

"You're strange in the head for making that up!"

Ares's mouth dropped. "Why I never! Why would you say that about me?"

"I know a man makes a funny face whenever he fibbing. You made a funny face. And why you sound different?"

Ares lowered her face. "I do not live on the streets. I live in a very fine house east of here, if you must know. And my name isn't Ares."

"What did you tell me all that for?"

"You said you wanted to play. I was playing."

"I supposing I did say that, but what's your name for real?"

"Meet me here tomorrow?" The girl whose name was not Ares poked her tongue out. "Then I'll tell you."

"Can't you just say it now?"

"Fine," the girl said. "Ruth." She turned down the side street and strode away.

"Your ball!" Ady said

"Keep it till next time!" Ady bounced the ball on the ground once, then caught it. *Ruth,* she said under her breath. When Ady returned the next day the girl was not there. This made a certain sense. Ares was mysterious, but there was one thing Ady understood about the girl. She was free.

5.

B Y THE FOLLOWING SPRING, as the daffodils began to bloom, Ady noticed Sanite's belly was growing larger with each passing day. Sanite's dresses, which were prettier and more elaborate than the ones she wore at Constancia, wrapped more closely to her body now, accentuating all her curves. Ady remembered women from the slave labor camp also called a plantation and knew what was happening.

They were together near the docks, where passing ships deposited flour, sugar, cotton, and every commodity a city could want. Ady read the painted signs, which advertised fruits, vegetables. A man was talking to Sanite, telling her the names of his children. At the name of one of his daughters, Ady raised her head and said, "That's my name!"

Sanite handed the man a sheet of paper.

"You've got a cheerful one there."

"Thank you, suh," Sanite said. She grabbed Ady's hand and they strode away quickly.

The man called after them. "I'll have those packages to your master's by evening."

When they were a distance away, Sanite grabbed Ady by both arms.

"You remember the name I gave you?" Ady found it a strange question. It was her real name, the name her mother had given her. She had just heard it and said so. Why wouldn't she know it?

Sanite slapped her. Ady began to cry.

"You can't be saying that to these white people," Sanite said.

"But why?"

"That wharf grocer works with . . ." Sanite glanced out at the water. "If word gets back to him that you ain't abiding his rule, no telling what he may do."

"But you were the one who told me not to forget my name."

"That's right, baby." Sanite brushed the wet from Ady's cheek. "And you bet never forget. But you have to be careful around them."

"Why does he get to say what my name is?"

"You know why. Don't go asking no dumb questions."

"What if I don't!"

"Because he has us!" Sanite said.

"You said nobody could own us."

Sanite exhaled, and then softer said, "I said that?"

"You sure did."

"I did." Sanite wiped Antoinette's face and kissed her head. "He has us, but I have you."

"But who has you?" Ady asked.

Sanite closed her hand around Ady's and said a prayer with words Ady only half understood.

"What did you say?" Ady asked.

"I asked him to protect you," Sanite said. "We have many protectors and many ways to reach them. Our ancestors, spirits, other selves. They have many names. As long as you show them respect, they will hear you."

. . .

During the time that Sanite was large with child, du Marche did not come to their quarters. One night, Ady sat on the courtyard steps watching the darkened window of their quarters where Sanite slept. Sanite had retired to their room early, having fainted earlier from the baby, exhaustion, hunger, or all three. Candles flickered in the parlor window of the townhouse. A Negro man, one Ady didn't recognize but knew belonged to du Marche, beckoned for Ady.

Du Marche had had guests, had made Ady serve them port wine. He had barked at Ady when she spilled on the table, soiling the white tablecloth the color of eggplants. But he and the guests clapped when Ady was made to sing for them. She sang even as her throat threatened to close. When the others left, he supported himself on the doorjamb. His tie was undone, one end trailed down his chest. He was often this way after a meal with visitors, full of spirit and rubber-limbed. She knew what was to come. This new activity as Sanite was often unable to fulfill his requirements.

Ady cleaned the dining table as quickly as she could, hoping that she could finish and scurry away. Or that he would fall asleep. But he didn't.

He called to her from his bedroom. She stalled just then, dragging a rag across the tabletop, but knew that she had to go in. Last time she delayed, he had struck her across the cheek with a thin statue that lay on his sideboard, knocking her to the floor.

"Get these off," Ady said as she pulled off his boots. His feet smelled of the streets they had walked.

"Would you like a new one?" he asked.

"A new what?"

"A dress, you fool." He stood and pulled off her sack dress, one of two that belonged to her, the only clothing she had other than the pair of old boots her feet had grown into since he bought them. She knew that she shouldn't, but Ady reached for her dress.

"No you don't." He shoved her with his stockinged foot. He grabbed the dress and pulled it apart with his hands. Fabric dust came into the air as the dress disintegrated.

He grabbed Ady's shoulders and pointed her so that she was facing his bed. She stood unclothed in the middle of his bedroom, shivering. He lay down and smiled.

"You're like a monkey in the wild." He closed his eyes, and a bubble of mucus appeared at the corner of his mouth. She heard a dog barking down the street. It was late, but she wondered if the free girl was downstairs. Much time had passed since she last encountered her. She could be anywhere. On a ship bound for some other place. Or beneath the window, wondering if Ady was present therein.

Ady waited until du Marche was sound asleep before she dared to move. She turned to view the balcony on the far side of the courtyard, where Sanite slept. This wasn't the first time. It wasn't the fifth or tenth time, for that matter. But Sanite was free of his embrace while Ady was with him. That was one good thing.

Ady slipped out of bed and walked back across the inner walkway to the quarters, the remnants of her dress pulled around her body. When she reentered, she was shocked to see Sanite awake and standing in the corner.

Sanite rushed over to Ady, who collapsed into Sanite's body. She wrapped her arms around her mother, and although she tried not to by shaking her head, tears escaped and Ady cried against Sanite's shoulder.

"That's all right," Sanite said. "I got you." Sanite leaned back against the wall and brought Ady closer. "That time he came in here and I had that meat cleaver, I wasn't thinking right. Never fight a man with a long knife. My mama taught me that. Your gramma." Ady, still crying, looked up at Sanite. Knowledge of her grandmother was a sore spot. When Ady was very small she often asked about Sanite's parents, and Ady's own father, to no avail.

"She said he gone have a longer reach and more strength. So, let him think he got you. They always want to rub against us anyway. When he ain't expecting it, you jug him with a short one. You only got to get him that one time for good." Sanite kissed Ady's head. "They never see it coming."

6.

ADY'S BROTHER WAS born in the middle of the summer on a night where rain threatened but did not fall. He grew fast. His eyes were blue and his hair came in red-brown. Sanite named him Emmanuel and slashed his forearm with a blade, just as Ady realized her mother had done to her when she was a newborn. Ady's mark was the length of her small finger and crossed her arm diagonally. When Emmanuel started walking, Ady would stick out her finger, which he took, and she would lead him around the courtyard. This morning, Ady was awoken by Emmanuel tugging on her hand. She roused and took him for a morning stroll. The weather was already hot for early summer and Ady felt like the first year of Emmanuel's life had blinked before she was back in summer again. Ady was pointing out the names of various trees, when she felt a small wave of pressure like a wasp pass her ear.

A boy of her age in a sailor suit was inside the gate. His wispy brown hair and ruddy cheeks marked him as one of John du Marche's. It was not lost on Ady that the boy and Emmanuel bore a resemblance. The boy was throwing pebbles at them. One struck her in the cheek. She touched the spot and found blood.

John du Marche entered the courtyard. "Johnny, leave them be," he said. Sanite came out onto the balcony by their quarters and watched the boy.

The courtyard gate squeaked, and du Marche led a woman

inside. The woman carried a girl on her hip, a girl who pulled at the bonnet the woman wore. The woman stared at Ady's brother. Her body turned away, but she continued to watch Emmanuel as if to see what he might do. Then the woman turned her gaze up toward Sanite and placed a hand at the crucifix around her neck.

That night, Sanite and Ady prepared food for du Marche's family, red beans and rice with sausage and buttered wedges of baguette. John du Marche and his son ate heaping spoonfuls, but the woman only drank black tea, which she insisted on making herself. She kept switching her gaze from her husband to Sanite, whom Ady followed from task to task.

"You should have some victuals to keep up your strength, my darling," he said. "They are adept cooks."

"This gruel won't do, John," Mrs. du Marche said. "The darkies feed better to the pigs back on our ridge."

Du Marche cut a piece of sausage and chewed it. "Jealousy does not suit you," he said. Sanite placed a cube of sugar into his chicory. She approached Mrs. du Marche with the teapot, which Mrs. du Marche knocked to the floor. The lid came off and hot tea splashed on Sanite's leg, but she kept her lips pressed closed.

"I am not envious of this creature." When Sanite bent to pick up the pot, Mrs. du Marche pushed her teacup off the table. It glanced against Sanite's head and shattered on the floor. Sanite reached to pick up the pieces and Mrs. du Marche pressed her foot atop Sanite's hand. Sanite yelped but Mrs. du Marche didn't move. Sanite swiped at her leg. The woman drew back, her face almost purple. Sanite backed into the corner, holding her hand.

"How dare you touch me, you beast!" She slapped Sanite,

but Ady's mother did not lower her head. Ady had never seen the look that she saw on her mother's face in that moment. It wasn't hatred or worry, but something else entirely. Ady saw that her mother was taller than Mrs. du Marche—the way a man is often taller than a woman—and that Mrs. du Marche was pale and delicate in a way that suggested she could be carried off in her skirts by a strong wind. Ady couldn't imagine what her mother might do. The kettle, the pot on the floor, the sausage knives on the table. They all gleamed with possibility. Ady went to Sanite and wrapped her arms around her.

"Enough!" John du Marche rose from his chair, which fell over backward. "You're not behaving in a Christian manner, and I won't have it."

"You're now concerned with the Lord's ways?" Mrs. du Marche said. "After you have lain with this . . . animal?"

"My dear," he said, "you should rest. You look like you may swoon."

"Don't you quiet me!"

"Respect me!" He slapped her.

Mrs. du Marche grabbed the chain that held her crucifix. She threw the crucifix at John du Marche and left the room.

For much of the night, as Ady lay next to her mother, she heard the voices of Mr. and Mrs. du Marche arguing. Her brother slept fitfully, kicking his legs. Ady and Sanite listened to the others breathe, as they both didn't sleep.

Several nights later, after the du Marches had returned to their slave labor camp also called a plantation, Ady was awoken by the sound of the heavy iron gate being opened. It was the middle of the night and she imagined she was dreaming, but she looked next to her and saw that her mother's eyes were wide. Her mother pinched her leg.

"Stay here," Sanite whispered, and grabbed the wooden pole she used to open the shutters around the townhouse.

Ady heard gruff male voices below in the courtyard.

"Why are you here?" Sanite had stepped onto the balcony. Ady climbed off the pallet and grabbed her brother, who was almost too big to carry on her hip.

"On business, madam," a voice said. "To facilitate a sale, to be particular about it. I promise this won't take but a minute of your time." From the balcony, Ady saw that there were four men. They wore thick pants and dirty hats similar to the ones worn by the men that had brought them to New Orleans years ago. The men were climbing the stairs.

"Get down inside," Sanite hissed. "And latch the door."

"I ain't leaving you to them."

"Go!" Sanite shoved Ady into their quarters and closed the door. The footsteps stopped. Ady could see large shadows through the slats of the shutters, surrounding her mother.

"As I said, official business. We were instructed by one Mister du Marche to collect a package from this here premises. I'd show you the bill of sale, but I don't think it would make any difference to the likes of you."

"You won't take me from here."

"Take her from here?" one of the other men laughed.

"You've misjudged the situation, I'm afraid. We're not here for you."

There was commotion outside. Ady heard Sanite's wooden stick hit the courtyard ground. "No! Let go of me."

"You made this hard, not me." Ady heard a sound like when Sanite pounded beef in the kitchen.

The door to their quarters shook and then a boot kicked it open. Sanite lay on the balcony.

"Mama!" Ady cried. Ady knew the men wanted her, wanted to take her from Sanite, but there was nowhere to go.

"I'll handle this one meself," the man who had been speaking said. "Stand up straight, you." He removed a blackjack from his pocket and that was the last thing Ady saw that night.

When Ady awoke, morning light washed through the shutters, and the crown of her head throbbed. She heard her mother heaving. Ady sat up to see Sanite sitting on the floor at the far end of the room. She noticed Ady. Sanite jammed the heels of her palms into her eyes. Then she stood up and dipped a rag in the tin bucket.

"Mama, the men." Ady's head was swimming like she was hanging upside down, and her eyes hurt, too. Her mother was looking down at her, holding a wet rag to Ady's forehead. The left side of Sanite's face was bruised. It was the color of a plum. Everything in the room felt wrong. A section of the shutter door was missing where the man had kicked it in with his boot.

"Be quiet, my daughter. They gone."

"What did they—" Ady did not see her brother. "Where is Emmanuel?"

"You are here with me, daughter. You are who I have with me."

7.

THEY HEADED OUT before eating, neither of them hungry. Ady stood next to Sanite at Poydras Market. It was a smarter market than the one by the river. The tables were draped in striped sheets and the sellers wore adornments, bright flowers in their vest pockets, ornate stopwatches on golden chains, feathers in their hat bands. He had told them to buy fine items for a celebration, tins of meat from France, reams of silk, sharply scented oils. Sanite had been standing before a table of polished stones for minutes without moving. They weren't precious. But someone had worked them to bring their color out. Sanite picked up one, a maroon oval stone.

"Fancy these jeweled pieces for your master?" the seller said. But Sanite said nothing, and the seller removed the stone from her hand. "If not, be off with you then. Your stench'll drive off my income."

"I'll take a bunch of the smaller ones."

The seller seemed taken aback. He squinted. "For delivery or carry?"

"I take 'em now." Sanite reached into the pouch she held at her waist. She counted coins into her hand. Ady wondered where the money had come from; du Marche bought on credit only, so this had to be Sanite's. For that matter, she had never seen her mother count. She didn't know she knew how.

"O' course," the seller said, allowing a smile that he only

partially resisted. He wrapped the stones in brown paper. Ady followed Sanite through the market. They made the expected purchases. Christmas was arriving. In prior seasons, they had bought for him and his family terrines of fine sweetmeat from Europe, boughs of holly for the parlor, and candies. All for delivery. But there were a number of surprising items Sanite took immediately. Dried pork, a tin pot no bigger than a fist, several canteens, as well as a machete, a cord of rope, and sheets, tightly folded and tied with string.

"Why you staring crazy, daughter?" Sanite said when they reentered the courtyard.

"What's it all for?"

"We leaving this place."

"Leaving?"

"He just left earlier. I figure he ain't coming back any time soon."

"Really?" Ady asked with a mix of excitement and terror. "But where we going?"

"We going home."

"That slave labor camp?"

"No, girl. That ain't nobody home."

Sanite gently shook Ady awake in the middle of the night. Sanite had told her to nap because once it was time to go they might not sleep for days. Ady was groggy but stepped onto the courtyard balcony, and she saw the mist of her breath when she exhaled. The sky was pitch-black but sparkled with stars. Closer to her, the clouds were illuminated blue gray by the moonlight. It must have been around two o'clock. Sanite came out of the townhouse. She gripped something in her hand.

Ady saw that her hand was wrapped in fabric. Sanite punched the window several times, breaking the panes. The action panicked Ady.

"Mama!" Ady said.

"Hush, child. You want them to hear? We got to throw them off our track. I figure if they think this a raid by some freejacks, buy us some more time." Sanite pointed at the balcony behind Ady. Ady hadn't seen the two parcels there. Sanite had tied as much as they could carry at the small of their backs beneath their dresses.

They left the courtyard shortly thereafter and Ady hugged herself from the cold as they walked the soggy street toward the river. Sanite warned that while slavers were still out, most of them would be too drunk to follow them far. Slavers preferred to sleep it off, gather their dogs, and mount up at first light. Their only chance was to get as far upriver as fast as they could. Indeed, Sanite and Ady walked through the night, accompanied by birdsong, hewing to the eastern bank of the Mississippi as they made their way along the batture.

They had long left behind the activity of the paddlewheelers and sailors near the city. The sun was beginning to rise when Ady tripped.

"I need to stop, Mama," she said. She had caught herself on her hands without letting her knees touch the ground. Sanite glanced around the area. The river was only twenty yards to one side. The bank was muddy and flat. Beyond that the trees gathered close to one another.

"I said no stopping," Sanite said.

"You said no sleeping."

Sanite laughed and a puff of condensation escaped her

mouth. "You right." Sanite rubbed Ady's arm. Ady realized she'd been shivering.

"All right," Sanite said. "And we can eat. But only for a short li'l bit." Sanite herself never sat, but spent their respite watching Ady eat a cookie. Sanite kept staring into the distance as if listening for something.

"You saw somebody?" Ady asked.

"Might be. There was a man awhile back. But I ain't seen him in a minute."

Ady looked around. Was it him already hot on their heels?

"What we gone do, Mama?"

Sanite placed a hand on Ady's shoulder. "For now, we gone mind our business and keep on our task. Finish your food."

When they started out again, they moved faster than before. Oaks gave way to gum trees and crepe myrtle, pigeons to pelicans. One looped overhead, its white wingtips quivering in the breeze. Ady saw no one. They moved quietly—Sanite had hushed Ady when she lifted into a tune before sunrise. No singing until they were far away. But that didn't stop Sanite from speaking under her breath, half to herself.

"This is the right way," Sanite said without breaking stride. "I know it."

"Where we going?"

"I told you before. Home."

"How do you know where home is?"

"They say that moss only comes in north, but that ain't hardly always true."

"Huh?" Ady stopped and turned.

"The place we going is west of where we came from. Southwest." Sanite patted the side of a tree. "This fuzzy moss is most likely on the north face of the bark. So what way would you go?" Ady pointed in the direction they had been traveling. Sanite nodded.

They picked through soft ground in an area swarming with elderberries and duck potatoes. Soon they came upon a vast field of saw grass, the yellow blades bowing gently in the wind. If she could have, Ady would have paused then to take in the swaying leaves, a serenity not found in the city.

Ady could see Sanite was heading toward a slight rise. She didn't care about the water seeping into their boots or the field mice scurrying close to their legs. Dark cypress trees sprang from the oily water for as far as the eye could see. At the top of the rise they stopped, and Sanite smiled.

"That'll do."

"Is this it?"

"Chile, we ain't halfway there, but at least we can get off our feet for a while. Let me get to your satchel." Ady lifted her dress, and Sanite removed the wrappings at the small of her back. Sanite pulled out the machete, the thin rope, and a small saw, which Ady had not seen until then. Sanite smiled in a way that Ady had also never seen before; there was a gleam to her. Sanite plunged into the water.

"We're gonna make a little ship. Not from scratch, though. See those?" Three logs lashed together were near the water. "Somebody left that there. I use to see them around when I was out here. Let's pull them out."

The log raft was heavy, so heavy that their feet sank into the mud as they clambered backward. Ady thought the logs, held together by disintegrating rope, were the heaviest things she'd ever tried to move. Ady fell on her knees into the slime, but Sanite told her to get up quick. No time to sulk. As Ady pulled, Sanite pushed. Eventually, they edged the broken raft a few feet onto solid, if not dry, land.

Sanite was quick with the saw, but it took some time to repair the raft. Sanite cut several logs, notched the hulls, fitted the pieces together, and tied rope in a complicated pattern. Ady tried to help as best she could, but Sanite did most of the work herself. Ady was amazed at her mother's skill. Sanite instructed Ady to find a long, tough branch—taller than them both. When Ady returned, they slid the raft back into the water. Sanite climbed onto the makeshift craft, but Ady hesitated, worried the raft might sink under their combined weight.

"Hop on," Sanite said. "If I drift off, I ain't coming back." Ady took her mother's hand and boarded. They floated into the bayou. "You've done this before, Mama?"

"Yes."

"What was it like?"

"It was like hope."

Ady waited for Sanite to continue. She knew that if she prodded too much, her mother would tell her to wait until some time later. Ady sat while Sanite stood, gripping the pole in both hands.

"Like this. I lit out in the middle of the night."

"What made you run away?"

"You ain't old enough to hear all my reasons."

"Aw, Mama! When I'm gonna be grown enough?"

Sanite laughed. "What you need to know for now is that it was just like this. I wasn't running away. I was running toward myself."

. . .

As the day passed, Ady saw the roots of the cypress trees that arched out of the water like ribbons. In the beginning of their journey, some of the water washed up through the gap between the logs at the end of the raft, which frightened Ady, but Sanite had fastened the wood together well. After over an hour on the water, Ady trusted that they were safe. Ady watched as turtles slipped from the branches into the languid water. At one point, an alligator passed within a few feet of them. Mostly, Ady watched Sanite, who now, as she did most of the time, was looking off into the distance.

"You still think a man out here?"

"Girl, they got haints and everything else out here. Ain't no telling, but don't you worry," Sanite said definitively, her lips set as if to say she didn't want to be bothered on it.

Instead Ady asked, "What's all that?" The trees had something that looked like spiderwebs hanging down almost to the surface of the water.

"Moss," Sanite said. "But your daddy called them zombiewigs." Sanite steered the raft to the bank and beckoned for Ady to follow her onto land. It was dark now. Above, Ady saw the lengthening shadows of the evening branches and birds. Beyond, the sky was dark purple. She felt the energy of her mother's body covering her like a blanket.

Sanite was suddenly quiet and grabbed Ady's arm and pulled them both down to their knees off the side of the path.

"I hear it too, Mama," Ady whispered.

"It's just one of him," Sanite said, through clenched teeth. "I was fine to let him be, but he done followed us this far. He up to no good."

As if called into being, a white man in muddy pantaloons walked past.

"Say nothing," Sanite said. "Stay here." Ady saw that same firmness in her mother's eyes from that night she waited for du Marche with the knife in her hand, but this time she wasn't thinking through whether to move on it. Sanite stood up and walked onto the path behind the man. When Sanite was within arm's length, Ady saw her mother produce the short knife. The sight of the sharp dagger caused Ady's mouth to fly open.

Ady's surprise manifested in a small, escaped sound. The man wheeled around and threw a punch that seemed to go through Sanite's face. Sanite and the man struggled, arm in arm, body over body, first standing, and then on the ground. The man's paleness flashed in the dusk, his belly like that of a fish.

He and Sanite tussled until he got his arm around Sanite's neck. Sanite had dropped the knife and was calling out. Ady wasn't sure if she was calling for her or the weapon. Birds flew wild in the canopy. Furred animals rooted in the foliage and made for their own escapes. Her mother was slapping the man's arms, but this changed nothing. He just grunted and pulled his arm tighter against Sanite's neck.

Ady threw herself at the man. The man knocked her backward, and Ady saw Sanite going limp, her eyes pinched shut.

"What to do, Mama?" she yelled. Sanite said nothing, but her eyes sprang open.

"Hshuckm," Sanite grunted. Ady was unsure what she had said, but saw Sanite was glancing off to the side. There, on the black dirt, the edge of the object twinkling like a jewel— Sanite's short knife. All of a sudden, Ady could hear the garbled language of her mother's desperation deep in her soul: *His stomach.*

Ady brought the knife down, but the blade glanced away, merely tearing his shirt. She saw his sweaty face, his teeth, demonic. He knew what she was attempting would kill them both when he gathered himself. She tightened her grip on the knife and thrust her whole body downward behind the hilt. Suddenly, the warmth of blood about her hands, the same smell as the butcher's.

The man yelled, "God . . ."

Ady dropped the knife. Sanite rolled free and sat on her behind, holding her own throat. Ady ran to her mother and hugged her.

"Thank you." Sanite was gasping and her voice was raspy, as she held Ady close. "Daughter." The man, for his part, spoke, but Ady didn't understand him and did not care to. Shortly thereafter, he was silent.

Sanite and Ady took off, Sanite still clutching her own neck as they ran to the raft. They were silent as they pushed off into the water. They had gone a considerable distance in the dark before they felt safe enough to rest. Sanite was still breathing raggedy, and Ady, with blood stained on her, had wild eyes and an exhausted body.

"We'll set up on that hillock for tonight." She brought the raft to a stop an hour later, and they undid their sheets. "Think you can climb up there and tie this to the end of that big branch?" Ady had vague memories of climbing trees at the slave labor camp called a plantation, but she was not used to the bark's rough digs into her legs, her hands' need to grip against the sweat they created. Ady climbed the tree trunk and looped the sheet around the branch. She tied it off.

Sanite worked to start a fire. Soon they both huddled close to the small flame. Ady didn't feel much warmth from it, but she leaned against her mother and that helped. Eventually, Sanite had boiled a handful of rice into which she sprinkled salt. They ate the rice with dried pork and hardtack. Ady had never felt so fully exhausted and so fully satisfied; she understood it was the unbounded nature of their surroundings. No city. No townhouse. No him. The one who had accosted them didn't work for him, but in a way they all did. And Sanite and Ady had gotten the better of that slaver.

The pork was tough and salty. The hardtack dry as oak. The rice gummy. But when had she ever eaten like this? Away and apart not only from him, but from all of them? Ady's nose was cold, and she wiped it with her sleeve. She began to sing, softly, a song that Sanite had taught her. Sanite hummed along. She realized as they climbed into the hammock that she had made—and Sanite tightened—that they had been in motion since the small hours. Ady fell asleep in her mother's arms.

The next morning went by quickly. Sanite's neck was bruised, but when Ady asked about that, Sanite told her it wasn't anything to be concerned over. The weather had not warmed up, but the frigid was gone, and they floated into an area with no trees, but thick marsh grasses sprouting from the water. Sanite wondered aloud if they would be able to make it through the dense grass, but when they did, they found themselves in another cypress forest where the trees seemed much broader and older. They hit a wide open expanse where the water cleared enough to see the creatures a few inches below the surface. Mosquitoes bedeviled them throughout the day but rarely bit. Sanite said it was because the insects knew they were traveling to freedom. They went the entire morning without the sound of another's footsteps. They didn't exhale, but Ady did let herself inhale deeply. Sanite brought the raft up on a muddy bank around noon.

"Come on." Sanite helped Ady off the raft.

"What about our boat?" Ady asked.

"We ain't gonna need it again. Maybe somebody else will get to use it like we did."

"I don't want to leave it for someone like that man."

"Pfft," Sanite said, looking at Ady with light. "That vessel is for the living." As they walked up the bank, Ady glanced back at the raft. It seemed so small in the distance. Had they really spent three days on it?

Their feet freshened by the rest, they moved quickly once again. They entered a wooded area, stopped to eat, and continued deeper into those woods, which were so dense that Sanite used the machete to cut through the foliage. Ady picked up a metal ball.

"That's a musket ball," Sanite said. "Probably from some fight between mens. Might be a hundred years old or more." The woods opened onto an area where the trees were younger and sparser. There was a scent in the air, sharp and sweet, from light green blooming flowers.

"Where are we?" Ady asked.

"Chitimacha land."

"Who?"

"Every place you've ever been is the home of a tribe of old locals."

"Like what . . . he was talking about back then?" Ady didn't want to say his name or provide a title to their connection. She also didn't want to be more specific about the circumstances of the night du Marche came to their quarters and lurked outside the door.

"Yes. But not like he was saying. We still in the bayou, not Florida, so it must be Chitimacha civilization. If we kept going north, we'd get to where the Houma and the Choctaw be."

"Are they like us?"

"In they way. I mean some of them in us, and some of us in them. These tribes lived here for a long time, but most of our people from across the ocean. Those tribes had their own lands for a long time too."

"I feel like I been here before, Mama."

"That's because I was raised here and you was born here. This is where we going, baby."

Ady spun around, but all she saw was a scraggly clearing with tufts of foliage sprouting. But there! She saw a pile of dark wood.

"All this old wood is huts. Burned huts. I always thought they might still been out here after we was taken. I figure they must have been, but . . . your daddy."

"My daddy?"

"We can't set up in this spot. No telling who out here," she said, looking around. "Let's go, there's a stream through those trees."

They walked across the clearing and onto a trail that wound down toward the water. Sanite pointed and they set down their packs by a large fallen tree. Sanite sat on the tree and patted the spot next to her, and Ady sat.

"I used to play on this old tree when I was younger than you. I was never shown where my folk came from because they ain't like to talk about it."

"They were Chiti—cheeti, uh."

"Chitimacha. Maybe. Either way those tribes often helped people like us. They called us Maroons. But names like that weren't so important. Everybody out here lived mixed together."

"You don't be liking to talk about it either, Ma."

Sanite watched Ady for a moment. She reached down and plucked a thistle, broke off the stem, and stuck it into the gap in her teeth. Then she began to speak.

She told Ady about how the village had over two hundred people living inside the enclave. Her father spent his days growing crops with the other men or occasionally hunting deer or fishing from pirogues in the bayou. Her mother was a storyteller. She kept the children and passed on tales of the village founders, the people who had come from somewhere to the east, joined with some of the Chitimacha. Sanite's mother had almost died in childbirth. She often joked that it was Sanite's job to be all the children she would never bring into the world. In a way, Sanite heeded this call. She was one of the best athletes in the village, and responsible enough to help the women with any task at hand, be it sowing seeds in the field, making clothes from the goats they kept, or cooking food. The women of the village had their own kitchens, but each family shared what they had, so that the meals were communal. When Sanite was old enough, she volunteered for night watch of the Easy Path, the entrance to the village. This was a duty normally set aside for men and boys, but she didn't care, even if some said that made her a boy. Most of the men and boys in the village fell asleep at their post—the village was remote, and unwanted visitors rarely found it. But Sanite had no trouble staying awake. One night she was a five-minute walk from the village, watching the Path. It had been said that the Chitimacha had been walking that trail for a thousand years. The trail ended at a colonnade of trees that led into the village. The colonnade was called the Hidden Veil because of how the branches, leaves, and moss obscured the path. Sanite would watch the trail from the comfort of a tree branch. Sitting on a branch with her back against the broad trunk, she could see minutes up and down the path. Could easily jump down and run for the village if something strange happened.

One night something strange did happen. She heard the sound of an animal in the underbrush, perhaps a hog or a deer, based on the weight and frequency of the steps. She did not run. Instead she climbed down from the tree and approached the shuffling and snorting. Hogs were sociable but easily frightened. If one appeared, she could regain the tree when the animal charged. And deer rarely traveled at night. But the young ones could become easily disoriented. She would wrangle it back to the village with rope she kept in the tree.

But the animal neither revealed itself nor scampered away. Sanite carried no weapon. Her work was in her feet, speed her weapon and her defense. She was beginning to understand that whatever the animal was, it had a strange consciousness. She saw two eyes in the bramble and beneath them the unmistakable form of a man, who rose and seemed to continue rising. Her inner voice screamed that she had best run, but she was also embarrassed to have mistaken a person for an animal, which made her angry.

"Come out from there," she demanded, motioning with

her hand. "Come from there or I'll call the whole village and all the ghosts of my mothers from the wide savanna to deal with you."

The man crawled to his feet. She saw that he was very tall, but also stooped from fatigue. His blouse and pants were tattered. He had no moccasins; his feet were bare. His face was handsome, his eyes soft, his skin a rich dark.

"I'm sorry," he said, "but I don't reckon I know most of what you just said."

Sanite realized he was a common man. She, her parents, and most of the village spoke in a way that was a mixture of their ancestors' language. It marked family from outsider. She would have to use simple words for him.

"Why you snorted like a hog?" she said.

"Oh." He scratched the back of his head. "I was walking this here path and had the premonition I was being watched. Couldn't tell from where, so I jumped in those briars to scare out whatever critter it was. Then you came down that tree, so I reckon it worked."

"Don't you be calling me a critter."

"Sorry, girl."

"You a runaway?"

"Yessum. All the way from Chatham, Alabama."

Sanite gasped in spite of herself. "Alabama!" The village had taken in runaways from all over Louisiana, even the Mississippi Territory. But never so far. She was impressed that he hadn't been caught, killed, or eaten.

"Call me Miss Sanite." She raised her chin. "I'm in charge of you now, so you have to do what I say."

The man smiled. "I can abide by that." He walked with her toward the village. "Miss Sanite." His name was James and his plan was to head down to Mexico and freedom. He had escaped from a cotton slave labor camp also called a plantation on the Mississippi-Alabama border with four other men. But they couldn't come to terms on which way to go. Two of them were set on heading north toward the Mason and Dixon line. The other man wanted to find his sister whom he believed to be in Mississippi. James had gone with the single man, but they were separated when some pattyrollers spotted them on a ridge near Oxford.

"Sorry about your friend," Sanite said while they walked.

"We weren't friends. His name was Duck, and he was grouchy for a young man. I guess we might have been friends eventually. That's what makes all this so backwards. Not a one of us gets to live the life they were supposed to."

The next morning, James carried her share of laundry on his shoulder. Normally, she slept through the first hours of daylight, but she wasn't tired. She had introduced James to the village elders, and, as was the custom, he had been given new clothing and a place to sleep in an elder's home until his future was decided.

A spring ran down the hill from the village. When they arrived, James set down the wooden tub the clothes were in and dipped the first garment in the water. He grabbed a paddle from the tub and beat the fabric in the water. Sanite smiled. She hated washing, even if she only did it every few weeks. Afterward, her arms felt like dead weight against her sides and her hands were bruised. When she had told him he had to wash clothes for her, she thought he would refuse. But now, as James slapped a garment against the rocks and then wrung the water out of the fabric with his strong hands, Sanite reclined on her elbows with a thistle in her teeth. No one had ever worked for her before. She enjoyed the feeling.

James did not leave for Mexico either that week or any other. He turned out to be as good at village tasks as anyone but focused much of his energy on shoring up the huts and cabins. Supplies were not easy to come by, but he made the most of the green lumber, nails, pitch, and tools that were available. One day, Sanite returned from the spring with a bucket of drinking water. Her parents were standing outside of their one-room cabin speaking to James. She could tell from their body language that they were talking about an important topic about which they all agreed. James had already been in the village for nearly a year then. She was not surprised when he asked her to marry him. She knew she would marry him the night they met.

Their marriage was officiated by the village elder, Thom Adebimpe. And Ady, named after the elder, was born the following year. Sanite had long since given over her portion of the night watch to the younger boys who were eager to prove themselves. But she would never shake the belief that if she had been out on the Hidden Veil the night the men arrived, she would have provided more warning to all.

She was asleep in the cabin that James had built for them when she heard the sound of gunfire and voices outside. Ady was only a few weeks old at the time, and Sanite was still recovering from a difficult childbirth. That was why she didn't run as her parents had always taught her to do in the event of a raid. There was always a chance to regroup in the marsh. But once caught, hope was extinguished. Instead of running, she gathered Ady in swaddling and went to her parents' cabin. It was night, and the path was chaos. The interlopers were well armed, whereas the village had only three old guns in addition to their cutting tools. James had gone to another village to trade for grain. As Sanite watched a bearded man point a rifle at her parents, she knew she would not escape that night. The raiders had looped a rope around her arms, rope so rough that it was already bruising her skin. She glanced up at the stars and thanked fate that her love, at least, was safe under those same stars ten miles away.

"That's how you went to that plantation?" Ady asked. Sanite stood from the log. She nodded.

"You got questions?" Sanite asked.

"I do, but . . ." Ady said.

"But what?"

"You look like you need to eat something, Mama."

8.

SANITE AND ADY built a lean-to on the side of the ridge that faced the stream. They fished. The catching was easy because the fish were plentiful, and the water was clean enough to drink. They cooked, ate, and walked the ridges and natural levees. Ady was amazed that Sanite seemed to know the name of every creature or plant they encountered. Ady learned to pay attention to her nose. She could smell when deer were nearby or when rain would fall within the hour. Sanite explained what plants to avoid and what flowers were edible or useful as medicine. Ady sang nonsense songs, adding the names of the flora as she went. *Peppermint for my head, spearmint for my teeth. Elderberry, groundsel, beautyberry, and sassafrassery.*

"Can we stay here forever?" Ady asked, sucking a thistle.

"No," Sanite said. "It ain't safe to live without anyone else like this." Sanite ripped a cotton plant from the ground. She brushed dirt from the root. "This one here. I messed up and ran out of it. If I had ground up the bark, there wouldna been no baby in the first place."

"It's all right, Mama," Ady said.

"Always keep some around from now on."

Ady nodded. "We going to find Emmanuel?"

Neither of them had spoken the child's name during their time in freedom.

Sanite doused the fire they had been using with the small pot of water. She stood up and brushed off her dress.

"We going to go to Mexico." Sanite said.

"But Emmanuel needs us."

"You think I don't know he need us? But where he at though? You think he behind those trees?" Sanite pointed. "Or maybe he in the river swimming like a tadpole. Where he at, Ady? Let's get him. I'll follow your way."

Ady was surprised by the tears trickling down her own cheeks. The world was big, she understood. Emmanuel could be anywhere in it. She understood that too. But the thought that they might never see him again had caught up to her.

"I figure we do what your daddy would have done," Sanite said.

Ady felt a tickle in the back of her mind like when she watched Sanite's face change when she talked about him being safe away from the village. It was a look of pain, but something else too.

"He was good and smart, for a man." Sanite wiped Ady's face. "Almost as good and smart as your mama," she laughed. "If he is down there somewhere, then maybe we can come back this way and find Emmanuel together, as a family."

"But where is Mexico?"

"West and down, my daughter. West and down."

They broke down the camp they had built and began walking west, keeping close to the river. Just when they had crossed a stream, still dripping with wet, Sanite grabbed Ady's arm.

"Again?" Sanite asked herself. From a cluster of foliage on the riverbank, they watched a side-wheeler boat chug downriver toward them. Men squatted on the flat deck, their eyes scanning the shoreline from beneath wide-brimmed hats.

"We gotta get," Sanite said, quickly pulling them over the

riverbank, but they stopped when they heard the sound of twigs snapping under boots.

"Morning, you," a Negro man said from the top of the ridge. He held a rifle on his shoulder and a Bowie knife in his free hand. "You two wouldn't happen to know where we could find an associate of ours? A fella about yea high? He's a tracker following two womens who ran off from their master back down in the city. Nimrod ain't talking about you 'cause Nimrod know you wouldn't do anything like that. You two are upstanding slaves. Nimrod can tell."

"We ain't who you looking for," Sanite said.

"That so?" Nimrod said. "Mama and girl traveling on foot alone. Mama tall and not too dark. Daughter tall too, a darky and not much to look at."

"We ain't do nothing!" Ady yelled.

"'Don't know her place. Tend to mouth off,' your master said. Take Nimrod's counsel. Be calm and gracious and ole Nimrod will keep them hicks from getting friendly up on you."

"Nim," said one of the white men walking across the mud. "If that's our catch, stop playing with our food. We get a bonus if we get them to his land before sundown tomorrow."

Sanite looked around. The other men were with the boat. When Sanite turned back to Nimrod, his rifle was pointed at them. She grabbed Ady's hand.

"We gone run as fast as we can," Sanite said between her teeth. "Come on." Sanite and Ady ran toward the same trail they had used to descend to the riverbank. Ady was amazed by her mother's speed. She had never seen her move so fast, and she had a sense that if the movement of her legs were not hampered by her long, damp dress, she would have run even faster.

They approached the spot where the woods opened onto the colonnade. "We got to go up there," Sanite said, "we get back to our raft we have a chance." The path up to the top of the ridge wound diagonally through the woods. They ran hard, dashing through the forest. They were rounding a large oak when a white man appeared. He wore a sleeveless shirt and had tattoos on his arms. He grabbed Sanite, but she twisted free. She yelled at Ady to keep moving. Once on the ridge's summit, Ady paused. Sanite was still at the bottom of the climb. The white man had been joined by Nimrod.

"Tell your li'l girl to come down from there," he said.

"No."

"Tell her!"

"Ma!" Ady said. She took a step down the ridge toward them.

"Antoinette!" Sanite said. Ady was thrown off to hear that name, a name Sanite had never issued from her lips.

"Come down right now, Antoinette!" Sanite said.

Ady knew that her mother was telling her to run away. But Ady stood looking at Sanite. They were both frozen in place.

"All right. All right. You hold on to that one. Nimrod will get the child."

When he started up the hill, Ady hesitated for a moment, then ran. She ran so hard that when she stopped minutes later, she had no idea where she was or where anyone else was. She wanted to go back and find her mother, but leaves crunched in the distance.

Ady looked for a sturdy tree with leafy branches. When Nimrod arrived, he stomped into the small clearing beneath her. From where she was twenty feet above the ground, he seemed small.

"Where you at, girl?" Nimrod said. "Don't you know there are beasts out here? Gators with teeth the size of your little hand and black bears that eat your guts while you nap. It's Nimrod's job to keep you from getting chewed up. You is important. That man is waiting for you. Worried about you. So come out from where you is. Nimrod knows you here. He can smell your tears."

And Ady was crying. But she knew that she couldn't let that fact control her. She told herself she would collapse into her mother when she and Sanite were safe.

"If you worried about that old tracker you kilt, don't. He was no friend of Nimrod. Nimrod woulda done the same to him before long."

Ady remembered Sanite's story about being in the tree the night she and Ady's father met. Sanite's voice calling her Antoinette echoed in her mind, reminding her of du Marche. Ady did not climb down.

"I know you're close by here," the one called Nimrod said. But eventually he turned and left.

Ady felt entranced. She should run away from the party of slavers, but Ady couldn't leave Sanite alone with those men. She climbed down from the tree and followed the men as they led Sanite through the forest. Her most present thought was never to lose sight of them, for she knew that if she allowed her mother out of view, she might never see her again, like her daddy, like Emmanuel. Her other thought was to keep her own body out of sight. The men were clumsy and slow. She struggled to maintain an adequate distance from them. At several points during the afternoon, she saw Nimrod turn to scan the woods behind him. She would flatten her body against a tree, her palms pressed to the rough bark, certain that they were moving toward her. But they never approached.

That night, they pitched camp on a hummock. Ady watched her mother seated before the glowing flames as the men jeered. Ady was not close enough to hear their words. But she smelled the bean and pork vittles they cooked in a pot. Her stomach groaned, though she didn't consciously register the fact. She kept waiting for the men to tip into sleep. She wanted to run to Sanite, then away with her. They were faster. They wouldn't be caught this time. But the men took turns staying up overnight.

When Ady woke up the next morning, it was in a panic. She ran to the crest of the hummock. They were all gone.

Ady wandered down from the hummock and into the tall grasses of a meadow. She tried to find their tracks, but it was useless. It seemed to her that they left the area days before. As she walked through grasses and shrubs, she became aware of several things that she had only been dimly aware of until then. She was barefoot and injured, having apparently run out of her boots during Nimrod's pursuit. Something sharp had torn the skin between her big and second toes. Dried blood coated her foot, and the pain caused her to wince as she walked. Sanite had packed a compact of salve and bandages, but they were lost—all the materials she and Sanite had carried were likewise lost, unless the slavers had confiscated them for their own purposes. And Ady was indeed hungry. As Sanite had showed her, the blossoms were abundant, but no easy food like apples or berries or seeds were to be found. As she limped through the woods, she saw lizards and daddy-long-legs and songbirds. Her stomach felt hollow—worse than that.

The walls of her belly ached. In her famished state, she wondered what each creature she saw tasted like. What would Sanite instruct her to do?

She hunted for a dip in the land. She was far from the marsh by then. The ridges were lush and covered, but she needed to find a trench. During the afternoon, she came upon a number of streams, but none had what she was searching for until she found one with soft clay banks. She waded into the water. Her feet sank into the silt until the current tickled the skin along the backs of her knees.

The mud smelled fresh, which made her hopeful. She wished she had a net or something sharp and metallic. But her hunger compelled her. There were silvery fish below. She saw one as clearly as if it were a fly on her arm. She struck her hand down into the water, the stream bubbling and churning around her hand. She missed! But she was hungry. She cast her hand down again and again. The fish had scattered. They were incredibly fast, more like spirits than mortal creatures. Her desperation was real. She thought she might climb out of the water—she was already drenched up to her elbows—and walk over to one of the trees and bite directly into the rough bark, but she stilled herself like a tree with two trunks. She crouched down in the water without opening her eyes and clenched her fingers. When she lifted her hand from the flow, she was holding a bluegill that furiously slapped against her forearm. Recognizing that she might lose it at any moment, she dived toward the muddy bank. That was how she caught her first fish.

It wasn't easy, but Ady worked to prepare a fire as she often helped Sanite do in the townhouse kitchen. She skewered the fish on a thin branch and held it over the flame, which flashed within the circle of stones. The fish was small, but when she bit into the flesh, her eyes watered at the flavor. She cleaned the bones with her teeth. She thought the simple meal might have been the most delicious of her life. But soon all she could taste was salt, from the tears that gathered in the corners of her mouth. She was worried about Sanite, and her worry spilled out of her.

This was how the next days passed. At night, she took off her dress and used it to tie herself to a tree branch. She dreamed twenty feet above the soil. During the day, she was hungry all the time. She became better at catching fish. Once, she used a trap to catch a rabbit, but she let it go because it reminded her of the townhouse, as if she were du Marche and she the rabbit.

She once saw white men with picks and hoes walking down a road, but she easily avoided them. Above them, Ady spotted large birds flying in the opposite direction from the men. She couldn't imagine an alternative plan, so she followed their flight for hours well into the night.

By the next morning's light, she saw structures in the distance. Shacks. A chill flushed through Ady. If Sanite were by her side, she would have asked her mother to confirm what she surmised. The way the shacks sat next to one another reminded her of her earliest memories.

This was a slave labor camp also called a plantation.

9.

WHITE PEOPLE—MEN, WOMEN, and children—milled about the shacks closest to Ady. The Coloreds and whites were separate on plantations, weren't they? She questioned whether getting closer was pressing the wrong side of her luck. But she knew going backward posed a threat. She had no alternative.

Ady ducked back into the woods behind the closest shacks. She worked through the underbrush until she heard voices. At a clearing, she saw that a large group of Colored people had gathered in a semicircle. Led by a man at the front of the group, they recited words and then sang in harmony. It must have been Sunday. Sanite had told her that their people were only allowed to gather thus on the Sabbath, just as they did in Congo Square. Ady's stomach troubled her again. If they were all together, then that suggested she could find food in their cabins.

She kept her distance from the congregation and followed a trail behind the shacks, which seemed to become shabbier. The planks were looser, the pillars more crooked, the windows cracked. This was their section of the slave labor camp also called a plantation.

The most run-down shack was at the edge of the property, almost in the woods. Indeed, foliage crept along the ground and surrounded the lower regions of the shack. She stood on her toes and looked into the one-room building, but the window was obscured by dust. She rounded to the front door and opened it partially. She quickly realized the room was full of people, but what she saw made her pause rather than run.

An old woman sat in a rocking chair with a girl lying against her. A dozen or more children were in her lap, sleeping on blankets, or playing together.

"You came to help?" the woman said. "I could sure use it." She laughed, and the girl who had been lying against the woman's shawl adjusted her body and continued to sleep.

"I came into the wrong house, miss," Ady said.

"Might as well stay now." Her name was Baba Cici. She was older than the country. Those were the first two things she told Ady. She didn't ask where Ady had come from, who she belonged to, or what her intentions were.

She roused the girl sleeping in her lap. "Samantha, go fetch that plate from the larder." The girl, who might have been seven or eight, rubbed her eyes and did as told. She placed the plate on the table. It held biscuits with a pat of butter.

"Go 'head," Baba said. "Have it all. We all ate good this morning." Ady crammed the flaky biscuits into her mouth, consumed them ravenously.

"Don't swallow too fast," Baba said. "You'll make yourself sick."

Ady inhaled the plateful, feeling the victuals land in her belly, heavy and warm.

"You've been out there alone, huh?" Baba said. Ady glanced over at Baba, who sat rocking. Ady was nervous and embarrassed. She had crumbs on her lips and butter on her chin. She wiped her mouth with the back of her hand. Where was she?

"That's okay, baby," she said. "I been there too." Ady stood up and wiped her mouth again, this time on her dress sleeve. She went to the door.

"Where you goin'?"

Ady saw beyond the door the great expanse of fields, and beyond them, almost too small to see, a big house. What now? She didn't know.

Baba was standing next to her. The woman was only slightly taller than Ady. Though she was very old, her face was mostly smooth, except around the mouth. Baba had a cloth in her hand. She dabbed at the wet around Ady's eyes, then wiped her jaw.

"You can tell me about yourself tomorrow. What you gone do today is find a spot over in that corner." Baba put an arm around Ady's shoulder and guided her to a thick blanket that lay on the floor under the window. "You gone sleep. Go 'head. Ain't nobody gone bother you none while I'm here. I promise you that." Ady did as told and laid her body on the soft blanket. It smelled of babies, the good and the bad. The flowery fresh scent of their heads. The pungent odor of their bottoms. Soon she was fast asleep.

The next morning, Ady awoke alone. She went to the window and saw Baba talking to a man. The conversation was animated, but they seemed to know each other well and were not angry so much as working through concerns.

"How my baby feeling this morning?" Baba said when she reentered.

"Who was that man?" Ady asked.

"You feeling better, eh?" Baba chuckled. "That was Bo. He my eyes and ears since I hardly ever go more than a few feet from my old house. Now, answer mine. Where you from, girl? You came like a spirit from the woods. But that's a city dress you got. Even if it's in tatters."

"New Orleans."

"I figured as much. Lived some warring times, but, Lord, I guess I do got fresh trouble today."

"How'd you know where I came from?"

"I was born in New Orleans my damn self. Carried a rifle more than once in uniform. Lived there till the Spanish gave it back to the Frenchmens." Baba spit out the window. "But listen to me. You old enough to understand, so you gonna have to make a choice. How old you?"

"I think I'm twelve."

"Good enough." Baba moved toward her rocking chair. Ady took her arm and guided her to the seat. "People like us ain't always got choices. That's for damn sure. Way I see, and listen to me good, you got two or three choices. You was out there on your own even if it was only for a short time. But you was free, understand?"

Ady nodded.

"Freedom ain't nothing to be sneezed at, I tell you that. So you can go back out there. Bo ain't 'bout to blab. 'Course life on the land ain't easy. I reckon you clever. But clever don't beat patrols sniffing around, to say nothing of the animals on four legs. But going back out might be your easy choice."

Ady rubbed her foot against her leg.

"I'm guessing you don't know. Maybe you ain't so smart then. I thought you was on her tail."

"Who?"

"Your mama."

Ady ran to Baba and grabbed her arm. "She's here?"

"The mens brought her in 'bout a week ago. From what I hear, ole massa was equal parts pleased and angry. He don't like the confusion runaways bring. But he must not have thought she'd turn up like she did, even if it was without her little daughter. You. Y'all share the same set of eyes. Ears too." Baba stroked the side of Ady's face.

"I know from your look you wanna see her. And that's where your other set of choices come in. This a big plantation. You could lay down and they might even not know you here for a bit. But eventually, you'd be singled out. Maybe you ain't so much to look at. But you a girl and you fresh and before long every man here be knowing you around. And that's what your last choice about. Massa looking for you, as I said. I don't owe him shit." Baba spat into her cloth. "And I know what kind of man he is. Done put his finger on just about every girl or woman on this land. His right, he thinks. But if you want to be safer he got to know you're here on his land. He'll keep the riffraff off. Until he change his mind. But at least you show yourself I reckon you get to see your mama. He might put you on field because you got beautiful dark skin and you sturdy. But he might put you in the house because you tall and have smart eyes. I don't know his damn mind. But I know you want to see your mama, true?"

"Where she at?"

"All the grown folk about to go to the fields for planting. Some of the chirren be here after while. Go outside and ask that little Samantha to bring you to the haystack when she show up."

Ady was outside staying in the boundary between the woods and the flat dirt road that went to the fields. Some adults brought babies to Baba's shack. Some of the children walked themselves and their younger siblings. Still, they were all very young, under five years old, Ady guessed. The rest of the children must have been working too. Eventually, Samantha came into view, and Ady realized from her self-possessed gait that she was no baby. Ady supposed that she was only a few years younger than herself, but significantly shorter. Why then was she not planting or hauling water to the people in the fields?

Ady called out to her, and Samantha turned off the path. When Samantha arrived in the bright light of morning, Ady saw that there was an opaque quality to her eyes that had been difficult to notice in the dimness of yesterday evening.

"Mama Baba Cici said you could take me to the haystacks."

Samantha giggled.

"What?" Ady asked.

"What you just called Baba sounded like a spell or something. Just call her Baba or Ba like everybody else do. You want to see your mama?"

"Yeah."

"I guess I would feel the same way if I was you. This is the way." Samantha wore no shoes. When she walked, she held her hands out slightly for balance and lightly dragged her feet along the dirt path.

"You don't work out there?" Ady asked.

"No. Most everybody treats me like I'm bad luck. Suits me fine. I get to help Baba with the healing arts and watching the little ones. That's better if you ask me."

"I think you're right. Those are cute babies," Ady said.

"Cute until you have to wipe their butts."

"Ha!"

"This is it," Samantha said when they arrived at the tall barnlike structure.

"You not coming in with me?"

"She's your mama. You want me to come in with you?"

"Yeah," Ady said. They entered the haystack, the interior of which was dark in contrast to the bright flash of outdoors. The stacks of hay were so tall that Ady couldn't see over them. They turned at one of the shorter stacks, and Sanite was laid out with a quilt covering her. Ady almost leapt at her mother.

"Be gentle. They whooped her something terrible."

"Who been in here with her like this?"

"Mass wouldn't let anyone keep her in they cabin. That was his word. Otherwise, Auntie Issa and Auntie Prune would have watched her in their place. Hell, they said even the overseer volunteered. But he's shit anyway. We all been checking on her in here. I was the last one to change her bandages last night after midnight. I made the salve myself."

"After midnight?"

"The dark don't affect me none." She waved a hand before her face.

"I guess not."

Before Ady reached her, Sanite opened her eyes. There was an awful bruise on her cheek.

"Adebimpe," Sanite said. She sat up, clearly in pain.

"Don't get up, Mama." But Sanite gathered Ady in a hug.

"Hush, girl. Can't nothing stop me from putting my arms around you."

"What they do to you, Ma?"

"Shhh." Sanite patted the back of Ady's head.

"I thought I lost you for good," Ady said.

"That can't never happen," Sanite said. "You found me yourself, huh?"

"Uh-huh."

"Spirits. You really are your daddy's daughter."

"What you mean?"

"Shhh." They sat hugging each other for a few moments. Ady felt someone behind her, and she realized it was Samantha, who joined into the hug.

"What you?" Ady asked.

"It's good," Sanite said. "Love is in low stock on this land, but not in this room."

"Someone is coming in." Samantha let go of them.

Ady couldn't see the entrance of the haystack for all the hay. But she heard nothing beyond the creaking of the rafters and, far in the distance, the swell and fall of work songs being sung by people in the field. But after a moment, the sound of bootsteps presented itself. Ady's skin prickled.

Du Marche came into view, a cane in his hand.

"My. I should have known."

"You stay back," Ady said.

"Is that my property in my property telling me to keep my distance from my property?"

"Look what you did."

"You two ran from my house. Those slavers disciplined her, as the law allows. I could have done the same. Although admittedly they went farther than I might." He walked closer. "In any event, you're both back where you belong. I would cart you back to New Orleans immediately, but the disciplining must continue, I'm afraid. You haven't had yours yet."

He punched Ady, and she fell to the ground. She saw stars on redness. He had never hurt her before. At least not like that.

Ady held her face. Her skin throbbed. His blow felt more honest than the other ways he had assaulted her. As though he were telling truth for a change rather than hiding behind words and airs.

"Don't touch her," Sanite said. She tried to stand, but Samantha held an arm around her.

"Mr. Travers is my overseer on the plantation. But I've instructed him to use a light hand for the time being. You." Du Marche pointed at Ady. "My oldest daughter will have a playmate. You'll come back with me to the house. As for you, good ma'am, I want you in the fields by noon."

"No!" Ady said.

"What's that?"

"I won't let you."

"She ain't near healed, mass," Samantha said.

"Oh hush, you sightless mole."

"I'll go now." Sanite stepped off the stack and stood upright, slowly. "Do like he say. I'll see you before long."

"No! No! No!" Ady said. He watched Ady for a moment.

Sanite grabbed Ady. Under her breath, Sanite whispered. "You'll have better in the future, I promise you that. But this what we have right now. I'll see you before long. I promise you that, too. Understand?" Sanite squeezed Ady's hand.

"Yes, Mama," Ady said.

"Thank you for looking after both of us, Samantha," Sanite said.

"Ain't hardly nothing you wouldn't done for me if I needed the same."

Sanite continued holding Ady's hand, and they walked to the exit of the haystack barn. He pushed his cane between their hands and separated them.

"Quit that," he said. He pointed toward the fields. "Your work is over there."

Ady watched Sanite walk slowly, with a hitch in her step, toward the fields. Ady trailed behind du Marche as they walked to the big house.

"I'd be good for you in the field," Ady said. He stopped and wheeled around.

"What did you say?"

"You want to punish Mama, put me out there with her. That'll hurt her more than anything. I ain't never picked a field." Du Marche cocked his head.

"You are most peculiar, little girl."

"I ain't used to being out in the sun like everybody else. I might just die."

"Go. I don't care."

Ady ran, favoring her left foot, the right still pained her, until she spotted Sanite, who was being helped to the field by a woman in a gray head wrap.

Sanite frowned. "Girl, what you doing?"

"Mama, I was off in the woods for days. There were all kinds of animals out there going about their lives, swimming, flying, fighting, and eating each other. I mean those alligators and coyotes and bears. Any of them could have got to me. When I laid down to sleep, I wasn't even worried about getting kilt. I was sad about being kilt without you knowing what happened to me. If something going happen to us, then it need to happen to us together."

"Girl!" Sanite said.

"You raised her right, I think, ha!" the woman said. Ady smiled.

"Hush now, Lua. You be giving my crazy girl more cause to

be that way." Ady stepped in to relieve Lua of the burden of supporting Sanite. The three of them walked to the fields where planting was in progress.

The one called Bo met them. He was thick around the middle and had a confused expression.

"He sent y'all out here to work?"

"More or less," Lua said. "We need them on light though."

"You know they ain't no light work out here."

"Ponder something," Lua said.

"Well, ain't this a mess. I'm glad it's planting instead of harvesting season. Take the middle rows. Overseer's crew pay the least mind to there. I'll get y'all some seed sacks. The water bucket get to you last though."

Ady and Sanite worked in close proximity, burlap sacks of seeds slung over their backs.

"Baby," Sanite said after they had been stooped over for the better part of an hour. Sanite's dress, the tattered one she had worn all the while they were in the Hidden Veil, was drenched down the back. Ady's arms ached terribly from the recurring motion of dipping her hand into the bag and pulling seeds. The row they were working seemed endless, as if they could follow it all the way to the end of time.

"Yeah, Mama."

"I want you talk to me," she said. "To pass the time."

"About what?"

"You always like chit and chat. Anything on your mind."

Ady knew that Sanite must have been feeling sickly to say such a thing as much as she hated being pestered with questions. But there were things Sanite had said that made Ady wonder what the truth was.

"Is my daddy alive?" Ady asked.

Sanite huffed.

"How'd I know you'd bring him up first thing?" she asked. "It'll go easy if we work in the same time. You moving too fast and about to kill me dead out here."

"Sorry, Mama." Ady followed the movement of Sanite's hand into and out of the bag as they stepped forward.

"Y'all two were here together?"

"No. But that slave labor camp was lot like this. Right down to the big house on the ridge. Maybe they all the same. That place was where I put that cut on your arm."

Ady didn't have to look at her arm to see the short sliver of raised skin just up her arm past her wrist. The wound had always been there. She had once thought it was a birthmark. But then she remembered what Sanite had done to Emmanuel. It was a claiming mark, not a birthmark.

"Like I told you. James, your daddy, wasn't around when I was taken." Sanite was at the slave labor camp called Constancia for a period of weeks. She was allowed to nurse Ady for a few days before they brought her to work at the house as a cleaner and gardener. James showed up weeks later. Causing a commotion on the road in. Sanite watched from the second floor of the house as two of the overseers walked James into the grounds. The overseers were smaller, but his hands were up and they carried their rifles pointed at his back. The master of the slave labor camp, whose name she refused to learn, met the men outside at the foot of the hill. Sanite later found out what the discussion had been. She was on the side of the house weeding the garden boxes when he appeared. She wrapped her arms around his waist. She couldn't believe that he had managed to find her. He said he would find her wherever she was in the world. She looked around to see if they were being watched from the house. He said they had time to talk due to the deal he made. James had given himself to the owner of the place for the right to be with his wife.

"You big fool," Sanite had said. "You put yourself into captivity to be with me."

"You and our daughter," he said.

"Why you men such fools?"

"We will find a way out of here. And we'll do it together."

James became an all-around man. He worked the fields and picked more from the ground than most. He repaired the master's carriage when a wheel came loose. He even put new siding on the big house. But his plan was flawed. The master had received a windfall, a slave who could do anything with efficiency. But he was willing to trade off his advantage on principle. He abhorred the idea of a Negro setting the terms of his own captivity. Within two months of his arrival, slave buyers appeared. They shackled James while Sanite fought to embrace him. She was thrown to the ground and held there. The last time she saw her husband, he was tied down to the back of a horse cart headed north.

Ady and Sanite moved to a cabin that had been unoccupied. It was in poor condition when they moved in. The roof had gaps as did the sides. When storms passed over, water rushed in through the gaps until Bo and some of the others came over with boards and straight nails.

"You still ain't take my word on this place?" Bo asked, as he hammered in place the last of the boards.

"That y'all say it ain't livable on account of it being haunted?" Sanite asked.

"That's right," Lua, Bo's wife, said.

"It's livable now," Sanite said.

"And haunted by us," Ady said.

"I ain't studying bout y'all, ha!" Lua said. "Y'all nutty as a fat squirrel."

That night, the first when the structure was secured from the elements, a Sunday, they had a gathering for dinner. Lua, Samantha, Bo, the aunties, a few others, even Baba Cici came and shared a meal of great smoking heaps of white beans with pork shanks, greens, cornpone, and sweetened butter after joined hands and prayer.

They didn't have a table, chairs, or plates. But the others brought their own tinware. And the group stood or sat cross-legged as they ate as much as their stomachs could hold.

Ady couldn't recall if she had experienced something similar. As far as she could remember, this was the first time she had shared a meal with anyone other than Sanite. She recognized the feeling in her chest as she watched Samantha use corn pone to scoop savory beans into her mouth. She felt ease, belonging.

Ady went to the pot that sat on the grease-covered potbellied stove. She shoveled more beans onto one of the tin plates Lua had brought. The plate was heavy in her hands, and although she was no longer hungry, the beans and pork smelled wholesome and good. She wove past Baba Cici and the small child holding on to her dress. Sanite looked at the plate in Ady's hand.

"I told you I didn't want any, baby. That little bit of pone I had was fine by me."

"You should eat, Mama," Ady said. Sanite's mouth moved as if to speak, but she nodded and took the plate from her daughter.

. . .

The hard days of summer in the fields came on and Sanite and Ady spent their time harvesting the early crops from just before sunrise to sunset. One blistering day, Ady was lopping corn. One of the small children had brought a bucket and ladle out onto the rows. Ady saw the waves of heat moving down the lane between the stalks. She felt as if she were frying. Ady grabbed the heavy bucket in both hands. She lifted it above her head and doused herself.

"Hey, gal," one of the men said. "You ain't supposed to hog the whole thing."

The next thing she remembered, she was lying on the porch of the big house. She had fainted. The corn field was closest of the fields to the manor. Ady didn't know where Sanite was, but she recognized the voice of the white woman standing over her.

"Land sakes, these lazy niggers always fall out during the summertime." Mrs. du Marche nudged Ady's leg with her foot. "Disgusting." She walked out of view, coughed, and called off the porch, "Jules, you come back here and get this dirty thing off of my porch. Take and lay her out on the back gallery. Next to Beth's place where the dogs sleep."

Someone poured water into Ady's mouth. Eventually, Ady heard her mother's voice.

"There she is," Sanite said. She kneeled next to Ady.

"Hey, Mama," Ady said.

"I know you ain't feeling right, but you too big to carry, Adebimpe. So you gone have to help me get you up." They got Ady up. She was out of sorts, wobbly. Her head throbbed. She saw that Mr. du Marche was a ways off, standing at the door to the gallery.

"Providence is what the faithful call it."

"Master," Sanite said under her breath.

"That sickness came back," he said. "I've seen it enough times over the years. The gals that run the house are all up in the attic with rags on their foreheads. Lady du Marche is starting to feel ill herself. I've felt better for that matter." He slumped against the doorjamb and pulled a towel from his suspender. Ady stiffened her spine as she imagined him falling all the way to the floor dead as a plank.

"You two will work the house until the others are off their sorry backs."

"You got better workers out there." Ady pointed at the fields. "I might got that yellow fever myself."

"That's right," Sanite said. "I came to get her back from falling out just now."

"I say where you go!" He coughed, then hacked for several moments before regaining composure. "A little bit of heat flush never killed anyone." He went into the house. Sanite waited until du Marche was gone.

"Don't go anywhere I can't see him. He's bad in New Orleans, but men like him be worse out here in the fields, away from they society. First thing you gone do is rest. I'll get them set up today."

Sanite had Ady lie on bedding in the back room of the first floor. Ady heard Sanite in the kitchen preparing a dinner meal for the house. She heard Sanite bring food up to the second floor where the du Marche family was. Mrs. du Marche yelled at Sanite for showing her face, but Ady didn't hear any dishes being thrown. Then Ady heard Sanite return to the kitchen for more servings. She climbed the first set of stairs and continued up to the attic, where Ady imagined the enslaved house workers were. How strange, Ady thought, as she stared at the smooth white ceiling, that wherever she and her mother went, they worked in service of his desires.

Over the next several days, Sanite and Ady took over running the house. Between the four du Marches and the other enslaved people, all of whom were in some state of sickness, there was always work to do. They'd never had much rest at the townhouse, there they worked all day and bedded down at dusk, but in the big house, they were always moving, even at night. Or rather, Sanite always moved. Ady didn't understand how Sanite seemed to work harder than ever. Beth, the enslaved woman who normally ran the house, issued orders to Sanite about how things were to be done. Ady herself couldn't force her hands or feet to move with the same swift determination. At night, they slept in a nearby shed, close by in case needed.

One day, Ady was carrying a heavy platter, and a saucer fell over the side of it. The saucer landed on the carpet and didn't break. Slowly, Ady squatted to pick it up.

"Don't drag on, daughter. The work goes easier if you keep moving," Sanite said.

"How can you do this when he stole Emmanuel from us?"

"Because I think Emmanuel might be here on this land."

Ady dropped the saucer again.

"Why didn't you say anything?"

"'Cause I don't know what's true. All I know is if no one in the fields know, then someone in this house know. Damn, he himself knows."

"He won't ever tell us!"

"Don't raise your voice."

Sanite caressed Ady's cheek. "We'll find out what we can. If we find out nothing, then we'll run away from here just like before," Sanite said, and then added, "As long as you ain't too scared for it."

"I ain't never scared." Ady smiled.

Footsteps were coming down the staircase and they turned and saw that it was Beth. Ady thought Beth was probably the same age as her mother, but her face was impassive so it made her seem older.

"What are you two lazing about down here for? Miss expecting her tea upstairs."

"You ain't got to hop when she say hop," Sanite said. "She too sick for more than a sip anyway."

Beth stopped and stared at Sanite. "Ain't about hopping. It's about doing the work we here to do. You can go back to the field right now. I can tell them you already out there."

Sanite sucked her teeth. "No call for you to get that way."

"You city Negroes." Beth continued into the kitchen. When she was out of sight, she spoke from the kitchen. "Come in here and show me that way you were talking about for the beans."

"I'm coming right away." Sanite made a mocking face. Ady realized she wasn't used to seeing her mother interacting with someone who could have been a friend in a different life.

Sanite moved to the kitchen counter with Beth next to her looking on as Sanite took a chicken apart with her fingers.

"You just need to get all the meat off the bone and then throw it all in the pot."

Beth hummed and chuckled at Sanite. "So you the one," Beth said.

"I guess I am."

"Must be nice."

"Not like I have a choice," Sanite said.

"You ain't lying." They both laughed. Sanite noticed Ady. "Girl, come in here and help us with this dinner." Ady adjusted her apron and entered.

Beth pointed at the counter where three tin pans sat. "Y'all can eat from those. If miss knew you were eating on her plates since y'all been here, she'd have a conniption. I guess things different where y'all stay. But we got to get back on track because I don't want no trouble."

She scooped white beans and meat into two round pans.

"We'll take this out to your shed and eat," Beth said. "They don't like us hanging around in here for meals."

"You ain't worrying about them calling for you?"

"They can survive for a few on they own."

They walked out across the back porch, where Beth slept. Her blanket was rolled up neatly atop a bench. Ady swatted mosquitoes as they approached the toolshed that had been their living quarters over the past days. The women stood near the window eating off their pans, but Ady seated herself by the back wall and placed her tin on her lap. But she didn't eat. Beth and Sanite were talking.

"You know what would go good with this biscuit?" Sanite said. "Some butter."

Beth nodded. "You know where the larder at." As Sanite left, Beth looked at Ady. "What's wrong with you? Plantation food ain't good enough?"

"Why you never tried to get out of here?"

"What you asking? Why I ain't run like you and your mama did?" Beth sucked the meat from a ham hock. Then she threw the pan at the wall where Ady was. If Ady hadn't ducked, it would have hit her in the head. She jumped to her feet.

"That's why!" Beth said. "I know the likes of you look down on me. You don't think everyone on this land want to get off it? But what that get you? My husband and son lit off with a tracker years ago. I heard they found their bodies in a creek. And all of us here had to pay hell for their disobedience. So don't you go asking me about running away!"

Sanite came back into the shed. "What's going on in here?" she asked.

"Nothing," Beth said. "I'm going to go check on miss. She like to start calling before long anyway."

Days later before sunrise, Ady followed Sanite from the shed. It was their first time away from the big house since they had been brought there. In the mist of the morning, Ady again saw the tumbledown shacks where the enslaved people lived. She knew that she too was enslaved, but she had not quite thought of herself that way, had heard from her mother stories of people who were forced at the blade of a whip to work the fields on days so hot the dirt burned their feet, but couldn't imagine that pain until she herself encountered it. She had only worked the fields for a few days before she passed out. And she felt embarrassed by her weakness.

They stopped by a field of sugar cane. "I only worked fields a few times," Sanite said. "They always liked me in the house on account of my light skin." Ady imagined she saw people walking down the rows of cane, swinging their blades. She saw the house in her mind. The people who had worked there even before Beth. Ady had a sense that this was what growing up was, this mixed understanding of what used to be and what was. She was nearly as tall as her mother. Growing up, she thought, was seeing what was always there but had been invisible before.

In the house, it was quiet. They checked the kitchen, but the oven wasn't fired, the food still packed away.

"You stay here," Sanite said, but as she moved toward the door out into the dining room, Ady followed her. She grabbed the fabric at the waist of Sanite's dress and tethered herself to the garment. Sanite looked back at Ady, first in confusion, then with an expression of understanding. They walked outside to the back porch. Beth lay with her blanket tossed on the floor. Her forehead was covered in sweat.

"This sick got me too," Beth said. "Y'all need to handle cooking and such."

"When is the last time you ate?"

"Just do what you came here for."

"Tell me and then I'll go."

"I ain't have an appetite yesterday, so it was the day before."

Downstairs, Sanite and Ady worked to prepare breakfast. There was a larder full of meats and breads, enough to feed a family for a week.

"What if we lived there?" Ady asked when they arrived at the chicken coop behind the house. But she was pointing at the big house.

"Girl, you too funny with that talk." Sanite said. Ady began placing eggs in the front pouch of her apron.

"But why?"

"You ask too many questions but I don't blame you. I would too. I used to ask the same kind of things when I had your years. Sit and don't break the eggs." Sanite wiped her hands on her apron. "The only thing I've ever wanted was life with a house and you and your daddy to be unbothered by the likes of white folk. But the older I get, it seems that ain't possible."

"You mean being free."

"I mean we can be where they put us or we can die."

"You saying you don't want to run again."

"I'm saying—"

"That don't make any sense. You always talking about freedom."

"I'm talking about the world. Do you know where I went when I ran away years back?"

Ady shook her head.

"That night I had a guide. She gave the signal by whistling 'Nobody Knows' from the woods."

"You trusted her?"

"I did. And I was right to. We ran for miles. But before long, I heard the dogs and the men on horses. She say we got to split. Go in different directions. They'll follow one of us. The other will go free, if that's God's word. So we did. She went up a ridge into the woods. I went down toward the sound of water. There was a little river. Just deep enough that I couldn't cross it. But I knew I didn't have to. I heard the men up the ridge, the dogs going wild. They had her. If it was you and me out there right now running from this evil house as fast as we could with dogs, men, and guns rumbling after us, do you think I could leave you? You couldn't leave me. You was free yourself."

"We just have to run faster next time."

"What I'm trying to tell you is it ain't her fault for getting captured. It ain't my fault for getting loose for a while. It ain't our fault for getting a taste of nature in that swamp and then getting took here. It's this world that's slanted. We could have kept going for the rest of our life knowing that any old white could bring us back. That ain't freedom either. You know what is freedom? You my freedom. My life out there don't mean anything. My life in here ain't much either. But you my daughter. My joy. That's why we here."

"You saying you don't want to do it. You afraid of running away again. But you know we can make it."

"I don't know what I'm saying. I just have a feeling I need to understand."

Sanite stood and they walked back to the house, eggs bumping slightly in Ady's apron. Ady took out an egg and threw it at a tree. It splattered against the trunk. Sanite took an egg from Ady and held it in her closed hand.

Inside the house, those who were able to eat were fed. Those who were too sick to eat were given spoonfuls of chicken bone broth. It was a strange thing to Ady. She was used to watching the way people moved, the way white people commanded Colored people around, the way Colored people were obliged to duck and scrape so as not to seem as powerful as they were. The du Marches were looking down always upon Sanite, Ady, and the others, but now he, the woman, and their children were on their backs, deflated, moaning.

And so were many of the people who worked the fields. Ady wanted to check on Mama Baba and Samantha and the little children. But Sanite and Ady were tasked only to the house and Beth because, Ady realized, Beth was considered by the slave masters to be no more than an extension of the house.

Sanite and Ady were dividing up care of the infirm. Sanite would see to Beth and to him, who had taken to a side room. Ady had told Sanite she would attend to the children and the woman. Ady didn't want Sanite to ever be at her whims again, if possible.

When Ady brought the woman a strong medicinal tea, the woman seemed daft. The woman's eyes were wet and she didn't move until Ady placed the silver tray on the small stand near the bed.

"Is that the best you can do?" the woman said, but she didn't seem to be talking to Ady, so much as through her. Ady served her.

"I thought you were your mother," she said. "Will you be another one like her? A beast? Or those buffoons at Harper's Ferry?" Sanite entered just then and the woman looked on at her and said, "I only want you to serve me." Sanite sent Ady downstairs.

On the third day, Beth was strong enough to cook. She moved with more strength and didn't hesitate as much. Du Marche and his son were back up and about, too, but not Mrs. du Marche. Ady was sweeping the parlor when a man in a suit and carrying a black bag entered.

"John," the doctor said, "I'm glad you're up on your legs."

"I am, but not the old girl. She's got no wind in her."

"Let's have a look."

When they came back down, the doctor put his hand on du Marche's back. Both of their faces were reddened.

"She's got a fight in front of her. I'll stop by again this evening."

After the doctor left, du Marche turned to Ady, although he could have been speaking to the wall behind her.

"Pray for my wife. They say the prayers of children are the most powerful of them all."

But Ady did not pray for her. For the next several days, Mrs. du Marche did seem to be fading from the world. She was too gone to scold Ady for being the carer. She was as sweaty as a wet dog and her lips stayed parched, even after Ady gave her drink. That night, Ady prayed only for Sanite and Emmanuel.

10.

In the early morning, Ady found Sanite passed out on the floor upstairs. She felt her mother's head, which was hot enough that Ady drew her hand back in surprise. There had been a shadow over the house, just like every place they lived. Ady wondered if some part of the shadow had entered her mother. In the long span since they had taken Emmanuel, Sanite seemed to shift from agitated to somber minute to minute. But this was different. She couldn't revive Sanite nor could she carry her. Ady had been sitting on the floor with Sanite's arm wrapped around her neck for some time when Mrs. and Mr. du Marche entered, the doorjamb creaking under his boot.

"And what is this?" he said.

Ady squeezed her eyes closed. "I just found her this way."

He picked up Sanite and carried her out into the chicken coop, Mrs. du Marche looking on. She was thin, having lost weight to the illness, but she stood upright, tall. She was on the mend. It didn't seem to matter that Ady had not prayed for her.

"No! Don't you touch me." Sanite's eyes rolled back in her head. He caught Sanite from falling and carried her to Beth's pallet. He rolled the coverlet back and tucked her legs underneath.

"What we do?" Ady asked. Beth joined them in the shed.

"I'll send word for Doc Hadley," he said. But Ady knew he intended no such thing.

"I could ask Mama Baba to make her something."

"Who?" he asked.

"She heals," Beth said.

"Never mind that," he said. "I'll not have you bringing that field witchcraft so close to my house. Let her rest and see to it she gets nourishment." He left.

"Child, you ignorant for a city girl. You ought to know better than to talk about that kind of work around the likes of him. White folk afraid of the natural ways."

"I'm going to see Mama Baba." ·

"No you don't." Beth grabbed Ady's arm. "You can't disobey him like that. It'll be hell on you."

"I don't care," Ady said.

"She done passed," Beth said.

"What you talking about?"

"Almost a week ago. The same day you was brought up to the house. I don't think she was so sick. I think it was just her time."

"I don't believe you!"

"Don't go down there, girl," Beth said. But Ady was already walking down the hill. She crossed the plantation and passed fields. White men on horseback watched her with rifles on their shoulders. But they didn't stop her. Perhaps it was her dress, that marked her as from the house. Or maybe they knew what she would find. When at last, Ady made it to the shacks, she saw that someone had hung a strip of black cloth on the frame by the door.

Ady went inside and saw children all around the room. Some at rest and others playing with each other. Samantha was on Mama Baba's rocking chair, holding a baby close. Ady crossed into the room.

"What you doing back here, Ady?"

"How'd you know it was me?"

"You walk a certain way on the floorboards. And you smell a certain way, too."

"I'm sorry about Mama Baba."

"She said she didn't want nobody crying over her." Samantha hugged the baby tighter. Ady saw that Samantha was crying.

"I never was that good at following what she said," Samantha said. "I thought you was up in the house."

"You don't know why I came?"

"I don't get visions, Ady. But I heard a bunch of y'all were getting that fever."

"My mama's laid up. I need to make her some of that tea you and Mama Baba would make."

Samantha stood up with the baby on her shoulder. "Ady," she said.

"Y'all pick those leaves on the edge of the woods, right. By the evergreens? I can get them if you don't have any."

"Ady."

"What?"

"That yarrow is good for a lot, but people all over here done had the fever already. It don't help that none."

"How do you know, anyway?"

Samantha sighed. She placed a hand on Ady's shoulder. "How is Miss Sanite?"

"Not doing good. And the sick done almost killed that lady up that house. And she had all the things that doctor brought for her."

Samantha went to the wooden box near the potbellied stove. She opened it with one hand and pulled out a folded cloth. She gave the cloth to Ady.

"That's about five cups' worth. Don't boil it more than five minutes or that'll kill all the good in it. And give it to her while it's steaming."

Ady hugged Samantha. "Thank you."

"You need to come help me with these children one day. They a handful."

"I will," Ady said.

"I hope your mama feel better."

Ady had to depend on the rhythm of the house to help her mother. When Beth asked what she had done when she left, she didn't answer. Together, they prepared breakfast for the family. When Beth insisted that she bring the food up to the du Marches herself, Ady took that chance to set the kettle on the hot stovetop. She was just pouring tea into a tin cup when Beth came back in.

Beth went to the counter and grabbed the cup from the counter. She sniffed it and shook her head. Beth was tilting the cup into the basin when Ady slapped her. Beth placed a hand on her own cheek. The cup fell into the basin.

"You little dog," Beth said.

"You can't do that," Ady said. She took the teapot and the cup.

"He said no witchcraft in his house. You working on all sorts of trouble."

"It's tea." Ady stopped at the door. She stared at Beth, who was still holding her face, and went out to Sanite in the coop. She was half awake. Ady cradled Sanite's head and smiled as she sipped the hot tea.

"How did you get this?" Sanite asked.

"I had help," Ady said. Sanite closed her eyes and grinned.

"It's good and sweet." Sanite coughed. Ady felt her mother's body convulse.

"I know you telling a tale, Mama. Everybody know yarrow taste like cabbage." Sanite grabbed the back of Ady's head and rubbed it.

Ady had left Sanite when she closed her eyes for rest. It was early evening and she was tidying the kitchen when someone knocked on the door.

"You get it," Beth said.

Ady went to the door. Two white men stood on the front porch, whom she recognized as overseers. They grabbed Ady by the arms.

"Let me go," she said.

"Shut up," one of them said. They carried her down the steps, her feet kicking against the air. They put her down but held her in place. Du Marche exited the house. He slapped her with the back of his hand.

"Was I not clear?" he asked.

"What you want us to do with this little one, boss?" one said.

"We could take her down to the creek."

"No." Du Marche raised his hand. "Put her on the pail." Beth brought out three pails, dragging her feet. Ady recognized the pails. She had carried them up from the river to the house for the past week. Two of them were full of water. One of the men turned the empty pail upside down and bade Ady stand on top of it.

Ady glared at Beth, who was behind the men, but Beth shook her head. Then she frowned and shook her head again.

"Give her a chance," du Marche said. "Pour some of that out. She'll never hold them full up."

The overseers poured water from the pails off to the side and placed the handles of the pails in her hands.

"Go on and hold out your arms like you're on the cross."

Ady straightened her arms. The pails were still heavy. But she wouldn't give Beth the pleasure of seeing her lower her arms.

"I'll take the crop." He opened his hand and one of the overseers tossed a riding crop to him. "Don't spill any of my water." He struck Ady's calf, and she felt a fiery pain. It was too much for her to concentrate. The pails fell from her hands and water splashed across her feet.

"You act like you're such a strong one," he said. He struck her again. Ady cried out and fell to the ground, pulling her legs against her body. He struck her legs again, and again she yelped. He dropped the crop and walked away.

That night, Ady lay on the coop floor next to Sanite. Beth was up on her bench wrapped in a blanket. Ady hadn't gone to sleep. Beth had wrapped her bleeding legs in cloth. But Ady didn't feel the pain.

"My daughter," Sanite said.

Ady rolled over to face her. "Yes, Mama?"

"You are always my daughter."

"I know, Mama."

Ady became aware of the stillness beside her. Sanite wasn't breathing.

"Mama?" she asked, but Sanite didn't stir. Ady shook Sanite. "Mama!"

Beth came in wiping her hands on a rag. "Girl, what's that yelling?"

Ady was on her knees, shaking Sanite. "She's not waking up, Miss Beth."

"What?" Beth said. She climbed down from the bench and knelt next to the pair. "Lord, Jesus. She gone."

Ady stood up. She would find help somewhere, but her legs gave out, and it was Beth who caught her and held her firm. Ady slapped Beth's arms, but the woman didn't let go.

11

Week ending Aug. 6, 1937   Milton P. Cole
              Identification No. 0328-2532
          Federal Writers' Project, Dist.2.
            WPA Project 3609, Mobile, Ala.

MANNY PHILLIPS, EX-SLAVE, SAYS HE
NEVER FOUND HIS MOTHER.

(Written by Milton P. Cole.)

The writer requested to ride with a group of workers heading north toward Harpersville on state route 25 allowing for an interview with an old ex-slave named Manny Phillips, who, when asked when he was born, said:

"Sir, I don't know the date but I sure recall the change 'round leading up to the Surrender. I was a babe when the cannon fire and such happened and Marster Henry got his cavalry uniform for fightin'."

They call him Drummer Boy Phillips in these parts on account of him being paired with his master's son, Henry, Jr., at the head of the war camp. Henry, Jr. Played a piccolo; Henry, Sr. was shot off his horse at Munford. Drummer Boy crossed the line

and wound up marching with the Union reg-
iment.

When the writer asked Drummer Boy
about his own family, he replied:

"I got four daughters and ten grand-
children and a few little ones just arrived."

When asked about his parents, he replied:

"No, I don't recalls much."

Drummer Boy looked down at his hands
and back up. It was then the writer noticed his light green eyes. He told the
writer that he was sold off from his mother
as an infant. After the Surrender, Freed-
men tried to find their loved ones, but he
was too young to even know where to start.
Later, after he started his own family, he
encountered a woman who, he said, "was
short as a house cat," and claimed to have
known his mother in New Orleans. She even
told him how he got the cut on his arm. He
went to New Orleans with the woman and
searched for his mother, but did not locate her. The woman gave him a written
journal, which he gave to his second
daughter:

"Because I never learnt to read."

12.

THE DAY AFTER Sanite died was a Sunday. Du Marche would not let Ady see her mother's body again, and because he was due back to the city that day, he tied Ady's hands and made her sit next to him in the uncovered carriage. And although Ady kicked and screamed as they rounded the bend and the slave labor camp plantation fell out of view, the carriage continued on.

They returned to the townhouse and Ady fell out of time. Her mother's words echoed in her ear. He had Sanite's body brought into town along with a shipment of supplies. There had been a funeral, in the cemetery by the swamp where they buried Negroes.

Autumn and winter had fallen upon the city like a dampening wool blanket. Ady felt that that was appropriate, that it matched her insides. She took to never stopping moving, but she no longer felt alive in the realm of her body.

By the time spring came, and with it the smell of coffee beans roasting as the sellers pulled their carts along the cobblestones, Ady was a wind-up doll, rising with the sun, whisking the dust off the slate-covered courtyard, preparing meals for him that she herself never touched. She lived off gray nubs of bread when she ate at all.

Yellow fever had visited the city several times since the same sickness took Sanite. Ady herself had a mild case once in the time after. For all his affronts, she couldn't blame him for what happened to her mother, but she could. The circumstances of their lives, their caging and enshacklement, were his doing. It was he who had enslaved them. Who still enslaved her. Perhaps another white man would have done as much—but no—it was he and he alone.

Maybe their lives would have been harder if they had run away many years earlier. A patrol might have come upon them in the swamps and shot them for sport or worse. Runaway slaves had value to the whites, Sanite had taught her that, but some patrols only wanted the slaves they were after. It wasn't every day they got to destroy someone else's property with no consequences. There was never a day in creation that a planter grieved for the loss of chattel.

But those would have been circumstances where Sanite didn't expire on the dusty floor of a shed at his big house. Ady's yarrow tincture hadn't kept death from reaching her mother. If only she had been taught more, had learned more from Mama Baba or even Samantha. She was ignorant, and her ignorance had contributed to Sanite's death. She knew hardly anyone or anything at all. She was without use or worth.

In town, Sanite and Ady had been a part of no kinship, no family, and all that Ady learned from people who were not Sanite had come from the man himself, his Knight cronies, or the brief exchanges with others in public, quick glances, or mundane talk over purchases for the townhouse. Sometimes she hoped to run into the scruffy girl she had met before she and Sanite ran away. At some point he had hired a woman whose duties were initially unclear to Ady. The woman, Mrs. Orsone, was a governess who had been educated overseas and acted like it. She sat as if a rod ran from her neck to her tailbone, and she spoke with her chin up, down through her nostrils. Imagine Ady's surprise when it was disclosed that Mrs. Orsone was to educate her, the commencement of which occurred immediately upon her second visit to the townhouse.

Though her body sat mere inches away from Mrs. Orsone's, Ady barely registered their sessions. The inner her, the real Ady, was off in the chasm between the blowing out of a candle and velveteen darkness. When the woman sharply criticized her pronunciation of high French words or slapped her wrist with a wand for not curling the loops on her letters elegantly enough, Ady watched it all from the grotto deep in the back of her skull. She was like a house from which all the furniture had been removed. Mrs. Orsone could restock it however she chose. Sanite was gone and her baby brother Emmanuel was gone and Ady herself was gone. She imagined Emmanuel picking and sweating on some ugly gash of land next to a white man's big house on a slave labor camp also called a plantation, and even though she'd hate it all the same, she wished to be there, to be with him, with blood.

None of it made any sense to Ady, the lessons and the pronouncements from the woman's nostrils. None of it seemed important.

"I shall require you to try harder," Mrs. Orsone said. She was prodding Ady to say the French word for locksmith. But instead Ady dropped her head and cried. In a surprising show of empathy, Mrs. Orsone placed a hand atop Ady's hand. She wore a jeweled ring on her middle finger. "My dear, I know what transpired in your life and the dreadful circumstances under which your beloved mother perished. The city has outlawed the teaching of the enslaved. My presence here may not seem like a blessing, but I suspect in some tangential manner, Sanite played a role in my presence. And she would want you to accept what is given you. I should want you to benefit as well."

Ady repeated "Sanite." No one had said her mother's name out loud for quite some time. She didn't know whether to be comforted or insulted. Mrs. Orsone was just that way. She ranged from strict to warm moment to moment. But she seemed to know Ady's mother. That was reason enough to try and do as she said.

Even less sensible were the actions of him. She had gone through a growing. As the scars on her legs faded, she watched her feet grow longer like cloven hooves, her fingers spread forth like palm fronds, her face ripen into sweetness. But she didn't develop a shape, like Mrs. Orsone or the woman who sold coffee down at Congo Square—not a prominent shape, anyway. Sanite had had little shape, so why would she have more? But she had taken her mother's height. By the time Ady was fourteen—she never did and never would know her actual birth date, but she was born in winter and this was the fifteenth time she'd witnessed the blooming of flowers that preferred the cold: witch hazel, hellebores, winter jasmine—she was almost as tall as he. Facts that barely registered within her consciousness. The same way she had once seen a magpie on the crepe myrtle in the courtyard day after day, for weeks on end. Then one day it was gone like the tree had cupped its leaves and consumed it. That's what happened to her child body. She figured the changes accounted for his new odd behaviors.

His wife had died that summer giving birth to a baby that itself did not live. He spent more time at the townhouse than before. When he had business that took him away, he would return with gifts for Ady, sometimes candies from the local sellers, or baubles that she had seen at his big house. But more often than not he brought clothing. In looking back, it began even before the death of her mother. After he ripped that sackcloth dress she had worn, he replaced it with a pair of linen dresses. They weren't fine by any means, but they were nicer than what she'd had. In fact, they were similar to what Sanite had worn most of the time. And then the linen dresses became more ornate and of finer fabric.

It was on the occasion of her presumed fifteenth birthday that he stomped into the townhouse with a long mauve box wrapped in pink ribbon. He told her to sit at the table and brought a pair of shears. Inside was a silver crucifix.

Ady thought back to the previous week, when he and she were outside the jeweler's and he announced, "You will call me Father." They were east of downtown, in the old Spanish district, the Third Municipality some people called it still. Another gift had been given. Ady's eyesight was poor; that had always been the case. That morning, he must have noticed her on the steps in the courtyard squinting at the copy of *The Swiss Family Robinson* that Mrs. Orsone had taught her to read from. She did that from time to time. Ady went back to that first text to see by what measure her skill had increased even though the townhouse was full of other books she favored. "That's how you should address me," he said. "Father."

Ady looked at him. He wore a full beard by then, trimmed to the length of an inch, flecked with gray at the corners of his mouth. There were moments when her mind felt as though it had rocketed off in several directions at once, like the time John Jr. threw a sparkler down into the courtyard where cats had gathered, as if plotting.

Ady had ached to know more of her father throughout her

life, and Sanite had only ever really given in to her curiosity during their pilgrimage in the swamp. Ady had learned more at the slave labor camp called Ascension, du Marche's plantation. From the details her mother shared in the off moments between meals or while climbing muddy trails or on the moldy porch where she died, Ady had finally fixed in her mind an image of her father, James, shimmering at the edges and translucent throughout, but fixed. He had been at the slave labor camp also called Constancia Plantation with Sanite when Ady was only an infant; he was loved for his size and the way he wrapped his big arms around anyone he liked. And he liked everyone. But he had loved Sanite. The owner had gotten the value of three others for him when James was sold to a newer plantation in Oklahoma.

Ady had reflected before on the nature of du Marche's presence in her life. She did not know her father, but he had existed once and possibly still did, like Emmanuel. Might even be free, her father. She had had a mother, had known her mother all her life and been loved by her; had loved her and then lost her. The work of a parent, Ady thought, was to in the first instance create the child and in the second instance to nurture that child. But she was enslaved to this drunkard businessman, landowner, and sometime man of the state government. She had never seen the papers with her own eyes, but she didn't need to. In her time at his big house she surmised where he maintained ownership documents for all the people joined to him by leg weights. She knew that in the fine cherrywood cabinet across from his bed was a ledger book inside which sat a leaf of paper covered in elegant handwriting and in between claims for cattle and milled grain was her name along with the age at which she had been acquired and the price of her body. Her mother's name too. In the books she read in the townhouse, Ady had encountered intellects and adventurers, humans of great wit and strength who traveled and overcame stupendous obstacles. Some of them even were women, but none of them were enslaved. She had read one book with an enslaved man's name in the title, but he was simple and dull and didn't represent to her anyone she had known or wished to know. Certainly not James.

But there were many Free Negroes, great hordes of them, in the Third Municipality. She had seen how they lived over the years. They owned haberdashers and bricklaying concerns. They attended and ran their own schools. They were free unto themselves. They reminded her, pointedly, of the whites who lived near the townhouse in their own townhouses, haughty, self-assured, in point of fact arrogant. She admired this aspect of their personalities because, after all, one needed to be free to be truly arrogant. Hnh. Self-possessed. That was a better word for it. A compound word, Mrs. Orsone would point out.

So it seemed to her—she had thought on many a night when Gulf storms brought sea-brined winds to the shuttered quarters where she still slept on her straw pallet, and she saw herself running away under a canopy of lightning—that the very nature of freedom was to nourish and of slavery to devour.

How then could this man presume to have her call him Father when he was destroying her all the time?

"Why would you want that?" she asked. She had been quieter of voice since her return to the townhouse. This was an effect of both her loneliness and Mrs. Orsone's tutelage. Mrs. Orsone, who was always remanding her to a lower volume. But there outside the shop, Ady's voice was sharp, clear.

This was unintended, but she cherished the feeling of it in the tightening of her chest, her neck pulsing, her fingernails tearing into the soft flesh of her palm. "On what basis should I ever call *you* my father?"

He titled his head at her and winced as if she had just ground her heel into his shoe.

A woman who stood under the painted sign of the store where he had purchased her glasses glanced over at them. She was a free Creole, Ady would bet her soul on it. They were nearly the same color, and their clothes were of similar quality, but the woman had the posture of someone who wasn't used to bowing and scraping. And the true marker of her status was the wrap about her head. She had a mass of hair, jet black and wavy-textured, piled high under an elegant tignon. Wisps of her hair showed about her ears. White women sometimes wore tignons, too, but the colorful fabrics didn't complement their skin. On them, the accessories seemed like nothing more than a common scarf. The free women wore it in a manner that even an unaccustomed person would see as regal. The woman looked away in the way of one who hadn't intended to eavesdrop but was in too deep to turn away in time.

"My dear girl." He grabbed her forearm. She knew what he was capable of. "You may not be my own flesh and blood, but I regard you as such. Surely, I treat you that way. I've always kept you close." Ady's face contorted, but he was already speaking again, "Come," he said. "I'll hire a cab. The clouds are gathering."

13.

NEW ORLEANS WAS CHANGING. Ady paid close attention to these movements. She thought they represented some aspect of her own life, though she could not say what. At the river, beyond the little market, the wharves had expanded. Gone were the scraggly piers where vessels had once docked. The piers were replaced by one massive continuous boardwalk of sturdy, uniform wood. The structure ran the length of the riverfront, so far down the curve of the Mississippi that she couldn't see its end. Walking along the boardwalk, she felt that nature had somehow been tamed, like when men came to a dense forest and, days later, left bare ground behind.

The market had been widened, the poles painted in garish stripes of yellow and green. Even the river was changed, or rather what traveled on it. More ships crowded its brown, seething surface than ever. She liked the vessels, the way in late winter they floated high on northern snow melted into water, so that she had to gaze up at them from ashore. When she and Sanite were in their first year in the city, a wharf building caught fire and burned to cinders her favorite boat, a paddle steamer called the *Natchez*, its wheel spinning even as it capsized. A replacement *Natchez* arrived perhaps a year later, and she always treated seeing the new vessel as a good omen, but she assumed it had burned again somewhere and that whatever prayer the boat used to resurrect itself had fallen upon dead ears.

The night the first one burned she saw the steamboatmen in their wide pants and flat hats running about the docks and on the smoking deck of the ship. That smoke smelled like charred grass. One of the men was in a state of delirium. He sat on one of the bollards they used to tie ships to land. His hands were on his face and his wrists were wet from tears. She had never seen a man cry before. Or since for that matter. That memory always came back to her whenever something tickled her throat and made her cough.

In the seasons since Sanite died, Ady was alone even when du Marche and Mrs. Orsone were present. Or perhaps more so when they were present. The general nature of her life with Sanite was one together. She could not compare her experiences to the enslaved at the slave labor camp also called a plantation. There was not a great distance between those experiences save for the fact that those enslaved people had a tight community around them. The city enslaved gathered only when allowed. Yet Ady felt the company of her mother was more than enough. They didn't talk much, or rather, Sanite didn't talk much, because that wasn't her nature. It was Ady's mouth that chattered. Ady remembered that she herself talked incessantly back then while they played finger games, or lay in bed together, or when, on clear winter nights, they named the stars above the courtyard—Bearnice, Roundjub, Marrowby—and made up new names for constellations changed by the presence of clouds.

Without Sanite, the townhouse, quarters, and courtyard were quiet. The townhouse felt like her walks through the cities of the dead, where the oven tombs and columbaria loomed. She had heard life beyond the walls of the cemetery vaults, winter sparrows on the leafless branches, packs of dogs barking in the beyond. This was how she felt now, life happening in the distance.

She had taken on all the responsibilities of maintaining the townhouse. Beyond cooking, cleaning and errands, she directed carpenters and artisans. She once asked about normal schooling not under the wing of the governess. But he reminded her that it was illegal for her to attend any of the schools in the state, even the Free Negro ones, and it was also a violation of the laws even to allow Mrs. Orsone to see her. She didn't want that to stop, did she?

"We are going," he said, one late afternoon. It had been a strange one. He had directed her to forgo her duties that day and stay at her writing desk. "Continue," he had said, hours after Mrs. Orsone left. "Practice those letters. I want them clean as a priest's hand." Ady was confused—she only rarely thought on the inexplicable nature of her captor pushing her to learn the alphabet and read literature even as she knew he hated anything that might cause the black race's advancement. Yet this wasn't the first time he told her to practice longer than usual. Ady did as she was told until he reappeared at the threshold in a top hat and silk tie and said we are going. In that very manner. *We are going.* As though it was the most mundane thing on earth. But it wasn't.

On shopping days, or if he required her to carry items, he always said where they would travel to in advance. Ady would make the journey in her mind. She would feel the psychic pain of walking the streets several paces behind him before they even left. The pressure of a basket perpetually upon her head. But *We are going* was different. It was for this reason alone she asked what she never asked.

"What should I wear?"

"Not your scullery rags. Don the gray one and look smart, if you are able."

They walked along the quiet side of the French Quarter. Beneath the quivering lamplight, cupfuls of water trembled in the hollows between the cobbles. She carried his satchel, which was heavy enough that she listed to one side. Ady wondered why he hadn't called a carriage, but didn't ask. One question was enough for the evening, she thought, just when he stopped in front of a building, a grand three-story house, the windows warmly lit by candlelight.

"I was beginning to believe you might never arrive, John." A white woman stepped down from the sidewalk. She wore a high-collared dress and had bright eyes. The light was dim, but Ady saw that his cheeks had reddened. He cleared his throat.

"Companionship is better when pined for," he said.

"Perhaps. But a few moments more, and I would have retired for the evening." The woman swatted at the air. "The midges are terrible tonight," she said, and then, noticing Ady, "What's this?"

"She belongs to me."

"Ah." The woman tilted her head and went to the door of the building. He opened it. After the woman entered, he glanced back. "Hurry, fool."

Ady entered, negotiating an awkward shuffle. He never held doors for her.

"Just wait by the walls."

Ady didn't understand what she was seeing. It wasn't a house at all. The room was quite large. Tables were arranged off to the sides, and at the center of the room people, mainly couples, danced to men playing fiddles and banjos in a corner. He and the woman were already locked in an embrace.

Someone grabbed Ady's arm and pulled her out of the way as the pair spun past.

"Get out of the path, darky," another white woman said. Her voice was almost drowned out by the music and chatter of the dancers. "You must belong to Ole John, I reckon that. Figures. You're his type for one in bondage." The woman was older and wore a simpler version of the dress the first woman did.

"What is this place?"

"Are ye daft? It's an inn and tavern."

"An 'in'?" Ady asked. The woman perhaps didn't hear Ady and continued.

"I don't much like Missy cavorting with the likes of him, but I haven't seen her this cheerful in a long while, I reckon that." Ady looked on at the talkative woman and noticed her clothes, less fine than the ones the white women who were dancing were wearing. She also had no makeup or jewels on. She must have been a maid or servant, free and paid to do the same work as Ady.

Ady looked through the flowing crowd for the couple, but instead her eyes fell upon a woman at the far side of the room. She stood like a rock in the jittering mass of people. Her smile was practiced, glowing. She wore a golden dress with embroidery and was watching Ady directly. Suddenly it dawned on Ady that she was the Free Woman that Ady had noticed outside of the jeweler's! It felt as if the woman had reached across the clutter of bodies and touched Ady's face.

Ady stepped forward, but the talkative woman grabbed her arm again as dancers twirled past.

"Watch it! You were right in the mix. Sakes, you really are daft."

Ady realized absently that her own cheeks were warm. She wanted to talk to the woman in gold, but what would she say?

The Free Woman's attention was taken by another woman, who wore a floral hat. The pair walked toward the back of the hall out of view. For the rest of the evening, Ady stood with her back against the wall. When the woman returned, Ady followed her movement around the room as she chatted with guests or seemed to direct others to carry out tasks.

"Why do I want to talk to her?" Ady said aloud this time.

"What?" the talkative woman, who had been speaking all night, said. Ady heard not a word. "Are ye possessed?"

Suddenly he left the dance floor with the woman he'd met at the door. The talkative woman followed the couple out of the building. Ady looked back over her shoulder as she left but did not see the Free Woman anywhere.

Once they returned to the townhouse, he had Ady turn down the bed and pour whiskey from the decanter for him and the first woman. The talkative woman took a cup for herself and went outside, presumably to the courtyard. But he told Ady to stay within the main house. She went to the kitchen and sat on the stool. As yelps of excitement came from the townhouse master bed, Ady thought back on the night. On control and power. He must have done this before, she realized. But on this occasion, he wanted a match for the talkative servant woman. The woman in his bed was wealthy, from a powerful family. He likely wanted to show that he had wealth and power of his own. Enough to have Ady stand against a wall and watch him dance. Enough power to know Ady could never tell. Enough to position Ady in a room adjacent to the one he was in.

Ady was tired of thinking of him. She opened the door to the courtyard and saw the talkative servant woman drinking as she sat on one of the wrought-iron chairs. But Ady didn't take this in very deeply. She looked up into the cloudy sky and waited for a few faint stars to reveal themselves.

14.

THE NEXT MORNING, the two women left in a carriage. And he left in his riding boots for the plantation. Shortly thereafter, Ady too left the courtyard, walking due south to the river. Fog sheeted the ground and before long she came to the edge of the boardwalk. Below, a crew of young men sat on the sooty banks, tossing stones into the water, probably mud clerks waiting for a ship to come in. When the fog cleared, she found that she was far down the river bend and the sun was a weak glow behind the clouds. She knew that if she walked far enough downriver, she would encounter forts from old wars, but she turned north into the Third Municipality.

She was no stranger to this part of New Orleans, but she had taken it from a different angle, from the river instead of through the bustle. Like staring at migrating birds through a pond's reflection, everything felt somewhat less familiar. The townhouses were grand, if only slightly less ornate than in the town's center. Broad stucco walls with arched carriageways repeated on most streets. Mule carts laid high with vegetables, casks of beer, whale oil, and wine.

It was midmorning by then and Ady realized she had been walking for a very long time. Her feet were sore in her shoes. A low stone wall surrounded a brick building. She would be thought uncouth to sit, but she rathered that than any more objections from her soles.

Seated there on the stone wall, Ady absorbed the vibrations of the city, the countless feet and hooves clopping along the cobbled streets, the pigeons pecking and cooing about the walk, the carts and carriages trundling, the woof of a steam whistle in the far reaches of her perception. Men, she imagined, building something that ought not to exist. And then, a chuckle of high voices above and behind her. She had taken rest beside a school. A second-story window was open and she heard the faint scraping of chalk against the board. The reply of the young Colored students. Free children, already learning things that she herself—twice as old as they—sometimes struggled to grasp from Mrs. Orsone's brusque instruction. Ady imagined herself up in that room, a giantess among the poppets, nearly as woman as the schoolmarm.

"Excuse me." Ady looked up to recognize the face looking down upon her with a reserved but unmistakable smile. Ady found that du Marche's face evaporated from her memory when he wasn't in front of her. And Ady even had trouble recalling Mrs. Orsone beyond the jeweled rings she wore on several of her fingers. But this woman's face stood out as if she had never turned away from it that first day outside the jeweler's. Her eyes remained with Ady as she went about her work, scrubbing, wringing, and folding. And here she was now, her face glowing in the daylight. The Free Woman.

"Are you well today?" the Free Woman asked.

Ady tried to stand, but the low height of the wall made the attempt arduous. She awkwardly fell back onto her behind. She was not dressed as well as if she were accompanying him, but she was still restrained. Her dress was what she wore for physical errands about town, the fabric coarse, the color dun, the pattern blank. She felt she must have looked as though she was going to purchase a packet of spice or perhaps a basket of oranges. The woman held out a hand, which Ady took.

Ady was surprised by the luck of it. There were many thousands of people in the city, to be sure. The chance of ever encountering anyone a second time was small, a third time minuscule. Ady was stunned to note that the woman, though still regal and composed, was not remarkably older than she. No more than five years separated them, Ady thought. Why then did Ady feel like a schoolchild in her presence?

"Are you?" the woman asked.

"I'm sorry?" said Ady.

"I feared you had heatstroke, doubly fearsome given the cool season, n'est-ce pas?" The woman gestured toward the wall where Ady had been seated.

"Oh, that. I suppose I'm just tired, is all." Ady's face was warm. She could suddenly hear her own voice, her own accent. She felt like a bumpkin. She was recalling all of Mrs. Orsone's lessons about deportment, how to carry oneself. She wanted to be worthy of the woman's attention, even if she wasn't quite sure why. Ady straightened her back and spoke crisply. "It seems I walked somewhat out of my range."

"I see. You can replenish yourself at my establishment. The distance is only two blocks, if you can manage."

"I can," Ady said louder than she intended. She cleared her throat, "I will."

In retrospect, even later that afternoon, Ady would not recall the walk, which was indeed short. But she would remember the strong pleasant scent once they stepped through the doors of the three-storied building: lemons, sawdust, cloves, beer, and warm bread. A wooden sign with a carving of a bird hung over the door. One wouldn't need to be able to read that sign if they knew what they were looking for: an establishment for the free and enslaved alike.

The first thing Ady thought upon entering was that the main room looked different in daylight. More open. Homely. Charming. Light through the large windows gave a good sight of all the people in the area, mostly Colored men, mostly in chaps and spurs. White men and a few men and women of other races sat here and there. And the women were, for the most part, unaccompanied by men. Ady had never witnessed anything like it. She could hardly believe it was the same room from the night of the dance.

Ady couldn't discern what the business was. The talkative woman had called it an "in." In truth, she rarely spent time inside any building other than the one where she lived and worked; she hadn't thought about the fact that he had not once leased her out since her return to the townhouse. She entered higher-order shops with him and visited the general provisioner on her own each fortnight, but the owner met her at the door—she wouldn't know the interior of a clubhouse from a jailhouse.

"I thank you, ma'am." A man with sideburns sat at a table with two others. He raised his beer stein. "The Queen of England doesn't sip this well."

"I appreciate your admiration, Cletus," the Free Woman said. "Just be sure to pay your tab before you swoon this time." The man and his companions chuckled and slapped their knees.

"This . . . business is yours?" Ady asked.

"Yes," the Free Woman said. "I have a partner, but I'm the

proprietor." The woman's eyes narrowed. "My dear girl. You have never been in an inn before."

Ady lowered her face. "I don't—"

"Will you have lemonade or root beer?"

"What?"

"I don't fancy you drinking champagne . . . this early." The woman turned toward the bar. "We also have tea if that's more your pleasure. Myself, I tend toward—"

"Root beer!" The townhouse's larder was well stocked, but he found root beer uncouth and forbade it on the property. Ady had never tasted the beverage. There was something particular about having the choice that widened her eyes.

At the door, several more people entered. Two Colored men, and three whites, one of whom was a younger man and one was a woman. They walked past her to the counter, their guns clinking in their holsters. Their leader, the tallest, who was Colored, pulled a scroll from his satchel. He wasn't the same man from the swamps who had pursued her and Sanite, but Ady didn't need to see the scroll to know what he and the others were there for. They were the same class of men who had transported Sanite and Ady to New Orleans those many years ago. Men like them had broken into the townhouse courtyard and taken Emmanuel. Ady found herself edging toward the corner of the room by the front windows. The woman's eyes followed her as she moved. Ady settled into a partial crouch, her shoulders wedged into the tight angle of the corner of the room.

"Pardon the interruption, all," the leader announced. "I promise you this won't take but a moment, and I'm just passing through from back east."

"Gentlemen," the Free Woman said. "I know what you're about to ask, and I must advise you we do not allow that kind of inquiry in my establishment. You should leave."

"I don't mean to offend, gorgeous madam, but trust we can make it worth your while. We can put all your girls to work."

"This is not a brothel," the Free Woman said through curled lips.

"The reward for the return of this property—"

"Hello, sugars," another woman said. She was standing behind a counter at the back of the room. She wore a tight bodice and a large red flower-covered hat. "Lenore asked you to leave, but you're still braying."

"Last I checked, the law is on my side." The man pointed toward the main door as if the law stood just outside. "We're duly deputized."

"And I have the right to refuse service to whomever I please," the Free Woman, Lenore, said.

"I've never drawn on a lady before, but I might be inclined to make an exception in your case." Ady looked to the door, which was only just a handful of steps away. But she couldn't move her feet. She had slipped down the wall and was now fully seated on the floor, her heartbeat speeding along within her.

The woman behind the counter coughed.

"Um, Smith," said one of the white slavers.

"What is it, Johnny? I'm kind of in the middle of something."

The woman behind the counter leveled a single-barreled shotgun across the wooden countertop. Several of the men around the room coughed one by one: each held a gun or a knife.

"You stallions should depart while you can," the woman behind the counter said.

Lenore gestured around the room. "Unless you would like Alabama and our friends to demonstrate how we make geldings."

Smith frowned at Lenore. He kept eye contact with her for a beat too long. He wiped his mouth with the back of his hand.

"Come on, boys," Smith finally said. "We won't find what we're looking for here." He knocked over a chair as they left.

"Ugh." The woman, Alabama, dropped the shotgun roughly on the counter as soon as they departed. "Has somebody been toying with my scattergun? I swear the only thing I hate more than a rude man is a greasy shooter." She wiped her hands on a towel.

Lenore approached Ady in the corner of the room. Ady presently remembered that she was sitting on the floor, in public.

"Miss Alabama," Lenore said, "would you have a look outside and make sure our unwanted guests have left the area?"

"They better have," Alabama said, walking to the door. "I won't ever let anyone run me away from where I belong ever again." Alabama glared over at Ady. "You better get your behind off them planks, sugar. You ain't a mop."

"Do not mind her. She's merely annoyed at the circumstance." Lenore offered her hand to Ady, but Ady didn't take it. She was too taken by replaying what she had just witnessed. The women had run off slavers! It seemed outlandish, like something out of one of the books she had read. And this Lenore. She was so unflustered by it all!

"Imagine me having to help you up twice in the span of half an hour," she said, and Ady took her hand and allowed

Lenore to help her to her feet, but she continued staring at Lenore.

"Are you all right?" Lenore asked, and instead of answering, Ady threw her arms around Lenore and kissed her cheek.

"Oh," Lenore said, chuckling. "What was that for?"

"You—stood up to them." Ady stumbled on her words, shocked by her own actions and those of Lenore.

Lenore was looking directly at Ady. "I did," Lenore said. "With some help from the others, as you saw."

Ady had the intense sensation that she was being seen, perhaps for the first time in her life. The beating of her heart against the inside of her chest confirmed this feeling. It was too much feeling.

"I should go," Ady said.

"To that man I saw you with the other day?"

Ady touched the handle of the door. "My . . . father may be looking for me." Ady wondered why she called him that. It was a bald-faced lie and the opposite of the truth. But she didn't want to admit she was enslaved.

"Wait," Lenore said. "What's your name?"

"Antoinette," she said, lying again, before exiting the inn and running toward the townhouse.

In the days that followed, Ady continued about her assigned tasks. But something flitted about behind her eyes. She hadn't seen or heard from him in a fortnight. Some nights, as she floated in that fitful domain between the waking world and sleep, she remembered his rough hands. Still, by morning light, she thought not of him, but of Lenore.

That was her name, the woman who owned the inn,

Lenore—a name that lifted and expanded on Ady's tongue. A name covered in the light of the morning sun. Ady's duties took her to the Third Municipality only once a month under usual circumstances. Yet she conjured reasons to walk the distance nearly every day over the course of a week. She would pass the inn or stand at the street corner and watch others pass through the sturdy doors. The sign above the doors swung on two hooks, a gray bird with white fringe painted on wood.

Ady could not explain to herself why she kept coming back without entering. She knew only that she couldn't help herself. One day, a woman in a bright pink dress and a large floral hat approached from down the street carrying a basket. That was Alabama.

When she neared the building, a man brushed past Alabama, causing the items inside to spill. The man didn't slow down even as Ady found herself yelling at him for his rudeness. The man glared at her from a distance. Ady covered her mouth.

"What are you staring at?" Alabama said to the man. "If you see something you don't like, take it up with my maker!" The man continued walking.

Alabama pulled Ady's hands from her mouth. She spoke through clenched teeth. "There's nothing wrong with saying your piece."

Alabama exhaled. She stooped to collect her goods and Ady went over to help.

"I swear the world gets wilder every day," Alabama said. "These were sent to me all the way from Boston."

"Apples?" Ady collected the overturned basket.

"You're pretty smart," Alabama said, sarcastically. "Crab

apples," Alabama added, snatching the basket from Ady's hands and beginning to pick up apples from the ground.

Ady's face warmed. "But you can get apples in just a four-minute walk."

"Not from Boston I can't."

"But they wouldn't last that long."

Alabama stared at Ady for a moment. "You must lead a pretty boring life, given how deep into my affairs you are."

Ady collected an apple that had rolled off to the side. Alabama snatched that from her hand as well. "Give me that." Alabama wiped the apple on her sleeve and opened her mouth to bite it but thought again. "If you're that interested, these are from a beau. He's a bit of fibber."

"A bow?"

"A male friend. They're a gift." Alabama opened the door to the inn.

"Oh," Ady said. "That's kind of him."

"Well," Alabama rubbed the apple on her sleeve, "I was kind to him, too." Alabama went to bite the apple.

"I don't know if you should—"

"Are you trying to tell me what to do with my own fruit?"

"No, it's just that—"

Alabama bit the apple and grimaced.

"—they're sour," Ady said.

"Just like him," Alabama said. "I guess I can put some of this in a cider."

Ady realized that they had entered the inn even though that wasn't her intention. The inn was less busy than when last she was there. In point of fact, it was nearly empty except for an elderly man in a brimless hat who seemed to be dozing off on a bench.

A pair of saloon doors at the back of the room swung open. Lenore entered.

"Antoinette! You've returned," Lenore said. She placed her hands on Ady's arms and kissed her cheeks. Ady's face flushed.

"Lenore, you're a fortunate one." Alabama tapped Ady. "Antoinette says that she's looking for work."

"But I—" Ady said.

"She has good apple-picking hands," Alabama said. "A body can hardly keep an apple to herself with her around." Alabama shoved the basket into Ady's hands.

"Is that so?" Lenore asked. "Fine. We'll bring her in as a scullery at half rate." Lenore turned her attention to Ady. "If we find your work satisfactory, then, after a sufficient time, you'll get the full rate with back pay. Does that sound fair?"

"Uh."

"I swear the cat has her tongue, teeth, and brain," Alabama said. "You should put her by the window as a mannequin. No one will know the difference."

"Be kind, Alabama," Lenore said. "Can't you tell the young lady is nervous?"

Ady's palms were sweaty and her forehead felt wet. Why was this Alabama so intent on teasing her? Neither of them seemed much older than she, and Ady was taller than both of them.

"Your sign doesn't have any words on it," Ady said. "What is this place called?"

"You can read?" Alabama asked.

"Yes," Ady said. "Can't you?"

Alabama's face twitched. "I've been here since the start, sugar. Lenore wanted to name it something silly, and she got her way because it's her party."

Lenore furrowed her brow at Alabama. "Welcome to the Mockingbird Inn. New Orleans's finest sleeping, dining, and leisure quarters for all people of good intentions."

"It's a real nice place," Ady said just as the basket slipped from her sweaty fingers, sending apples across the plank floor. Alabama rolled her eyes and stalked off.

Over the next few days, shuttling between the townhouse and the Mockingbird, Ady considered the situation she found herself in. He was often away, and it wasn't that she couldn't work for others, but she hadn't gotten permission. He alone had the legal right to decide the particulars of where she went, and any earned remuneration was to go to him. In theory, she could save money in hopes of buying her freedom, but he'd ask where the money came from, Lord knows he didn't give her any, and if Sanite had some, it was taken after she died; besides, Ady didn't believe he'd ever let her go. Still, she was astounded by these women. Their confidence and self-possession. Their vibrancy resonated within her. She felt joy, even, and for the first time decided she deserved to indulge in that. Though it made no sense for her to accept the work, this opportunity was far too delicious to reject.

The Mockingbird Inn was a perpetual motion machine. Downstairs were the main hall and draught room where new arrivals negotiated their stay and were served whatever food and drink might be available. An office that Lenore and Alabama used was down the first-floor hallway, behind the counter. The hallway led to a courtyard with a kitchen and three-stall outhouse. The second and third floors were lodging rooms, four per level.

On the first day, Ady rapidly cleaned the townhouse and lit out across town. She arrived at the Mockingbird Inn with a scarf wrapped around her head and an apron around her body. Some women were walking out when Ady entered. But she didn't see Lenore or Alabama, so she started sweeping the stairs, humming softly.

"Hello there." It was Lenore. "Where are you going so early?"

Ady looked toward the front windows. Sunlight was just breaking down the dusty street, painting the surface gold. Her ears were warm, little daybreak lanterns. "I thought I'd get started on the rooms after this."

"I appreciate your eagerness, but Mrs. Gaines attends to the rooms."

"Oh. So, I won't be cleaning?"

"I didn't say that. You will be, but not so much. Tell me. Are you good with people?"

"Good with people?"

"You strike me as someone skilled in the art of hospitality."

"Well, I—"

"I'd like you to be our hummingbird."

"Hummingbird?"

"Our helper. There are many tasks to be done here in the lobby. Yes, we have to keep it clean and organized. But someone has to watch the desk at all times. And marshal the kitchen activities. And ensure that the guests upstairs are well taken care of. Alabama tries to do too much on her own, and I often have other concerns around the district to attend to."

"Does Alabama have a bird name?"

"The Dove of Peace," Lenore said.

Ady recalled Alabama leveling that long gun over the counter at the slavers. Ady couldn't stifle a laugh. "Her?"

Lenore raised an eyebrow. When Lenore walked away, Ady continued sweeping. "Dove of Peace," she chuckled to herself.

Ady quickly became acquainted with the many people of the Mockingbird. There was Courtland, the cook, who specialized in Creole stews; Mrs. Gaines, a large woman who sometimes brought her young daughter, Greta, with her to clean the rooms; Mr. Houser, the elderly man, who kept a room by the second-floor stairwell—he only left the building for evening constitutionals; and a British girl, younger than Ady, who ran errands. Her name was Molly. Several young men worked as stockers, including a fine-featured Negro who seemed also smitten by Lenore.

People came in at all hours of the day and night. From Mississippi, Texas, and Georgia, but also Virginia, New York, and Holland. Ady was not allowed in any of the hotels farther north than Elysian Fields. Nor would Lenore have been, which Ady found ironic considering she owned her own place of lodging. But everyone was allowed in the Mockingbird.

Sometimes she read his newspaper that hung on a wooden bar in the townhouse parlor. *The Picayune* had articles every now and then about the proper establishment of slavery, its God-given place in the world of man, the separateness of Coloreds from whites being a necessary part of the good maintenance of society. They said riots would break out if the Northerners had their way. But the Mockingbird was in a constant state of exchange, and Ady could no more imagine a riot breaking out there than Ursuline nuns running naked along the riverfront.

There were other interesting reports in the newspaper, too. The almanac column anticipated crop yields upstate. And the occasional crime tale appeared. A planter had gone missing just the other week, his abode seemingly untouched except for missing bushels of crops an associate claimed he had come to town with.

One afternoon, Ady came upon Alabama standing atop a chair. She held gold bunting but was having trouble hanging it on account of her lack of stature.

"What are you doing?" Ady asked.

"I'm minding my p's and q's," Alabama said. She wobbled on the chair and nearly fell. Ady caught her by the arm. Alabama shrugged her off and jumped down.

"Did I do something to you?" Ady asked.

"You couldn't do anything to me if you tried," Alabama shot back.

"Well, why don't you like me?" Ady asked.

"Who said I didn't like you?" Alabama asked. She sighed and twisted the bunting. "Fine. You're so timid. It makes me nervous, sugar. You need to have some iron in your spine if you're going to survive at all."

Ady frowned, recalling crawling through the mud of the swamp on hands and knees as hungry animals, including men, circled in the bush around her. "I'm not so frail, don't you know?"

"You don't have to prove anything to me, but I saw you when those slavers were up in this place. There's nothing wrong with being afraid when something like that happens, but you can't let people make you forget you're a person." Alabama handed the bunting to Ady. "Go ahead and put that up. You're tall as a giraffe."

Ady climbed onto the chair.

"See, that's what I mean!" Alabama said. "You're too ready to jump when people tell you."

Lenore entered. "What are you two doing?"

"We're working very hard, Miss Lenore, to be ready for tonight's festivities," Alabama said, sweetly. "Our hummingbird was just showing me the correct way to decorate."

Ady climbed down and gave the bunting back to Alabama.

"I think she's much better at it than I am," Ady said, and left them both.

That night, the Mockingbird's hall was full of people. Lenore had hired additional staff to serve the crowd, and musicians played. There was a piano in the corner of the room that Ady had only absentmindedly noticed before. A man played it, accompanied by a fiddler and a woman who played banjo. The crowd stomped their feet to melodies Ady had heard in Congo Square and at the slave labor camp also known as the plantation. During the fourth or fifth song, Alabama, in full skirts, danced, kicking her legs high, her floral hat flashing across the room. This was how the inn had looked the night he brought her. The improvement now was that he was not present.

Lenore touched Ady's arm and shouted over the rumbling music, "I'll need your assistance in a moment, Miss Antoinette." Ady gritted her teeth at the sound of the false name she had given. Lenore pulled Ady toward the musicians. Ady realized Lenore meant for her to sing.

"I can't," Ady said.

"Now, there. Courage! I'm just a mean singer myself. No one will judge you. But I've heard your voice. It's very sweet!" Had Ady been singing in Lenore's presence? She didn't remember doing so. She realized that she hadn't intentionally sung, even for herself, since her mother died. Lenore gave a signal to the musicians who started into what sounded like "Oh, Susanna."

"No, Lenore, I couldn't—I don't know the words," Ady said.

"Just listen to the verse and repeat after me." Lenore sang the verse and led the audience in clapping along. But when the verse came back around, Ady merely clapped along as well. She was wet about the eyes. When she became aware of the sensation, she quickened toward the stairs.

"Antoinette!" Lenore said. But Ady climbed the stairs. Kindly Old Mr. Houser was standing by his door, just back from his nightly walk. He held his hat in his hands.

"Evening, ma'am. I hope you're well tonight. Say, you aren't upset over a fellow, are you? I'm old, but I still have a fist if'n you need it for him."

"Thank you," Ady said. "I'm just having one of those nights."

"It must be going around," he said. "I heard a mess upstairs just now. Some other person having a bad night, I figuring."

Ady gave Mr. Houser a small smile and climbed the stairs to find some privacy on the third floor. She checked a vacant room to ensure it was clean but kept wandering. She then walked to the room on the east end of the building, when she heard voices in disarray. Although her mind told her not to intervene, her hand opened the door.

Alabama was in the room. Her dress was ripped and her face bruised. A large white man in his cotton underclothes stood across from her. He lunged at Alabama. They fell to the floor. The man was atop Alabama and held her by the arms. Her kicking motion had no effect.

"I go for a bath and you go through my belongings!" he said. "I'll teach you some manners and leave you for the dogs."

Ady's spine was pressed against the wall. She was perfectly still. Unable to budge. Breathless.

"Girl," Alabama said, "help me!" The man didn't seem to notice her words or that Ady was even in the room. He pulled at Alabama, ripping her dress.

Heat coursed through Ady's veins. The sight of the man over Alabama had dislodged her. With speed beyond thought, she grabbed the chamber pot and struck the man in the head. He collapsed to the floor, and Ady hit him again. And again. The pot flew away, but she continued using her hands. A thought pulsed through her. A wordless thought in the color of *He will pay*. She was vaguely aware of being pulled bodily from the man.

"Miss Antoinette, stop!" Alabama said. But Ady struck him again.

"Hummingbird!" Alabama cried out, and at that Ady stopped and fell to the floor. Alabama slumped onto her. The two women sat breathing heavily. Ady went to touch Alabama's face. But blood was under her own fingernails. She withheld her hand. Her fingers fairly throbbed.

"What did I do?" Ady said.

"You saved my life."

"Is he— Did I—"

"I think he's done for this world," Alabama said.

"No," Ady said. "That can't be right." She winced.

Alabama pulled Ady in for a hug. "Shhh. It's all right."

"What do we do now?"

Alabama climbed to her feet. "I'll go fetch the lady of the house. She'll sort it."

"No!" But Alabama left the room. In addition to the body, the man's possessions were scattered across the room as though by a gust. A pen over here. A small wooden box with an ivory lid there. Drops of blood. Ady wondered what Lenore would think of her when she saw what she had done. Lenore would be disgusted. She would banish Ady from the inn. It dawned on Ady how much her time with these women had come to mean to her. She needed to stop Lenore from finding out, but it was too late. Alabama returned shortly thereafter with Lenore, who closed the door.

"Sweet Lord." Lenore covered her mouth. "The pair of you really did a number on him."

"Not the pair of us," Alabama said. "I just watched."

Ady stood. She noticed a small pool of blood that had formed near the man's head.

"I'm so sorry," Ady said. "He was on Alabama. I— I couldn't let him."

Lenore smiled. "Are you apologizing? Don't."

"We have to tell her," Alabama said.

"Tell me what?" Ady asked.

"No, it's far too dangerous."

"Yeah," Alabama said. "Dangerous for them. Besides, if you ain't noticed, she's already in. That's Thomas Barker lying dead on your floor!"

Lenore looked on at the man, in thought. Her eyes darted around the room.

"All right, fine," Lenore said. "Don't yell." She turned toward Ady and said, "Antoinette, my dear. Would you please have a seat at the washbasin?" Ady did as she was told, and Alabama began to straighten the room, collecting the man's things in his bag, spilling water across the blood. Lenore found a washcloth and took Ady's hand gently. Ady felt like someone had smashed her knuckles with a hammer. But she withheld any expression of pain. She didn't want Lenore to think her touch gave her displeasure.

"Am I hurting you, love?" Lenore asked.

Ady shook her head.

"This will sound rather fanciful," Lenore said, "but it's true. That man is—"

"Was," Alabama said from across the room.

"That man *was* a spy. And we"—Lenore motioned to Alabama and then to herself—"we are spies as well."

Lenore stopped wiping Ady's hand and dabbed ointment onto her bruised knuckles. She wrapped Ady's hand in cloth, talking the whole time. Lenore explained that the man on the floor was a Northerner who was sympathetic to the expansion of slavery into the western territories. He had been in town meeting with like-minded men. There were women like them across the nation—some enslaved and some free—who kept watch and passed on information to their sisters. This had been their work for generations.

"Spies for who?" Ady asked, sounding incredulous but not knowing who else they could belong to. "The president?"

"The man in Washington don't even know we exist, sugar," Alabama said. "I prefer it that way myself. I don't trust a one of them."

"This is about our power to help," Lenore said. "If a person needs safe harbor, we provide it. If they must run, we provision them."

Alabama held up the chamber pot. "And if a man needs an attitude adjustment—"

"Alabama, please," Lenore said.

"But if you have all this help, why are you here?" Ady asked.

"I don't understand," Lenore said.

Ady stood up. "You're telling me that you have those connections. You could have run from this city and never looked back."

"This is my home," Alabama said. "I ain't trying to flee anywhere."

"Yes," Lenore said. "And besides. If we weren't doing this work, the Coloreds of this community would suffer even more than they already do. Someone has to look out for them. For us. There are women in Houston, Jackson, Memphis, Atlanta, and beyond who feel the same way."

Ady sat down.

"Alabama?" Lenore asked.

"Yes, ma'am."

"How tall do you think the gentleman was?"

"He only had a few inches on me, so five and a quarter."

"And how big is that rug?"

"Six by ten," Alabama said. "I would know. I was the one who bought it at the market.

"Then we have our method."

"Shame to lose a good floor covering."

"Alabama!" Ady said.

"What?" Alabama said. "It is."

The women cleaned the blood from the floor and wrapped

the man's body in bedsheets. Then they coiled all of it in the rug and hoisted the assemblage onto their shoulders.

"Daggum this is heavy," Alabama said from the front, as they descended the back staircase.

"No need to state the obvious," Lenore said. She was in the middle. Ady was at the back because she was the tallest.

"We should have tossed this in the fireplace," Alabama said.

"Hush," Lenore said. Soon they deposited the rug in the narrow alley next to the outhouses. Alabama stooped to catch her breath.

Lenore dusted her hands. "I have just the man to remove that from the premises."

"What do you want me to do?" Ady asked.

"My dear." Lenore took Ady's hand. "I would like you to go home, rest, and forget that this ever happened."

Ady nodded, thinking she should get to the townhouse. It was not as late as Ady imagined. The sky was dark purple to the west. She walked down Good Children Street in the direction of the townhouse. Her mind was clouded by the events of the evening. She had killed a white man. Was there a hell for that? Or had she directed herself onto a new path? And Lenore and Alabama were spies, Colored women spies! She had read of double agents in the Revolutionary War who assisted the rebellious colonists against the British. There was even a short note about an unnamed woman spy. But that was sixty or more years prior. Ancient history. Practically fable. She had told Mrs. Orsone as much.

Still walking down Good Children Street, she saw a commotion. People were gathered in a partial circle and whooping as if wagering on fighting cocks. She did not want to approach the rabble, so she instead stepped onto the walk, which allowed for a better view. Two men were at work in the center. They wore suspenders for baggy pants like railmen. One of them held a cane that he was drawing down toward the ground. Moments passed before the view was clear enough for Ady to see that the cane was striking a third man, dressed in a black frock.

"That's enough, mate," one of the attackers said, grabbing the other's arm. "He's got his instruction."

"That'll learn him to come around here with that tripe." The second man threw down the cane and spat. The crowd was dispersing even before the man turned away. Ady was turning away herself when she heard the priest speak.

"Mercy," he said. Ady crossed into the street, aware that she was being watched. The priest was older, but not quite elderly. A bill calling for abolition lay half-crumpled on the cobblestones. She had seen men fight in the streets over the topic, had seen guns drawn. She found those confrontations amusing since none of the belligerents on either side knew what it felt like to be enslaved. Blood streamed down the side of this man's face, which made her nauseous. He was lucky to be alive. He would only need the gashes on his head cleaned and salved, assuming he had no broken bones.

"You trying to die, Father?" she asked.

"Aye, if that's to be the way," he said. She placed a hand under his arm and braced him to his feet. "Thank you. Perhaps I'm not the only one courting death today." The priest glanced over his shoulder.

"They'll just think you own me."

"What a disgusting thought, ma'am."

"Don't call me that. Might get them started again." She

guided him up the street. Soon they came to the townhouse. She opened the carriageway door and brought him through, then up the stairs. He was unsteady on his feet, so it was a slow climb. Inside, she sat him on the divan and went to collect water from the cistern. When she returned he was lying across the divan.

"I'm down from Massachusetts, Brookline to be exact. I'm expected to meet with peers from the archdiocese at first light. Those fools are unwilling to join our call for an encyclical against human bondage."

"Waving around that paper wasn't wise."

"I wasn't waving it. That goon must have seen it in my duffel. Where is my duffel?"

"I didn't see one."

"It doesn't matter. All that matters is that we end slavery. What's that face you're making at me?"

The nature of the situation was suddenly upon her. She had brought a stranger into the townhouse, a white man. And now this man was asking her opinions. Out on the streets, she was only rarely addressed by them and, rarer still, replied. She had no practice at it beyond her time with du Marche and no use for it generally, now that she considered the matter. Still, he had asked her a question.

"Why does that matter to you?"

"People are meant to be free. Your people are creations of God just like the rest of us. And frankly, if we don't sort this out, I fear another war ere long."

The door from the courtyard swung open. It was him, who Ady realized at that very second she had not seen for nearly a month. He stomped past them and went into the bathroom. He came back out. There was something different in his affect that she could not quite place. He was agitated and disheveled. The smell of beer caught her nose. She saw that he was wearing a gray uniform with a double-breasted top.

"The water pitcher, girl," he said. "Where is it?"

She had placed it on the floor by the divan, not having had a chance to attend to the man's wounds. Du Marche followed her eyes. He picked up the pitcher and took it into the bedroom. She heard him splashing his face with water from the bowl. He returned again.

"I'm sorry to invade your abode, good sir," the priest said.

"Think nothing of it. Even if you are a papist." He handed the pitcher to the priest, who drank from it. "Though, you are toeing the line with your freedom for the slaves talk. Though I imagine you paid enough of the price for today. You foreign priests should know better. I encountered one of your party this morning."

Ady wondered then whether the men were acquainted but couldn't pursue the thought before he barked another order.

"Fetch a jug of ale. Those Comus revelers threw quite an inaugural. But their mead was mud." When Ady returned with fresh water and ale, the men to her surprise were laughing and already smoking cigars.

"Oh heavens no," the priest said. "While it is true that our dark siblings should be unshackled, I do not oppose allowing new states to democratically decide whether slavery is correct for them. And I certainly don't advocate for giving darkies the voting franchise. Could you imagine what would happen if they decided who ran the country?"

Du Marche exhaled. "I wager we would have chimpanzees in the Senate before long."

"You mean we don't already?" the priest said. They laughed.

Du Marche stared at Ady. "Don't let this man of cloth die in my house. See to him." Ady wished to leave the room, to get out of their earshot. The priest could take care of himself. Of course, that wasn't an option, and she hesitated a moment too long. Du Marche sighed loudly.

The priest motioned for the pitcher Ady was holding. When she lowered it, du Marche took the rag from her hand and dipped the rag into the spout. He shook out the rag and applied it to the priest's temple.

"For Pete's sake, girl," du Marche said, "hold it fast." Ady pressed her hand to the priest's head. He moaned slightly and spoke.

"You don't seem cross that an abolitionist such as myself has spilled blood on your floor en route to a conference on the matter."

"Let the best men win, I say," du Marche said.

"Eh?"

"Your ilk would have the legislatures of our land free people like her, which would destroy our way of life and no doubt the future of the nation. My brothers see a different future. If our wishes prevail, the Southern way—the way of honest dominion and commerce—will run down to the lowest tip of old Mexico and in a circle across the Caribbean. Our rights will be expanded internationally rather than curtailed on this continent."

"I say that is a wretched plan."

"That is your opinion, but I'm already gathering men to the cause. This battle of futures has been tossing back and forth from the time when Old Hickory was in curls. My point is that one philosophy must win. Maybe not the release of our lessers that you plead for. Or the golden circle of freedom I might expect. We'll talk and talk. But I'd bet my lands that this ends with a clashing of the sword. That's when the better man will take the day."

Ady stepped outside and into the courtyard. Even in just the last half hour, the temperature had plummeted. The chill of February. She could have merely gone into her quarters. They would call her for orders. Instead, she wrapped her arms around herself and descended the stairs to the ground floor. She walked to the carriage entrance gate and leaned forward against the iron bars. It was late evening, and Ady exhaled. She had done her daily work in the townhouse that morning and spent most of the day at the Mockingbird. Her body ached, and her encounter with Alabama's attacker already felt so distant. Had it really just happened?

She heard the men upstairs laughing. A shiver ran down her back, and she realized that she was barefoot. When had she removed her shoes? The stone beneath her feet was cold and damp. All those things he had said upstairs just then. Absently, Ady realized that he had made similar statements in the past, but she rarely paid him any mind. Yet it struck her now that she was in possession of information most people were unaware of. He had been under her nose all the while preparing his schemes. Now she had someone to relay her knowledge to. Lenore would be pleased. Ady would make herself useful to the cause.

A horn began playing nearby. Beyond the gate, she heard heavy steps. A bugler in plain clothes passed first, followed by a small number of uniformed men with rifles on their shoulders. They couldn't have been slavers, she thought, but trained militia. A crowd was trailing in the wake of the militiamen. Behind her, new noises caught her attention.

Du Marche and the priest appeared at the far end of the carriageway and approached the entrance.

"See, Clarence," du Marche said. His uniform matched theirs. "These are the men I spoke of. True defenders of the South, Grand Knights of the Golden Circle."

"Sounds like a good bit of chaos," the priest said.

"One man's chaos is another man's Heaven. You may wage a war of words. But we'll use the rifle. Which do you reckon will win?"

That night, the priest went on his way. Ady wouldn't return to the Mockingbird for several days, when du Marche took his leave again. The day he left, she followed his carriage a good distance toward the edge of the city. When she was satisfied that he wouldn't turn around, she walked in the direction of the inn.

"Did you lose your way?" Lenore asked as Ady walked in. Ady hesitated. She rubbed her foot on the floor.

"No, ma'am." Ady called her ma'am that way sometimes. She felt Lenore deserved respect that perhaps she didn't get enough of.

One of the young men who worked in the inn walked over to ask Lenore a question. But she barked at him. "Not now, Darrow!" The young man frowned and stormed off. He slammed the door to the courtyard on his way out. Lenore turned her attention back to Ady.

"It's no mean feat running this establishment. Employees

often disappear as quickly as they come on. Some of them are shiftless and on no account by nature. Others are unreliable due to circumstance. People often assume that someone else is the proprietor. Some older gentleman with a curled mustache. Not an unmarried woman who just turned twenty. The Mockingbird cannot succeed if you're not willing to be accountable." Lenore stopped. Ady's face felt as though the sun were shining on it at full force. She had let Lenore down, which suddenly seemed the greatest possible betrayal.

Lenore inhaled and turned away. "I appreciate you hearing my thoughts on the matter. I must tend to the books. You'll assist Alabama." She went into the office and closed the door solidly.

Ady glanced at Alabama. Alabama smirked and picked up a wooden tray.

"Oh, don't cry and don't mind her none. She gets extra proper when she's worried."

"I'm not crying!" Ady said more loudly than she anticipated. She readjusted, "I was surprised. I didn't know she could be that way."

"She was terrified that a slaver carried you off."

Ady inhaled sharply, taking in the thought. She assumed that Lenore might be cross at her unexplained absence, but she didn't think the woman *cared* about her, at least not deep enough to worry over her. Ady realized that she didn't think anyone cared about her. Not since her mother died.

"Our friend's disappearance the other day"—Alabama pointed upstairs—"has the local gunslingers in a tizzy. But never you mind that. Of course, she imagines all of us will get carried off. Me, especially."

"Why you?"

"Listen, I'm sorry for how I was treating you before. I guess I was jealous."

"Jealous of me?"

"I'm a runaway. When I see someone like yourself who is free but shy as a kitten, I get mad. Like you don't know who you are. There's pride in freedom. And you should own that pride."

"But I—I," Ady said. Ady couldn't take Alabama believing that she was free, but Alabama kept talking.

"I was on a plantation up 'round Natchez. My folks didn't want to leave, but I ran as soon as I could hold my breath underwater for six minutes."

"Six minutes!" Ady said.

Alabama sat on a chair by one of the tables, the tray on her lap.

"Lenore says I tell this story too much, but it's true and worth telling, if you ask me. My brothers and me played hide-and-go-seek in the wood just off the plantation. They couldn't find me because I was small enough to crawl into a hollowed-out tree trunk or get under a big pile of leaves. When you don't breathe, people are less likely to know a person is there, I figured. So they never caught me. And when I saw I could hope my breath in the water, that's when I knew what to do. Those overseers were always catching runaways who panicked in rivers and splashed about. But I thought if I ever saw them coming, I could just stay under 'cause they ain't have much patience anyways, you know?"

"Hope your breath."

"What's that?" Alabama asked.

"You said 'hope your breath.'"

"Oh. Well, it's the same thing, ain't it?"

"It is." Ady smiled.

Ady had become quite good at her work for Lenore at the Mockingbird. She believed that if she impressed Lenore enough, then Lenore would be happy to tell her everything about the spy network and let her help. Ady had taken to arising before the roosters crowed to tend to the townhouse. Then she trekked to the inn. There was an omnibus line in that direction that she avoided. While there was no law against Coloreds riding, she saw the looks that some riders gave her as the mules snorted by, their harnesses and chains tinkling, their hooves clopping. As it stood, Ady mastered the trip in just over twenty minutes on foot.

At the inn, she found the clientele she served charming. Lenore's rules and the general appearance of the establishment seemed to filter out troublemakers. The rules were painted on a sign just outside the front door: No spitting, no cussing, no violence, and no thieving. The men and women who sought to rest there weren't the upper crust by any means, but they were generally respectful. That seemed to be the larger meaning of all the rules: to act toward others with respect.

Ady served the occasional meal. She took in guests. Locked their belongings in the large iron safe in the office. She communicated to Lenore or Alabama on behalf of the other staff whatever pressing needs they had.

But her favorite work involved the guest roll. It was kept under the counter, the one Alabama had defended when the slavers came. There was no value in the guest roll, for the pages were no more than a list of names, the amounts they paid, the places they came from, and the rooms they claimed. Still, it was not long after she had been trained on the workings of those pages that she received her first compliment.

"You write like one of them French girls," Alabama said as Ady completed an entry on a warm spring day. "So pretty. Oh la la!" Ady laughed and turned toward Alabama. "What it is?" Alabama asked.

Ady's face was warm and she knew that tears were again in the corners of her eyes. What was it about the inn that pulled her feelings onto the surface of her skin? She wasn't that way anywhere else. Not at the townhouse. Not at the slave labor camps also called plantations. Not even with her mother in the swamps. Inside the four walls of the inn, she felt like a turtle without its shell. But shockingly, she felt all right with that. She wasn't sure how to respond to Alabama's compliment because Ady knew the compliment came from a deeply personal place within her. Yes, a simple thank you would suffice. But that didn't feel adequate. Mrs. Orsone made laudatory comments when Ady was proceeding through whatever lesson was being taught. But there was something mechanical and necessary in that transaction. And he made complimentary statements about her when guests visited him seeking political favors. Or in the after times, when his belly was full of brandy and his hands were warm as half-chewed pork. But she did not accept his statements. She said thank you, but that was merely her mouth providing the required response.

Alabama wasn't required to say anything, and she wasn't trying to curry favor. It was quite the opposite. Ady wanted to impress Lenore and Alabama and all the other denizens of the Mockingbird. The guests received room and board at a rate of

$2 per week. And Ady received that same compensation for six days of work. She earned that money from all her duties, including writing legibly in the guest roll. To be thanked for using her own skills. It was too much for her to properly parse. Ady nodded at Alabama and continued writing.

Molly, the white girl, who was younger than Ady, was working alongside her today. Molly was spritely with scruffy brown hair and a winding accent that sometimes made it difficult for Ady to understand her. Molly often ran messages through the inn or handled simple tasks of procurement from local vendors. That afternoon, Ady noticed Molly giggling. She had been giddy most of the morning and giggled more whenever Ady passed by. Ady entered the work room to hand over a guest fee to Alabama, and as she returned back to the main room, she heard Lenore behind her. Ady turned back to Lenore. Lenore's brown skin was a darker shade, reddened by blush. She was holding back a laugh.

"What is it?"

Lenore pointed toward Ady's midsection, but Ady saw nothing out of the ordinary on her dress. Lenore made a motion with her finger for Ady to turn around. Ady did so, and as she peered behind her own body, feeling like a mutt chasing its own tail, she saw there was a tail. A furry tail pinned to the back of her dress. Ady turned to Lenore to apologize. Lenore's mouth was covered, and she continued to chuckle. But Ady noticed she was looking behind toward the door. Molly stood there. Her giggle was a full belly laugh.

Ady's mouth fell out.

"Happy tail day!" Molly said. Ady reached for her, but the girl scampered away.

"What's all this crashing around here?" Alabama asked, but

she saw the tail on Ady's derriere and burst out laughing. Ady glanced back and forth.

"I don't understand," Ady said. Lenore and Alabama shared a look.

"It's April Fools' Day."

"I—"

"My dear, you've never been pranked?"

"I think our Molly favors you."

"She does this to people she favors?"

"You ought to see what she does to the ones she don't," Alabama said. The front door of the inn opened and two men entered with a crate. "No, no, you goons!" Alabama shouted. "How many times do we have to tell you deliveries come through the alley?" She stormed off toward the men.

"I want to be like you and Alabama," Ady said.

"Is that so?" Lenore said. "As you can see, it takes effort and some good fortune to run an establishment like the Mockingbird, but with time you could do well in the business."

"No, Lenore." Ady grabbed Lenore's arm. "I want to be a spy, like you." Lenore's eyes went wide.

"Not out here," Lenore said. She looked around the room, then back to her office. The two walked into the chamber, as Ady closed the door.

Lenore raised her chin and stared down her nose at Ady. "What we do is not a game for children."

"I just want to help. Everything that happens in this city— I feel like I'm just watching it all. I want to do some good."

"Antoinette," Lenore said. "All of us have to mature quickly to survive. But you're just a young woman, a child. What happened to you the other night was a terrible accident. I fault myself for allowing you to be in such a position."

"Child!" Ady said. "Child." Ady thought of her mother, the man who owned her, the many times she had been mishandled. That wasn't the life of a child. She'd never been granted that pleasure.

"Lenore, you're only a few years older than me. You talk about people underestimating you because you're young too. How is this any different?"

"It is dangerous, Antoinette! People have died. And not just men like the one upstairs. Women have died. Or worse."

Ady pulled up the bottom of her dress so that she could reach her lower leg.

"What are you doing?"

Ady removed the folded sheet of paper she had tied to her shin with twine. "Have a look at this." Lenore put on her glasses and reviewed the sheet, mumbling to herself.

"Rifles. Bullets," she said. "This is a ledger for the purchase of war weaponry."

Ady sat on the front of Lenore's desk. "It's from last month. That note at the bottom says there are more shipments to come. And men will follow. Militiamen."

"I'm not entirely unfamiliar with some of this information. How do you know about this?"

"I'm not at liberty to say." Telling Lenore the truth would mean telling her who Ady really was, her circumstances. Ady wasn't ready for that—not yet.

Lenore shook her head. "I'm sorry, but I don't want you to become any more entangled than you already are. And don't sit on my desk, please."

Ady stood and walked to the door.

"Are you a churchgoer?" Lenore asked.

"I can't say I am."

"Why not?"

Ady said nothing. She had been to church regularly when she was small. She remembered from the slave labor camp also called Constancia, the little wooden tabernacle deep in the woods where the others gathered. She recalled the swell of voices, that feeling in the air itself that some force was moving among them. The old women rocking on the rough-hewn pews. The men stomping their feet. All clapping hands. It seemed so long ago. Like a memory not from her own life. He had caused them to attend church in town on rare occasions, if they could be said to have attended. He went to the front and seated himself. Sanite and Ady stood against the back wall where other Coloreds waited for their owners to partake in fellowship after the service. He rarely attended now.

"Well, this Sunday is Easter Sunday. I'd like you to join us."

Ady said nothing. Could she dare to go?

"St. Moritz." She knew the church. It was only a few blocks away. But she also knew that he would be back by then. He had written her a letter telling her so, with a list of things he needed readied. He'd return on Sunday, if not before then.

"I can't."

"Why on earth not?"

Ady lowered her head.

"Well," Lenore said. "You should come if you can. We'll have a feast of ham, turkey, and pork loin at my home after the service. Alabama will be there, and so will a few of our patrons like Mr. Houser."

Ady raised her head.

"What is it?" Lenore asked.

"What do I wear to Easter?" Of course, Ady had been to church with him, but those visits tended to occur after nights she preferred not to remember. He used to bring his family to town for high holy days, but that had stopped in recent years.

"People tend to wear white, my dear," Lenore said.

Ady knew she wouldn't be able to be with them on Sunday, but any chance of hope was lost when, back in her quarters, she saw that he had given her instructions for which goods to buy to restock the townhouse. Most of the provisions were standard, but the quantities were larger, which meant he was bringing others with him. Worse still, the request for licorice meant he was bringing his son, Johnny. It had been some years since Ady had seen the boy, either at the townhouse or during her time at the plantation. She didn't know what his inclusion might mean.

Most nights, she saw Lenore in her dreams, moving smoke-like and fleeting. When Ady awoke, her own hand still between her legs, she could practically taste Lenore's skin. But that night Ady was too frustrated to close her eyes. She lay on her pallet, muttering. How dare Lenore say that she was too young to help them fight the slavers! Ady had probably encountered far more slavers in her lifetime than Lenore. Ady's stomach growled. She realized that she hadn't eaten that day. She wasn't one to eat very much, but dreams of Lenore's family table circled her mind. She envisioned a great oak table as wide as the room she slept in and atop the table the most succulent foods anyone could possibly prepare. Knives ripping into leg of lamb, tongs grabbing braised potatoes, spoons cupping figgy pudding. She didn't even like lamb or pudding! She grabbed her face and rolled off the pallet.

Out on the courtyard balcony, she tilted her head back. Dozens of stars slipped across the velvet of the sky. The food meant nothing to her. Those hands grabbing at the food interested her. She could hardly fix in her mind what Lenore's family might be like. Sanite had been the entirety of her own. Her father—her true father—was only stories, incomplete ones. And Emmanuel— What had Ady been allowed to know of families? Just as often as she saw families together, she heard stories of whole families being sold off. The only family she had interacted with across time was his. Even if the mother and youngest daughter of the house were now dead. Senior and junior had each other and their homes across the state, and a community of folks at their ready.

Ady went back into her quarters and dug in the wooden box that held all her clothing. She had two other dresses. One of burlap she wore for her most difficult work, scouring the townhouse floors, carrying root vegetables back from the market, chopping meat for the family. The second dress was much like the one she wore now. Simple, durable cotton dyed brown. If she were going to St. Moritz, she couldn't wear either one. She turned toward the townhouse. The dresses he bought her were in there hanging inside the tall chifforobe. She was only allowed to wear them when she accompanied him around town, when he handed her one. All three dresses only touched her skin with his permission. None were white. One was a mild blue with cornflowers along the neckline. Another was green with a white panel at the front. The last was the one he most often told her to wear. It was the color of pink roses at dawn with an elegant trim, ruffled sleeves, and a crimped upper section. She held the pink one up, and as soon as she did so she decided she would go and this was what she would wear.

On Easter Sunday, Ady tortured herself, pacing with indecision. He was an early riser, and it was possible he would show up before the sun was fully risen with his son and their guests. She was already dressed for the service—the pink rose dress, white cloth pinned to her hair, and the boots she always wore, she didn't dare wear the fine calico shoes. If she had to run, they wouldn't allow it. And they were delicate. With him there were always carriage rides. On her own, the cobblestones of town and dirt of the Third Municipality would do their work. She would never be able to explain.

After the meal, she would leave Lenore's family no matter the situation as soon as possible. She would arrive back in the townhouse in time to stow the dress and make sure that everything was in order. Did she believe she could do this? As she stepped deliberately out of the courtyard and closed the gate behind her, she thought she saw something out of the corner of her eye, but when she looked back for it, she saw nothing. Her hand was shaking.

At St. Moritz, Ady waited outside, standing near the bottom of the steps. The morning was cool but not chilly. It would be the type of day that increased in brightness but not heat. She watched the other patrons show up. People of such variety she had to stop herself from ogling. The Free Creoles were always a sight, but their ordinary appearances were nothing compared to now. The men wore silk top hats and the women dresses in the colors of spring flowers, their hair architectural in complexity, wrapped in tignons of serene pinks, oranges, and yellows.

Ady saw Lenore walking up the street in a magnificent long white dress with matching hat. She carried a parasol and held the arm of a well-made older man. Several others, including Alabama and Mr. Houser, followed behind. It hadn't occurred to Ady to go to her house and meet them there. She was disappointed that she hadn't had the opportunity to be with them, if for no other reason than to see Lenore emerge in that dress.

"Antoinette! You're here!" Lenore said, coming straight over to her.

"I suppose I am," Ady said.

"This is Antoinette," Lenore said to her father, who bowed. Ady winced yet again at the sound of her lying name. Of all the people in the world she wanted to be truthful with, Lenore and her family were first among them.

"You will be joining us at our home for a meal?" Lenore's father, Mr. Pasquel, asked.

"Yes, sir," Ady said. "Thank you."

"Wonderful," Mr. Pasquel said. "Our cook makes a succulent ham. I'll make sure you get the first cut."

Alabama tapped Ady on the arm.

"Well, aren't you just the belle of the ball!" Alabama said. Ady couldn't tell if Alabama was teasing her. She felt plain in her clothes. Alabama wore a brilliant blue dress with lace panels on the foresleeves.

"Your dress is beautiful."

"I reckon it should be. I made it myself." Alabama slightly lifted the sides of the skirts.

"You're a seamstress?"

"I'm quite a few things." Alabama winked.

"Didn't Mrs. Gaines or Courtland come?"

"Lord, no," Alabama said. "They're Baptists. And you can forget about that Molly, too. She's a heathen. She would turn to dust if she entered." Alabama leaned in to whisper. "Come to think of it, I've committed a few sins myself. Maybe you and the rest should go in without me."

"Is that Darrow?" Ady was noticing Lenore's brother off to himself.

"Yeah. He put something in his hair to slick it. Trying to look like a rooster 'stead of a chick," Alabama said, and let out a bark of laughter.

Lenore's group moved to the front of the church. They took up most of the third row. Lenore insisted Ady sit next to her. Lenore touched the pewter cross on her own neck and said a silent prayer. It was strange to sit so close to the altar. Ady, for a change, could see the priest enter from the rectory, followed by an altar boy swinging a smoking pot of incense and another altar boy carrying a golden staff. She knew little of God in this formalized expanse and even less of Catholicism as a faith. But she couldn't deny the peace of the experience. The priest's voice chanting words of a song that she could not interpret but that Lenore's family and Alabama responded to. When they knelt on the knee rests, so did Ady, at Lenore's smiling urging. Although Lenore bade her remain behind when the congregation met the priest at the front to receive the sacrament.

On the walk to Lenore's family's house, Ady found herself furtively glancing for any sign of trouble. If she stayed at their house too long and he came searching for her—

"Are you all right?" Alabama's asked. "You seem skittish as a mouse in a lion's den."

Ady shook her head and straightened up. "I'm fine. What language was that in church?"

"Latin," Alabama said. "It's an old way of talking. My grandpa spoke some language. Not Latin, but from the continent of Africa. My folks spoke some too, but I never learnt . . ." Alabama stopped midsentence.

"What is it?" Ady looked in the direction that Alabama was looking. A pair of men stood across the street from the church. They weren't town types, but the kind of men who spent much of their time on horseback. Their chaps and spurs suggested this. They had been with the slave catcher that first day in the Mockingbird.

"Nothing to get worked up about," Alabama said, just as one of them lowered his head so that his wide hat brim covered his face.

Lenore's family home was a three-story stucco building with an elegant green awning over the red front door. They entered the home and Ady was immediately pinched by the smell of freshly baked bread. The furniture was covered in lace. A man named Edmonton in a black suit ran the affairs of the house. Mr. Pasquel called out directions to him as they entered, and Edmonton responded in a clipped voice that reminded Ady of Mrs. Orsone.

"The tea will be served shortly, I imagine," Mr. Pasquel said.

"Yes, sir, it will."

"And the ham is well-done?"

"Of course."

"I trust we have enough blueberry pie."

"Certainly, sir."

Ady took a seat at a long banquet table, next to Darrow, who had inserted himself between her and Alabama. Ady saw Darrow's hand beneath the tablecloth holding Alabama's. It was clear to Ady that they were being careful not to let their contact be observed by the other Pasquels, including Lenore. Ady looked up. The grandfather clock in the next room struck, and Ady's cheeks warmed. She asked Alabama what time it was and she said, "I reckon it just struck one o'clock."

Edmonton and one of the servants entered with platters of food, just as Ady shot up.

"Antoinette," Lenore said. "Is everything all right?"

Ady looked around the room at the dozen or so people gathered around the table. So promising and happy in their Easter best.

"I'm uh, I'm not feeling well," she said.

"Young lady," Mr. Pasquel said. "You're welcome to use one of the bedrooms upstairs to restore yourself."

"I'm very sorry," Ady said as she dashed to the door and out of the house, with Lenore calling after her.

She sped along the sidewalks, avoiding people who were traveling from their own churches. She needed to return to the townhouse before he arrived. Still, that wasn't the true reason. Lenore's family seemed wonderful, kind, but—

Just then, at a corner several blocks from the townhouse, a hand grabbed her shoulder and roughly swung her around. Breathless, she saw a tall, bearded white man before her. He was one of the men from outside the church. A slave catcher.

"I ought to carry you in," he said. "There's a hefty fee for runaways like yourself."

"What is this? Leave me be. I—I have an owner." Her heart sank as she said this. She avoided ever speaking those words aloud. But she had no other defenses. Who could she turn to?

He stood watching her, smiling. Then it struck her that he was not a complete stranger. Those eyes. Those were his eyes.

It was du Marche's son. Grown up.

"Johnny."

"'Magine Pa wouldn't be pleased to know his house wench is prancing around with uppity Creoles." Johnny spat and absentmindedly tapped the gun strapped to his belt. Ady said nothing.

"Come on," he said. They walked at a deliberate pace back to the townhouse. Du Marche wasn't there yet. Johnny demanded coffee. "Quickly," he said. "And fetch the washbasin."

Johnny undid his gun belt and laid it on the small kitchen table.

After starting the coffee on the stove, she brought in the basin.

"Get some water, dummy."

Ady kept her mouth shut. What did he want? How would this play out? She found the paddle to remove his boots and poured water into the basin at his feet. She gave him the coffee as he sat.

"I been in town for days. Figured you were up to something." He drank it all. "More." Ady filled his mug.

"I hooked up with a crew and been bringing runaways back for some time. Our chief was shot dead, though." Johnny pointed at his boots and Ady set about removing them.

"You saw him at the inn that time, a darky like you. I think you would have liked him, if'n you knew him. Surprising number of darkies in this line of work." Johnny was at the inn that day when Ady met Lenore. Ady had been so afraid of the men that she didn't see their faces. She felt especially foolish to be too scared to look Johnny in the face. Ady forced the paddle down into the back of his boot. "Easy! I got flesh in there! So when my crew broke up, I decided to change tactics and go for high-dollar catches."

Ady was on her knees. His boot came off and the funk of his foot assaulted Ady's nose. She removed his tattered sock and put his foot into the basin.

"Shit, some of these planters will pay double value for the right head, and wouldn't you know chance was on my side." She pulled off his other boot.

"Why you telling me all this?" Ady asked.

"I don't know. Maybe it's a kind of thanks. I've been hunting from Texas to Missouri over the last couple of years. I never thought you'd be the one to bring me to my best payday."

"I don't figure what you're talking about," Ady said.

"Your friend-gal. The short darkie in blue today. She run off from the biggest house in Mississippi years back. I mean a long time ago. Back when Jackson was pres. The owner of that big house had a soft spot for her and never forgot her."

Alabama.

"Why do you do it?" she asked without thinking.

He smiled, cocked his head. "That ain't your calling to know." He drank more coffee. "But I'll tell you this. Sure, Pa's land and all that'll be mine one day. But every real man needs some work of his own. I like getting my hands dirty. Don't matter if it's out on the range or in the cities." He stood up. "Just like Pa, I guess. Apple don't fall far. He don't like that I'm out there. Calls it beneath our station."

The carriageway gate clanked downstairs. Johnny stood up and stepped out of the basin, water splashing on the floor. Before she could react, he pushed her against the wall, his hands searching her dress.

"What are you—" she said. "Stop!"

He stepped back, laughing. He had bills in his hand.

"You ain't the first biddy to keep money hidden on her person."

"You—"

"I what?" He raged toward her and chuckled. "Way I see it, this your earnings for the week at that inn, am I right? I won't tell him about your little adventures. Long as I get at least this much when I come a-calling. And I will come calling."

"Why won't you tell him?"

"'Cause it's more fun to hold it over your head," he said. "But hear this—you try to warn your friend that I'm coming for her and I lose out on my bounty, that'll be a bad day for you, and I ain't talking about selling you off somewheres."

He released Ady, and she quickly stepped onto the courtyard balcony, away from him. Du Marche turned the corner and climbed the stairs. He pushed past Ady without slowing and stomped into the house.

"Howdy, you old skeleton," Johnny said.

"Hello, my biggest mistake. There's no percentage in laying about here. To the tavern." Ady watched the two walk back out, Johnny's left hand stuffed in his pocket, fingering all the money Ady had.

15.

Days later, Lenore turned to Ady as Ady wiped crumbs from the tabletop. The guests, men in town to purchase shipments of whale oil for a company upriver in St. Louis, had devoured their breakfast of fatback and grits with a lustiness that made Ady's stomach pulse. Darrow was at the inn, too, Lenore said she had asked him to help fill in for the stocker, who had gone missing. Ady realized that Lenore was standing quite still, just outside the stock room. Her face moved as if she wished to speak, but she tilted her head down for a moment. Ady stood straight and cleaned her hands against her apron.

"Why did you run off that way on Easter?" Lenore asked.

"I—I can't tell you." Ady had anticipated this question and yet still did not know how to answer. There were so many things Ady wanted to reveal to Lenore, about the danger Alabama was in, about her own life. Lenore didn't know that she wasn't free, didn't know that she had been shipped like cotton from his land. But Ady sensed disaster just beyond her imagination.

"That's all right. I'm your employer, not your sister." Lenore continued to stare at Ady.

"What is it?" Ady asked.

"There's something . . . I'd like you to see."

"What?"

"Come," Lenore said. Ady followed Lenore into the partially covered courtyard behind the Mockingbird. The sky was overcast, but the sun was peeking from behind the clouds, casting beams of light here and there about the yard. As Lenore moved, she exploded into the light. She had done her hair differently, had spun her long dark hair into buns along the side of her head in the manner of a white spinster. But the style was enchanting on her. She looked—and Ady didn't think it was possible—more like a queen than usual.

The back of the courtyard was bounded by a low wide building with two doorways in the front. Ady had been in the right-side doorway often. The dry goods were kept therein: rice, hominy grits, lentils, crackers. But she'd never had cause to inspect the left side.

Striking a match, Lenore lit a candle on a hanger inside the door and handed it to Ady. The room was dark and smelled of grease and dust that made Ady absentmindedly tap her nose. Heavy white sheets were draped over most of the objects in the room.

"What is this?"

"Hold that over here for a moment, would you?" They stepped toward the far corner of the long room.

Ady wasn't sure what she was illuminating. Lenore grabbed hold of a rod and spun her hand quickly. Shutters opened. Suddenly sunlight washed into the room. Lenore grabbed one of the heavy sheets and pulled it away from a stack of canvases.

"I don't spend very much time in here," Lenore said. "At least not as much as I'd care to. But this is where I—"

"You're a painter!" Ady said, surprising herself with her volume.

"Well," Lenore said, "I wouldn't say I'm a painter, but I am acquainted with the use of a brush."

"I can't believe it. Can I see them?" Lenore nodded. Ady laughed. She squatted and began to pick up the canvases in turn. There was a table against the wall, and Ady laid each of the canvases atop the table. The sheer variety of subjects dazzled her. Lenore had painted a table—not unlike the one before her—but the surface was larded with a feast of turkey, beef side, ham (with the bone jutting from it), and a cornucopia from which spilled oranges, lemons, grapes, berries, and, surprisingly, cherry cordials. Another canvas featured a slender dog, standing on three legs, pointing to something unseen with his paw. And yet another was a portrait of the city as if painted from a balloon high above, so high in fact that clouds obscured some of the buildings, though the Cathedral was plainly visible atop the square.

"How did you do this?"

"My father took me to France several years ago. While he was handling his business affairs, I studied under a master of the form along with my other schooling. We were there for the better part of a year. It's not something they enjoy seeing women do—I'm not very good."

Ady found the last canvas in the stack and brought it into the light. It was a representation of women, who looked like relatives of Lenore. They were on a city street, their hair wrapped in colorful scarves, the bright pleats of their dresses practically leaping off the canvas.

"You're incredible."

"You think?"

"I can't draw a stick figure, but these—they all look like life. Real life." Ady stopped and looked around. "But why are they in this moldy old room?"

"Father doesn't like them in the house. The smells. The

clutter. I don't think he thought I'd take to it the way I did. After all, I learned to play the clavichord and piccolo in Saint-Germain-des-Prés and I rarely—"

"When was the last time you made a new one?" Ady had placed her hand on Lenore's. They were closer to each other than they had ever been, so close that Ady felt Lenore's breath.

A voice called from outside. Lenore retook her hand and backed away.

"I—I haven't painted in months. My brushes are positively deplorable, and it's been so frantic around here and, well, I simply haven't."

"Halloo," the voice called from the main room of the Mockingbird.

"We should return." Lenore edged around Ady. She grabbed the rod and began closing the shutters. "Would you cover those?"

Ady glanced at her own hand, which felt as warm as if she'd held it over a fire. She draped the sheet back over the canvases on the table. She and Lenore waited for a moment in the dark. Lenore's eyes glistened in the light of the candle, which had remained quivering the whole while. Ady held out the candle to Lenore.

Lenore blew out the candle, placed it back on the stand, and stepped out into the sunlight.

In the following weeks, Ady often thought of the way she felt that day. She felt a new disappointment each time she left the Mockingbird, when she left Lenore, and a new keenness every time she made her way back.

One morning, there was a festival at Congo Square, which left the Mockingbird particularly quiet. Lenore was behind the

center counter paging through a copy of *Godey's Lady's Book;*
Alabama and Mrs. Gaines were out at the market; and Ady had
taken to slowly shining the silver utensils.

"There is an article in here about the men who patrol the
Midwest searching for runaways, but there's no mention of
the moral depravity of the enslavement of humans." Lenore
saw that Ady was giggling. "Do I amuse you?" she said.

"You get that way anytime you read that thing. I think you
read it just to get upset."

Lenore closed the magazine. "You might be right. But I'm
right too."

"I didn't say you weren't."

"Let's walk in the park."

"Oh—you sure?" Ady said, looking around where no one
else was.

"Did I murmur?"

The park was small but gracious. Whereas the manors west
of the city with their spacious meadows attracted and wel-
comed the white citizenry, the Coloreds of New Orleans had
a prescribed section of the Square, which was legally of use
only on Sundays; the swamps, which were always illegal; or the
postage-stamp parks like the one a stone's throw from the
Mockingbird. There were several of those parks in the Fau-
bourg Marigny, the largest of which they now stood on. Ady
stood at the entrance, looking toward the end of the path only
yards away.

"You don't seem impressed," Lenore said, stepping into
the park. "I gather taking a morning constitutional does not
suit you." Others were walking farther along the stone path.
And a couple sat on a blanket, drinking from a flask.

"I love to walk," Ady said. "Mama and I used to do that all the time. I walk whenever I can." Ady stepped onto the grass and relished the give of the ground beneath her boots.

"Let us stay on the path," Lenore said. Ady glanced down at Lenore's fine shoes, which were of suede and ornamented with stones, though Ady couldn't tell if they were real. The amethyst gleamed in the morning light.

"You're right. I wouldn't want to get those dirty."

"Where did you walk?"

"Oh." Ady suddenly felt self-conscious and lowered her head. She couldn't place her finger on the issue exactly, then just as suddenly the cause became apparent. No one had ever asked her about her private moments, the habits and situations she realized only then that she held dear.

"You do not have to tell me," Lenore said.

"No. It—it's not that." How to explain anything about herself? Her enslavement? The lies she had told Lenore and all the others? They were halfway up the first path. There were many such paths that crisscrossed the area, meeting at the center. Beyond the wrought-iron fence to her left, Ady saw a city patrolman heading down the street, a baton dangling from his waist.

"There are not many places safe for us to walk unbothered," Lenore observed. "We have to worry over the patrols on the one hand and men in general on the other."

"I like the markets," Ady said. "I walk along the river, especially around sunset. Sometimes I even hike down to the muddy banks and feed the gulls." Lenore stopped and stared at Ady as if she were mauve. Ady's inertia carried her forth several steps, so that she paused awkwardly and turned back to Lenore.

"What?"

"I cannot imagine."

"You think I shouldn't?"

"I mean, scampering about in the mud at dusk."

"It's not like I'm rolling in it!"

Lenore began to walk again. "It is just that I have never strayed more than perhaps six city blocks from home or the Mockingbird without male accompaniment. My father would have turned me into an anchorite if he found out I was—" This time it was Ady who stopped walking.

"You're serious," Ady said.

"Of course."

"But when you have something to do out of range, how do you do it?"

"My brother Darrow usually takes me. Father does when he's around and has the inclination. But he travels a great deal."

"I don't understand. You run your family's business. You've gone to the other side of the world."

"Correction. The Mockingbird belongs to me through and through. But my father's shipping holdings make the inn look like a bauble. He and my brother do not believe I am as sturdy as I am. They do not know about the bandits I have scared off with that old scattergun at the Mockingbird. They can't imagine that I have seen lifeless bodies."

"Bodies?"

"I meant what I told you that time. There is danger in what we do. I've faced my share of cruel men."

Ady thought about her own enslavement. The destruction of possibility it had wrought, was wrecking. There were most certainly different varieties of slavery. Some sanctioned by the state for the benefit of those of white lineage. Others prevalent for how many long-ago generations based upon the whims of men in relation to women.

"I'm sorry," Ady said.

"For what?" Lenore asked.

"For what they done to you."

Lenore grabbed Ady's hand. "Thank you," she said, and just as quickly let go of Ady's hand. "Finding male accompaniment shall not be difficult for me soon enough. I am to be married off."

Ady said nothing.

Lenore turned to her and said, "You look very surprised, Antoinette. Do you think me unmarriageable?"

"No," Ady said quickly, "of course not." She turned away from Lenore. "Anyone would want to marry you— I just meant, well, who is he?"

"A man from Philadelphia. He is the son of an acquaintance of my father. Papa waxes poetic about him. Calls him my knight in shining armor."

"What's his name?"

Lenore laughed. "Does it matter? I think he may be called Monsieur Mare or some similar name. And he is not too old. Perhaps just over thirty."

"Thirty!"

"I believe."

"Do you want to marry him?"

"My dear, a woman does not want. She simply occupies a realm and leads her life according to the parameters of that realm."

"You don't believe that in your heart."

Lenore paused. "No. No, I do not."

Ady stared at the Virgin Mary pendant around Lenore's neck. "You don't have to live this way."

"Who are you to tell me which way I am to live my life?" she said, as she started walking again. "My grandmother was wealthy and free. She sold coffee and built her life according to her designs." Lenore pointed toward the west end of the park. "She was so powerful that she caused that schoolhouse to be created. My mother took her portion of that wealth by skirting the laws against inheritance by free women of color. She made pacts with those she had to. Mother married Father, who was not poor, but he was not as well-off as she was. Then her empire became his by dint of matrimonial law. It never bothered her. She's trusted their union under God."

"What happened to her?"

"She died—of cancer." Lenore touched the pewter cross at her neck. "This was hers. From her mother."

Ady produced a lace handkerchief from her pouch. "I'm sorry."

"Thank you. I don't know what plans she had for our lives. Father has possession of all that was hers now. Darrow will take the lion's share one day. My dowry goes to whichever man most appreciates my charming face. So why not this Brewston or whatever his name is? It is all the same in the end. Is it not? He will take his position in the home he gains from me." Lenore was yelling now. "Then he will enter a business trade and I will give him children and rarely see him as he jaunts about swapping beef shanks for bales of hay! And maybe I'll end up just like my mother!"

"I'm sorry," Ady said, not knowing what else to say. "I'm sorry."

"Stop saying that. I am not one to be pitied."

"You are right," Ady said, affecting Lenore's accent. "You are not."

Lenore laughed. "You are such a ragamuffin. I apologize for my outburst. These are not situations I discuss."

"What if we quit talking and just walk around the park one more time?"

"Ah'd very much like-a that," Lenore said, trying to sound like Ady.

"I don't sound like that!" Ady said.

Lenore squeezed Ady's hand. "I am aware. I was aiming to get a rise out of you." Lenore grinned.

Ady stared at Lenore. The mischievous look on her face rekindled a memory. "Ruth."

"What's that?"

"We met before, didn't we, when we were younger?" Ady says, suddenly shocked, the words rushing out like a waterfall. "You gave me that rubber ball."

Lenore smiled and slowly nodded her head. "I did."

"You called yourself Ruth then," Ady said, laughing in shock. "We were always meant to meet again." Ady didn't realize she had said the last bit out loud, but Lenore's eyes shone, even as sadness overtook her face.

"That was her name. We had buried her around that time. She would send me out on . . . errands. My father didn't constrain as much when she was alive."

"That was the only time you breathed on your own terms, wasn't it?"

Lenore nodded. "Come along," she said, and then added "poet," while she smiled, crookedly. Ady had never seen this face on Lenore. Unguarded and girlish. It seemed truer than the face Lenore wore unthinkingly. They stepped onto the dew-covered grass, and Ady tilted her head back, the warmth of the morning on her cheeks. She began to sing.

She hadn't heard her own voice tremble that way since before Sanite's death. Indeed, she had not sung with careless abandon even once since her time on his plantation, not even in the moments before she fell asleep as had been her habit. Now her throat felt thick and heavy, her pitch was somewhat lower, but the difference was more than that. The timbre of her voice was altered as well, she noted. It seemed to her the difference between a sparrow standing on the ground and a sparrow in flight. Lenore was watching her with eyes wide in delight. Ady finished the line she was singing, then halted the song, lowering her eyes toward the dandelions, her throat captured by Lenore's gaze. Lenore took Ady's hand. Ady's embarrassment mounted. How had she sounded? Like a garden frog perhaps. She disentangled her hand and rubbed her throat.

"You called yourself Ruth then," Ady said, switching the focus away from herself. But Lenore said nothing. Instead she took Ady's hand back, squeezing it, and remarked "That was beautiful."

16.

ADY ALMOST LOST her way while walking to the Mockingbird that morning. The streets of the Marigny were clogged for the festival, throngs of bodies filling every curbside and every banquette. By the time she pushed her way into the Mockingbird's main room, her back was cold with sweat even as her stomach felt furnace-warm and achy, as if full of sour grapes.

Alabama greeted Ady with a loud hello and a quick hug. Since Ady's encounter with Johnny, he had made no move. Du Marche was again away, traveling by carriage to other southern territories, but she'd seen Johnny every so often. He stayed elsewhere, in the city somewhere. Ady had thought on how to help Alabama and come to no good conclusion. If she warned Alabama about the danger Johnny posed and she ran, what would become of her? She felt ashamed every time she asked that question. What was so important about her own life that she would leave her friend defenseless?

"It's going to be a big morning," Alabama said. "The rooms are full, and guests are sure to come down with empty stomachs. They drank late."

"Ain't never an easy morning around here," Courtland said. "I got some grits and hog maws will be ready soon enough. Come get y'all's portion when you want."

The thought of eating anything didn't sit well with Ady.

"What's that face for, baby?" Courtland said. "You know you love my vittles."

"Oh, I do," Ady said.

"She's looking mighty peaked, if you ask me."

"I'm fine," Ady said. "It must have been something I ate," she lied. She had eaten nothing. She wanted to lie down, perhaps with a cool rag across her forehead. She wondered if she was coming down with fever, maybe even The Fever, again, but this was different. She had none of the general lethargy that characterized the sickness, even in its initial stages. No, this feeling was centered low in her body and felt as though someone had tied a garrot around her interior and was tightening it by turns. Ady went to the counter and exhaled. She realized then what was happening, and a flash of embarrassment crossed her face.

The full flush of business crested midmorning with every table of the main hall occupied and several patrons standing with metal dishes in their hands. Ady was overwhelmed. Between feeding people and removing refuse, she barely had a moment's respite. Lenore was present, assisting. She had taken on temporary help to supplement the work Ady was doing. A young man dropped a stack of tin pans. He looked at Ady sheepishly.

"Ady," Lenore said, "join me in the kitchen." The kitchen was intolerably hot, but Lenore was preparing tea.

"This will help, dear." Lenore handed Ady a tin cup.

"What is it?"

Lenore smirked. "Cramp bark."

Ady laughed. "Is that what you call it?"

"I'll allow that it is an overly obvious name, but what else, pray tell, does one call it?"

"I've made this before," Ady said. "Thank you." She sipped from the cup.

"How old are you actually? I've called you a child, but I'd like a number."

"I don't exactly know. Fifteen. Maybe sixteen. Why do you ask?"

"I suppose it's because you are adept at many things. More than most."

"Thank you." Ady grinned. Lenore was so kind to her, more than almost anyone else in her life. If she couldn't talk to her, then who could she talk to? She would tell Lenore about Alabama's predicament. Johnny be damned. She would tell her the truth about herself also. Her actual story. "There's something I need to tell you."

"What is it?" Lenore asked, her face bright and hopeful.

But Ady remembered Johnny grabbing her shoulder on the street Easter Sunday. She remembered his father's hand on her inner thigh. The smell of sherry on his breath. The slaver Nimrod chasing her through the swamp, bats floating through the tree canopy. Her mother's body in the chicken coop, the spark of her gone. Ady vomited.

After she cleaned herself up, Ady convinced Lenore she was fine and that she just needed to go back home and rest. On her way out, Ady stopped at the patron's counter and ripped a page from the register and began to write in block letters. If she couldn't tell Lenore directly, she had another plan. It was gratifying to express a thought in the written word. Why didn't she do this more often?

After drafting the note, she felt a release, like the uncorking of a long-plugged bottle. She longed to continue placing ink to page.

When she arrived back to the townhouse, she exhaled when she confirmed he was not back yet. She went into the study and searched the shelves. Dust leapt from the gold trim of the books she pulled. Mrs. Orsone was away for the winter, visiting family up north, and they rarely used this room otherwise. She opened the parlor cabinets but found nothing. She knew it was somewhere. She had taken pains to hide it. Johnny had not been back to soil the room. He was likely carousing with his mates, shacked up in a room across town.

Finally, a notion caught. She went into du Marche's room, which was immaculate, as she had made it days before. The bedsheets neatly folded back at the top. The curtains parted and held back with thick velvet rope. A quill pen sticking from the inkpot on his nightstand.

Ady approached the foot locker at the end of his bed. It was one of the few places in the compound that she never touched, for she knew what was under the lid of that chest. She knelt before the chest. Then she grabbed the lid handle and held it between her fingers. Scooting her knees closer to the chest, she felt the metal bolts along its surface pushing through the fabric of her dress. She unlatched the chest and lifted the top.

A series of smells swelled from the hide-bound interior. The scents of dust, fabric, leather, and sweat. She recalled that his old military togs, not the ones he paraded in recently, had lain atop the stack of clothes and documents, but the uniform was no longer there. Perhaps they were the same uniform? Perhaps he'd had it altered? She lifted a pair of jackets out of the way, and knew before she saw it that she was touching

Sanite's dress. When she stood up with the dress, it unfolded to the floor, the scent of her mother returning to her with such force that Ady wrapped her arms around the garment and hugged it as if the woman were still within.

She pressed the fabric to her lips and sniffed the neckline, immediately recalling that fiery, apple-tinged underscent that Sanite carried regardless of whether she had worked a day without rest or had just emerged from a bath. Ady placed the dress on the bed. She stuck her hand into the bottom of the chest, she felt the pages nib at the pads of her fingers.

The notebook had been given to her by Mrs. Orsone, who had made express instructions that she use it only for writing about her deepest desires. She said it would be good for her. This idea had felt so alien to Ady that she didn't know what to do with it. For a period of days, she carried the notebook on her person in the hipsack where she kept supplies at the time. He had even asked her about the notebook once, to which she had replied "Writing practice assignments." Ady had never understood why he didn't object to her schooling in the alphabet, penmanship, and comprehension—there were many laws against it and he was an agent of government—but she didn't care about his reasons. Still, she found no use for her ability to place her thoughts upon a page. Thrice she had sat and began to write upon the pages, and each time she paused with pen tip to page like a statue of a girl by some odd sculptor. Eventually, she decided to secure it for the day she might want to revisit the matter. She didn't keep the notebook in her quarters because he sometimes searched that room and removed whatsoever he wished. Too, her quarters were dank. The notebook would likely be ruined after a few weeks. It was all she could do to keep her few clothes in a constant rotation of washing and drying on the line to prevent mold in the fabric.

So she chose the chest. The notebook wouldn't attract attention the way it might on one of the shelves. Before she stowed it those many months ago, she believed she had to write at least one word inside the covers to call it her own. In looping curls, she laid down the three letters of her name, knowing full well that he would object if he came across it. He allowed her schooling, but the voicing of opinions was another matter. She wrote her true name anyway.

Now she held the notebook in her hand, examining the word of herself and noting how those letters pressed into the following page and the page behind that one. A small imprint on the face of the world.

She brought the notebook to the half table in the nook where they prepared food for serving. She sat on the narrow straight-backed chair. She lifted the quill and rubbed the excess liquid against the lip of the inkpot. And then she wrote.

She was thinking about Lenore as she moved from the first page to the next and the next and the next, but what she wrote was not about Lenore—at least not yet. She teased out from memory the day she and Sanite were brought down to the auction, the day they were purchased by him, the day the townhouse became her barracoon, the city her open-air penitentiary. She wrote onward, her hand skidding across the mild beige page. When she finally stopped writing several hours later, her hand was cramping. She shook out her fingers and blew on them. She hadn't stopped of her own accord. She heard the gate below swing open, and heavy boots trod down the carriageway. As calmly as if she were crossing a river of glass, she neatly placed the quill and inkpot in the precise spot from which she had taken them. Then she tucked the notebook into a hidden pocket she had sewn into her dress. Until then, she had only placed small tools or food items there. But now it held something else entirely. She would find a way to protect the notebook.

17.

Excerpt from the unpublished, undated, untitled
Memoir of Doris H.

By the time a year had passed, my vision stopped
improving. With my Coke bottle glasses, I could read
again, provided the print was close enough, and I
had gained enough confidence to walk without my cane.
Faces were hard though. So was anything that moved
fast, and bright lights, too. Yet, I was thankful
that the world wasn't black as it had been right
after the attack. I knew for example that my light
sweater was blue and that my fashion sunglasses from
Krauss' had a tortoiseshell frame.

Best of all, Diana, I could see my baby again.
She was growing so quickly, not just physically, but
mentally. One day she was three and now a teenager!
She was doing well in school, and, to my surprise,
one schoolboy or another would walk her home.

I invited them in to see what they were up to.
One of the boys was from a good family and smart,
Jermaine, but he was a boy like the others, and
Diana, bless her, was so much like Ella. She and my
sister were nobody's fools, but they were good
girls, naive to a fault.

That Jermaine stopped coming around. I asked
Diana what happened to him, but she only said "noth-
ing," which I knew meant something. One day, I found
Diana sitting cross-legged on her bed with great-

grandmother's notebook on her lap, crying. How far into it had she gotten? I had read it more times than I could count.

"Mama, is that man our ancestor?"

"What man?" I asked.

"The one who did what he did to Mama Ady and to her mama."

"Hand that to me."

Diana didn't move, her face wet from tears. I should have hugged my daughter. I should have talked to her. I know that now. I should have sat next to her and put my arm around her and pulled her to me. Instead, I snatched the journal from her.

In the den, I sat on the sofa and old Ed Sullivan was on the Zenith. I flipped through, ripping out pages as those mop top boys yelled.

18.

I N ORDER TO keep the townhouse in working order, Ady continued to run errands as before. She'd never had a reason to like the tasks set before her, but suddenly her work became far less tolerable with Johnny around.

"I reckon I apologize," he said. They were outside of the butcher's; he had taken to following her on errands. Ady didn't ask him what he meant. She didn't care to know.

"You still have the mark," he said. Ady saw herself in the glass. Her reflection was faint, but she understood he was talking about the scar near her eyebrow.

"It was rude of me to throw that rock at you way back when."

Ady strained not to react. She had forgotten about that day. No, she had not forgotten, exactly. The memory resurfaced from time to time and she kicked it away with her boot each time. She wished she could kick him.

He snatched a newspaper from a boy.

"Hey!" the child said.

"Go on," Johnny said. He held up the paper. "That's something."

"What does it say?" Ady asked.

"How would I know? I can't read. I've taken lessons but don't have a mind for it. You can't read, can you?"

Ady shook her head.

"All I see is this drawing," he said.

The drawing showed a building on fire.

"This kind of thing has been happening a bit lately."

"Must be the lightning," Ady said. He cocked his head and eyed her. Ady felt uncomfortable under his gaze. He looked at her for a beat too long and then announced that he had business and that he'd be seeing her around. Ady didn't like that, but she watched as he walked off, waiting until he turned the corner before she made her way to the Mockingbird. In the courtyard of the Mockingbird, Ady saw Alabama helping Mrs. Gaines and Molly wash the linens. As soon as Ady approached, Alabama dropped her allotment and walked away.

"Why are you acting so strange?" Ady asked Alabama. Alabama stormed into the building. She crossed to the far side of the draught hall and raised the bundle of rags from the wooden bucket of soapy water. That corner of the hall smelled of spilled beer. The stench turned Ady's stomach.

"Why are you following me?" Alabama asked.

"Yesterday you said I was out of sorts, and now you are."

Alabama pushed Ady's shoulder.

"Hey," Ady said. She pushed Alabama back.

"Get away from me!" Alabama said.

Soon Mrs. Gaines and Molly were in the room standing between them.

"What goes on down here?" Lenore said, coming down the stairs.

"This goes on," Alabama said. She reached into her dress and pulled out a slip of paper. Ady knew instantly what it was.

Lenore read the paper.

"She's trying to run me off," Alabama said.

"That's crazed, that," Molly said. "You two are like two muffins on a stove."

"You don't cook muffins on the stove, girl," Mrs. Gaines said.

"Oh," Molly said.

Lenore read the letter out loud: "Find safety. Man named Johnny du Marche wants to sell you at market soonest." Lenore stared at Ady. "Is this true, Antoinette?"

"Don't you fib," Alabama said. "That paper is from the book on the counter. That's your handwriting."

"Poor child," Mrs. Gaines said. "You must be scared out of your skin."

"I'm not afraid of some man coming for me. I kept myself free all this time."

"I'm the confused one then," Molly said. "Why are you so cross at ole beanpole?"

"I just don't like being lied to."

"But the letter is true, Antoinette, non?" Lenore asked.

Ady sat on a chair and lowered her face to her hands. She cried into her palms. "I was worried and didn't know what to do."

Alabama relaxed at the sight of Ady crumpled. She placed her hands on Ady's shoulders. "I'm not that mad. Don't you cry on account of me."

Ady sucked in her breath. "It's not that." Her lip quivered. "My name isn't even Antoinette. That's just what the father of the man in that note calls me."

Lenore laughed. Ady looked up. Lenore continued to laugh.

"Child!" Alabama said. She laughed too, and so did Molly.

"What are we laughing about?" Molly asked.

"You all done lost your heads," Mrs. Gaines said.

"We knew someone had papers on you," Alabama said.

"That is true," Lenore said.

"I ain't know," Mrs. Gaines said. "Y'all don't tell me nothing, but I reckon that's why friend-gal work such skiddish hours, popping in and out like a broke cuckoo clock."

Ady looked at them, astonished. "But Alabama said she was jealous of how free I seemed."

"I was," Alabama said. "I reckoned some man had you. But you came here. That means you're free where it counts."

Ady shook her head. "And you let me lie to you about my name all this time."

"I still don't know what your name is!" Alabama said.

Lenore placed a hand on Ady's shoulder. "My dear, most of the people who work here use aliases. It's the nature of our society that demands it."

"I'm Hagar," Alabama said.

"My last name is Smith on documents," Mrs. Gaines said. "But that was the slave man name so I left it behind when I bought my manumission."

Molly pushed back her rumpled hat. "Molly was the name of the girl I shipped over from England with. She didn't make it. Scurvy got her. Me mum named me Edith."

Ady covered her face with her hands. Her shoulders shook. The others closed around.

"Lying ain't nothing to cry about." Alabama rubbed Ady's arm. Ady tossed her head back and laughed. "Hagar? Hagar! That name doesn't fit you one bit."

"That's how I felt about it," Alabama said.

Ady walked away from the women and sat on the steps. "I'm . . . Ady."

Lenore approached. "Ady. Is the man who holds your papers looking for you right now?"

"No," Ady said. "Not this minute."

"Good. Then I only have to make arrangements to Canada for one of you."

Ady looked from Lenore to Alabama. "Arrangements?"

Alabama pointed at herself. "I ain't going nowhere."

"I'm afraid you are, my friend."

"But—"

"I know about this Johnny du Marche and his associates. They've been holed up at a house of ill repute by the river. He's dumb enough to be dangerous."

"You know about him?" Ady stood up.

"It's my business to know all sorts of things."

Ady stared at Lenore. "But that would mean—"

"Mean what?" Mrs. Gaines asked.

Alabama stomped her foot. "Y'all listen to me right now and listen good. I don't care if every slaver in the State of Louisiana is hunting me. I made this life for myself. And I ain't leaving it on account of fear. I'd rather die first!" Alabama whirled around and crashed through the door to the Mockingbird's courtyard.

"Alabama!" Lenore said. Lenore began to follow, but Ady stopped her. She and Lenore watched each other for a moment. Lenore nodded. Ady went out to where Alabama was sitting on the dirty slate, picking leaves from a stem. Ady sat down next to her. Alabama wiped her own face.

"Why don't you just mind your own business?" Alabama said. "Ady or whatever you're called."

"You don't got to be rude," Ady said.

"It's not fair that you're taller than me. You giraffe."

"Who said life was fair?"

"When I first came down to the city, I stole food from

carts to keep from starving. I slept under a quilted coat in the place where they keep the omnibuses. One day, I walked past a run-down old building with a girl standing outside. She was so young, but so serious. I was covered in soot. My dress had holes in it. She told me that she was going to turn the building into an inn. And I told her that I never heard of a child doing such a thing, but I believed she could pull it off. I saw it in her eyes. I went inside and started straightening up the chairs and such that were left behind. I never really left this old shack again. We cleaned it up real nice, don't you think? I never wanted a husband or children. I only wanted to be a part of something good. Something more than hoeing a field on some little man's plantation."

Ady put a hand on Alabama's. "If Johnny catches you, he'll send you back."

"I know that, sugar. I don't want to leave and run off to Canada, but I ain't got a choice. I probably ain't never did."

Alabama stood up quickly and helped Ady to her feet.

"I'll go, but only if you promise me something."

"Promise?"

"You tell Lenore the truth about you. I mean the whole truth."

"I don't know what you're talking about."

"Oh, my friend. I know what he done. And I ain't talking about slavery. There's a way to kill a body without stopping their breath."

How did Alabama know, she wondered. "You always knew, didn't you?" she said.

"From the first time I laid eyes on you."

Ady lowered her head.

"Don't you do that!" Alabama said, picking up Ady's chin.

"I was wrong about this place. What I was trying to tell you is that I thought being a part of the Mockingbird was about running it. But what I really got from my time here was family. That's what I'm actually going to miss." Alabama turned away. "Lenore acts like she's such a mature person, but remember she's barely past being a child herself, despite what she says. Look out for her."

Over the course of the following weeks, events in the city had become quite chaotic. The body of a white man, believed to be a Northerner, had been found under the wharf, his body bloated from the waters. Meanwhile, the Colored newspaper on the other side of the Third Municipality had been ransacked. The owner was taken out into the street and beaten senseless by uniformed men. During her work at the inn, Ady watched Lenore who seemed more taciturn than usual.

Ady was entering the hall from the kitchen area when she bumped into Lenore, who dropped the tea set she had been carrying.

"Dear," Lenore said under her breath. She picked shards of teacup from the floor and placed them on the tray. Ady didn't bend to help her.

"It's all right if you cry," Ady said.

"And why, pray tell, would I do that?" Lenore stood up. Ady took the tray.

"Because life is awful," Ady said, exasperated. "To you! To me! To Alabama!"

A guest entered from the courtyard. He passed them on the way to the front door.

"Ladies," he said, nodding at them.

"Mr. Sharpe," Lenore said, putting on a face for the man. "I very much hope you're enjoying your time at the Mockingbird."

"Yes, ma'am," he called back. "It's heaven's nest."

Lenore grabbed Ady's arm. "How dare you? Alabama is going to a new life in a free land. I've never been happier for her."

"You're fibbing," Ady said, shrugging off Lenore's hand. "You haven't mentioned her even once. Her leaving pains you, just like it pains me."

"Fine. If you must know." Lenore stepped to the side. She lifted her chin. "I've cried often. Are you happy to hear that?"

"I'm not happy to—"

"Alabama is my oldest friend! I'm positively falling apart, Ady. Father thinks I'm having some kind of hysterical collapse. I fear he may commit me to the asylum."

"Why didn't you tell me anything?"

"Am I not allowed to wallow in privacy? Do I have to perform all my emotions on a stage!"

Ady watched Lenore. She felt for her, wanted to wrap her up in her arms. But then Lenore's lip quivered, and Ady guffawed. How would Alabama have reacted? Ady batted her eyelashes. "If Mr. Pasquel sends you to the madhouse, I'll visit you sometimes."

"Very humorous." Lenore had a queer look in her eye, a cross between mischief and good will. "Follow me, employee. I have a plot to cheer myself up."

They climbed the steps to the second floor. The halls were quiet. Visitors tended to avoid the city during the summer, in part due to the heat, which would only worsen in the coming weeks, and in part due to the risk of yellow fever, which flared along with the temperatures. Room number four was rarely used, or rather it was the last to be let. It was drafty and guests from time to time complained of disembodied voices in the night within. Once inside, Lenore began to set up an easel. Nearby stood a low pedestal covered by a sheet and behind it a small bouquet of flowers in a clear vase on a table.

"What is this?" Ady asked.

"Have a seat, please," Lenore said. Ady went to the pedestal and sat. She was unsure of how to perch on the platform, as its outer dimensions were obscured by the covering. She didn't want to miss the edge and slip to the floor.

"Shouldn't I be downstairs?"

"You are too on the spot, Ady. Relax. You know as well as I do that we are likely in for a quiet day." She picked up her palette and began to paint in broad strokes. "I'm going to paint you."

"What? I don't know about this. No, no, that's all right."

"About having your portrait done by me? Do you think I will make you look like a grizzly bear?"

"I've never seen a painting of someone like me. Them people, but not someone like me."

"And who are you?"

Ady worked her mouth for a moment. "Let me do what Alabama did. Let me help."

"Are we returning to that again?"

"Lenore! Don't you see what's happening? The beatings, people being carried away, buildings torched?"

"None of that is your concern!"

"It's my only concern. They want to terrorize us. I want to do my part to shove them back."

Lenore took Ady's hand. Ady stood up and Lenore guided her to the end of the bed, where they sat on the quilted cover.

"You're not going to forget about this, are you?"

"I'll pester you until your last breath."

"Incorrigible," Lenore tsked. Ady threw her arms around Lenore and hugged her tightly. Lenore hugged Ady back.

Ady felt safe in the embrace. It was as though in that room on the uppermost floor of the Mockingbird, no evil could enter.

Lenore stood up. "Now return to your seat. I would not want to lose this light while we have it."

The following week, Lenore took Ady away from the inn in a carriage during the late afternoon. It was sunny out, and the breeze from the movement of the carriage felt pleasant on Ady's face. But the sun was falling. Darkness would come on soon enough, her need to get back to the townhouse beat within her chest.

"Where are we going?" Ady asked. She was concerned about their distance from the center of town. Whatever they were about to do might mean she wouldn't return until well after dark. And though Ady did not expect to encounter him that night at the townhouse, as a practice, she avoided such needless risk.

"Is it very much further?"

"Patience," Lenore said. They were heading east, downriver, almost out of the First Municipality. The blocks were less populated with buildings. Lenore glanced at Ady. "You're worried about du Marche, n'est-ce pas?"

Ady couldn't help but wince at hearing his name out loud, especially from Lenore's lips.

"I'm sorry," Lenore said, shaking her head. "You're such a

courageous person, a lioness." Lenore leaned forward. "Driver. You may stop here."

Lenore nudged Ady, who climbed out. Ady helped Lenore down from the seat. Lenore scanned the streets as if looking for someone.

"Ain't nobody out here."

"Precisely," Lenore said. "Follow me closely and don't make a spectacle of yourself."

They walked for several blocks. Ady was completely unfamiliar with the area. The buildings were brick and wide. After turning several corners, they came to a large set of rolling doors. Lenore rapped on the door with a peculiar rhythm. Like the sound of feet tripping upstairs. They waited there for several moments. Ady wondered if anyone would come, but then a rap came from inside the door.

"For our mothers," Lenore said. The door rolled to the side just wide enough for them to enter. Inside, several women were at work on looms. Ady couldn't tell what they were creating. She followed Lenore deeper into the interior. The woman who had let them in didn't acknowledge them, but walked ahead at a determined pace, her boots scuffing the ground.

Ady's eyes got large. The law didn't allow Coloreds to congregate. It was one thing for someone like Lenore to own an establishment near the heart of the city. But this was different. The building wasn't a public establishment. The thought of the women working unseen by the masters of the city thrilled Ady even as it unsteadied her. Lenore placed a hand on Ady's shoulder as they continued walking apace.

"I understand the danger you're under. But you asked to participate, and such dangers are a central fact of our endeavor." They turned to enter a side room.

"I don't understand. What is—"

Several more women were inside the room. Ady recognized some of their faces, but she didn't know their names. At least two of them she had encountered long ago when she and Sanite were tasked with cleaning the offices and homes of the city's elite.

"Who is this one?" a large woman said. Ady recognized her, too. She had stopped by the inn many times for breakfast but rarely spoke. She was taller than Ady, which was a rare encounter for her.

"Aw, calm down, Tremaine," a woman who wore an apron over her dress said. "If Sweetness brought her in, you know dang well she's all right."

"I don't know shit but that those mens trying to find this barn."

"Sweetness?" Ady giggled.

Ady ignored her. "Ladies," Lenore said, "this is Ady. She will be joining us."

"So she here to replace Alabama," Tremaine said.

"I'm not replacing anyone," Ady said.

Tremaine glared. "Don't you talk back to me or I'll fold your narrow behind, gal." Tremaine shoved Ady. Then she pressed her fists together. Ady wondered what the woman did beyond the walls. She seemed like she could wrangle a bull with those hands.

"I— I ain't afraid of you." Of course Ady was afraid of Tremaine, and this embarrassed her. She wondered where inside her she could find the rage that allowed her to destroy the man who tried to defile Alabama. She had none of the fire Tremaine was looking down on her with. Indeed, she realized, she'd never had a thought about hurting another Colored woman. She couldn't do it if she tried. "You do what you want. I will talk any way I please."

"Ha!" Tremaine clapped, and the other women, including Lenore, laughed. Ady watched them in confusion.

"The look on your face," Lenore said.

"This was some kind of test?" Ady asked.

Tremaine threw an arm around Ady's shoulders. "It's good to know how someone acts in a truly perilous situation. You can't be one of the Daughters if you can't maintain yourself."

"Daughters?" Ady said.

"Nah," Tremaine said. "*The* Daughters."

"In honor of our mothers," Lenore said. "It's one of our codes for identifying who is in our number."

One of the other women placed a basket on the table. "I made sandwiches. Enough chitchatting, we ain't got much time as is. Let's sit and work."

"Sandwiches?" Ady asked.

"Miss Sonnier makes the most delicious refreshments," Lenore said. She turned to Ady. "You can't expect us to mother a revolution on an empty stomach, non?"

"I guess not," Ady said.

"Let us do what we've come to do," Lenore said.

"Let us do it through and through," the others chimed. Ady stood next to Lenore as the others began to introduce themselves and their ideas for the future. Tremaine ran a stable in Jefferson City for her master. The other women cleaned manors, cooked; one was a mistress to a slave labor camp owner. She wore so much makeup she seemed like a fanciful painting of—what, wondered Ady. A sunrise? A butterfly?

There was strength in her eyes. Tremaine started a song, and the others joined in. With women like these on the issue, failure didn't seem possible.

Ady would not return to the textile building. The women met only rarely, due to the danger of being discovered. But she had come to know of things that she was previously unaware of. Of battles in Kansas. Of slavers' hopes to expand to the new west. Of uprisings across the nation that were put down, but not before their legends were passed on. The suppressions had caused the women to go underground, to conduct their affairs behind barn doors and under the canopies of evergreens.

Now there was talk of a possible war between the states. Those up north had been arguing for the end of enslavement. Those in New Orleans and across the South vowed such an end would never come to pass.

The Daughters, who had many aliases—Daughters of Elysian Fields, the Mum Bett Society, Cecile Fatiman's Women, the Wheatleys, among others—had been operating locally since Napoleon handed the territory off to Thomas Jefferson— if not before. Many of the Daughters had been killed in their clandestine endeavors. This more than anything was why she had never heard of them. Whatever actions they took— whether successful or failed—were elided from all records. There were no reports in the periodicals of a young woman named Mary Ann who lured a bear into her owner's house, and the bear devoured much of the family, who had been slathered lovingly in French honey. No speeches by orators inveighed against General Desirée, who was said to have fought in men's clothes alongside the British against the Americans in 1815 and used her war wages to buy her own freedom and that of her extended family. Why would their so-called masters ever want to admit that the women—mere African American women—were capable of organizing and opposing their desires? The women were well aware that whatever the Daughters accomplished would be forgotten for all time. Ady knew that she, too, would be forgotten.

Yet instead of discouraging Ady, this knowledge steeled her resolve. She was dedicated to her mission. To gather as much information about his preparations as possible. And in every moment, this was her first purpose. When he was present in the townhouse, she lingered while cleaning the rooms so that she could overhear his conversations with visitors. She hovered over his desks, scanning the documents for useful notes. A shipment of cannonballs was being sent down from a foundry in Kentucky. New uniforms were being woven for the latest additions to his force of men. Even, a steamer vessel was being converted to war purpose. It would patrol the Mississippi and engage Northern warships. These were only some of the plans that Ady became privy to. But more importantly, he was in alliance with many other men around the city, and they all agreed that they didn't have the required funds to complete their defense against interlopers.

One Sunday afternoon, he shouted, "Why are you still in this room!" and slammed his ledger shut. Ady was applying polish to a silver pelican that was perched on his bookshelf. He approached.

"And where is my letter seal?"

"I haven't seen it," she said without looking at him.

He grabbed her wrist. "It seems like you're always underfoot these days. I don't recall you ever paying such attention in the past." It was true. She'd never polished any of the metal objects. Indeed, she'd had to purchase a special liquid at market to do so. She'd also gotten a duster and wax for the desks.

She looked up at him without raising her head. "Your visitors touch things," she said. "They leave smudges. I'm only trying to keep them how you like."

He tossed her arm away. "Just get out! I can't think with you hovering like a night owl." He turned away.

Behind him, Ady smiled. She raised her chin, gathered her supplies in her copper pail, and walked onto the interior balcony. When she closed the door, she threw her head back and laughed.

By evening, he had left for his plantation, and Ady took a direct route to the river. She waited where she was told and watched for her signal. The auction house where Sanite and she had been sold was across the street. Someone whistled and a large figure rode by on a mule-driven cart. Tremaine. She wore a wide-brimmed hat, which she tilted at Ady. Tremaine gave a look with her eyes that made Ady search the street near the curb. A parcel rolled across the ground. Ady ran to the spot where the parcel landed. Some small children approached it, but she shooed them away.

The parcel was hastily wrapped in brown paper and twine. Frayed along the edges. Tremaine must have wrapped it herself in that stable. Indeed, it carried a musty scent.

"What is that?" said one of the city patrolmen, rounding the corner. He looked familiar as if he had questioned her in the past. But then something remarkable happened. One of the children kicked him in the shin. He raised his club and gave chase to them. One of the girls called back to Ady, *For our mothers.*

Ady stared at the girls before she realized that it would be best for her to leave as quickly as possible. She headed straight to the Mockingbird.

As soon as Ady entered, Lenore approached and took her hand. They walked into her office behind the guest roll counter. Behind the closed door, Lenore sat at her desk. Ady handed over the package and Lenore cut the twine with shears. Ady helped remove the wrap. Lenore carefully unfurled a piece of correspondence and a small stamp.

"What is it?" Ady asked.

"This"—Lenore held up the stamp—"was from your insight. We plan to give them cause to make some onerous expenditures."

"I don't follow," Ady said.

"You said that many of these slavers are short on funds, most especially the vice mayor. A sealed letter from one of the upriver slavers asking him to acquire costly provisions for the troops—I hear that beef is especially high at the moment—should do the trick. This correspondence"—Lenore pointed at the unfurled letter—"shall provide a sample of said upriver slaver's handwriting."

"That's clever."

"We have neither money nor the force of law on our side," Lenore said. "Clever, I'm afraid, is all we have."

"When did you start on all of this?"

"I was born into it. So were my mother and grandmother. Tremaine's too. We've always been here, ripping them apart from the shadows. It was one of us," Lenore grinned, "who helped Governor Claiborne drink himself into St. Louis Cemetery Number One."

"The Lord's work," Ady said.

"Yes." Lenore took a clean sheet of paper from her drawer. Ady held out her hand.

"Can I try?" Ady asked.

"Have you ever forged a slave master's writing before?"

"No, but I'd like to try." Lenore offered her seat to Ady, who studied the loops and crosses of the words. She dragged the pen carefully across the page. As it went, Ady discovered a new skill. She was an expert forger.

"I couldn't have done better myself," Lenore said.

"Some young girls helped me today."

"Is that so?" Lenore said, smiling.

"I guess all of us are trying to get free, huh?"

Those late summer and early fall weeks were filled with success. Ady heard reports from Lenore and the Daughters as well as du Marche himself of the chaos created by their actions. A ship laden with cotton from one of the upriver plantations caught fire on the river. One of the Daughters had knocked over a kerosene lamp in the hold. A local tobacco merchant and supporter of slavery went bankrupt when he purchased a huge shipment of overripe bananas from Central America. Lenore had heard of the shipment from her father and made sure that she casually said to Miss Ady, within earshot of the merchant, that she would have bought the lot herself, were she in such a position. And a slave hunter was arrested by a Louisiana marshal on charges of train robbing out west. The charges were real, but an anonymous letter to the marshal informed them of where to find the man. That was Ady.

Ady was now part of a community that she could only see a small part of, but that she could feel stretching across the nation from the streets of New York to the frontier. The Daughters were wreaking havoc from toe to crown.

"Oh, they steamed. That's for sure," Tremaine said to Ady one day at the inn. Tremaine was drinking beer. It was early. This was after the turn. The slavers had started a counter-offensive. The only Colored jewelry shop in the district had gone up in flames the prior night.

"They can't tell who tearing them up." Tremaine laughed. "So they lashing out at anyone they can. Not like they weren't already."

"Pipe down," Lenore said as she approached.

"Pipe down why?" Tremaine asked.

"Because we're all of us being observed. Don't stare." A man in a bowler hat sat at a table halfway across the room.

"Hnh," Tremaine said.

Ady walked to the man's table. He had elaborate facial hair and was drinking a café au lait that she had prepared.

"Excuse me, sir," Ady said, affecting Lenore's manner of speech. "Is your drink satisfactory?"

He lowered his hat closer to his eyes.

"May I take your hat? I should have offered when you entered. I know a gentleman such as yourself would not want to appear uncouth."

"I'm fine." He pursed his lips. "Thank you . . . young lady."

Ady leaned close to the man. He leaned back.

"Would you care to join the establishment's owner and that stable woman at their table?"

"Pardon me?"

"You seemed interested in the conversation."

The man rose from his seat and exited the inn.

Tremaine slapped her knee. "That's one way to handle the nosy ones."

"Why did you do that?" Lenore said, her voice angry.

"I didn't like the way he was staring at you . . . Sweetness."

"This isn't a joke." Lenore gritted her teeth.

"Lighten up," Tremaine said. "Someone get me another beer."

"It's ten in the morning, ma'am!" Ady said.

"Don't call me ma'am! You'll give ma'ams a bad name, gal." Tremaine held out her empty mug.

Lenore grabbed the mug and slammed it on the table. "This isn't a game. All of our lives are on the line."

Ady stared at Lenore, who was trembling.

"Lenore, we have to—" Ady said.

Lenore held up a finger. "I find nothing funny here." She grabbed the mug. "I shall fetch your beer, Tremaine."

With autumn came a change in the city, both in the weather and in the slavers' activities. The militiamen, in their colors and boots, had been seen marching the streets in formation and running war exercises along the marsh. They began in small numbers with sticks, hoes, and batons. But their numbers had swelled and most of the men had graduated to long guns. Presently they were posted on street corners in groups of two to five. And it appeared to Ady that many of the men no longer had other employment—working on the docks or in carpentry—but were full-time belligerents.

Ady saw the men from on high. They numbered in the thousands. They stood out to her like the heads of dandelions. She blew and hoped the men were washed away by the strength of her breath. But when she opened her eyes, the men were still there. Tremaine had reported that she was being followed by the same man in the hat, had seen him stalking her on several occasions. More worrying, Miss Sonnier, the sandwich maker, had disappeared from her kiosk near Poydras Market. Ady had offered to go search for the woman herself, but Lenore had forbidden that. It wouldn't do to have two local Daughters unaccounted for.

"Are you tired?" Lenore tapped Ady's leg. They were in a carriage heading east. Lenore was wrapped in a magnificent violet coat with a fur collar. Ady wore a dark cloak. She was cold and sat in the carriage seat with her hands on her lap.

"Sometimes I wish that I could change everything in a blink."

"It may come to that," Lenore said. "I wouldn't wager against it. Driver, this is the establishment." The vehicle slowed to a stop. The driver hopped down from his perch but, apparently noticing Ady and Lenore's back-and-forth, did not open the door. He was now brushing the haunches of the horse.

"I've never been to a performance," Ady said. Lenore had described the method to her. People in costumes would act out a story that someone had created. It sounded like the madness of small children. Ady was delighted. "What are they doing?"

"My dear, I have no idea. I simply show up, and they entertain me."

"Before we go in . . ." Ady coughed and reached into her bag. She produced a parcel wrapped in brown butcher paper.

Ady had never given a gift. She'd seen gifts given to him by patrons. And at the inn she'd witnessed friends and lovers exchange gifts. Lenore had given a parcel to Alabama as she left. But Ady had never had any money of her own until the Mockingbird. And she'd never had anyone to give a gift to until the Mockingbird, either.

"What is this for?"

Ady placed her hands on Lenore's. "Do I need a reason?" Ady smiled.

"Ady . . ." Lenore said.

"Open it."

Lenore opened the package. Her face brightened.

"A paintbrush set!"

"You said you needed new ones. I didn't want you feeling like you shouldn't do your paintings because you didn't have the right tools, and—"

Lenore kissed Ady fully on the lips. The kiss lingered. And during that moment time seemed to stretch. Ady felt every part of her own body in the moment; alive! Her face was flushed, her stomach fluttering, stars spreading behind her eyes. Every drop of blood accounted for. The ecstasy she felt from this new kind of touch stirred a section of her spirit that she didn't know existed. A new world was unfolding within her. Had Ady died in that moment, she would not have had a single regret.

Lenore pulled away and took a breath, but Ady threw her arms around Lenore and continued the kiss. Eventually, Lenore pulled away.

"I love you," Ady said.

"I apologize." Lenore licked her lips. "I don't know what got into me."

"Don't say that."

"Ady, I can't." Lenore stared out of the carriage window as if searching for onlookers. "We shouldn't."

"Is it because I'm younger?"

"You're not so young." Lenore placed her hands on Ady's shoulders. "I'm but eighteen."

"But I thought—"

"Haven't you learned that no one in this city tells the truth? The truth is hazardous." Lenore seemed smaller, more delicate just then. It was as if she had taken off a mask.

"What are you saying?"

"There's too much you don't know. Too much I can't tell you."

"Why? Ain't I good enough for you?"

"You're the very best, my dear. That's why."

Ady saw that Lenore's eyes were wet. Then Lenore straightened her back and raised her nose. She seemed to mature, taking on her normal attitude, through mere body language.

"I'm going to enter. Follow me if you wish." Lenore opened the door. The driver helped her down. He tipped his hat. Ady followed.

Lenore had stopped at the entrance, where a bill was stuck to the exterior. Lenore was frowning.

Ady saw that it was a wanted poster for . . . The Daughters.

"An insult." Lenore raised her nose. "They're only offering fifteen thousand dollars for the lot of us."

Ady smiled. "We could use that money."

Lenore didn't smile. "Come in."

The hall was drafty, but warm from the body heat of the free people of color who filled it. Everyone seemed to know Lenore.

"Mademoiselle, comment ça va?" a man said inside the entrance, kissing her cheeks. He was thin and wore a colorful suit that the low lighting reduced to shades of gray.

"Comme ci comme ça, Henri," Lenore said. "What will be performed?"

"Our director is just back from England. We're doing Lear."

Ady smiled.

"Your tall young friend likes that," Henri said.

"I'm old enough to have read it."

"Oh. Well . . . pardon me then, petite chérie."

As they walked toward the front of the seating area, Ady spoke. "Why do people always think I'm a child?"

"It must be your baby cheeks and large eyes." Lenore laughed and flourished her hand across her face. "I use a small amount of kohl under mine so that people will refer to me as a woman rather than a girl."

Ady frowned.

Lenore took Ady's hand. "I'm sorry if I appear cold to you. Perhaps we can finish our conversation another time." Ady nodded. Lenore touched Ady's cheek, and Ady smiled despite her confusion at the events of the night.

The stage play began and Ady felt flushed. To be indoors with a score of other Negroes. To be safe and warm. She smelled wellness in the air. Perfumes. Flowers attached to dresses. Hair pomades and aftershave. The actors were game. They crashed onto the stage before the footlights and filled the room. Through their characters, Ady saw that they were enjoying the experience of performing for the audience. Until.

Someone screamed at the back of the room. The production stopped. Many of the audience members were on their feet just as quickly.

"Nothing to worry about, ladies and gentlemen," Henri said, coming through the double doors. "A hooligan left a flaming sack at the ticket booth."

Lenore grabbed Ady's hand and pulled her out.

"Why are we leaving?" Ady asked.

But Lenore said nothing. Out of doors, Ady saw there was a peculiar bustle to the streets. People moved with disorientation, as if they'd been roused from their beds. She breathed deeply to catch her bearings. She could feel the presence of the river to the south, aching past the town. In between, the park sat only three blocks south of their present placement. It was full dark by then, an overcast night. The thin clouds lay across the sky like rags. And over to the south, the sky glowed. The glow reminded Ady of the way the wall across from the hearth at his big house appeared. The glow warmed that den. But neither Ady nor the other enslaved were allowed to rest there. Something was in the air. She inhaled again. The stench of char.

Above the tops of the mansard roofs, Ady saw dark plumes lit by the edges of the flames below.

"No," Ady said out loud to Lenore. She didn't want it to be true. But as their legs carried them forth toward the street where the Mockingbird was, the fact became incontrovertible. A block from their destination, the unpainted bricks of the nearby storefronts pulsed with light. Ady felt the heated wind brush against her face. Like dragon's breath from one of the old English books Mrs. Orsone had provided.

"Oh!" Lenore said when they stopped a stone's throw

from the burning frame. Ady recognized several employees of the establishment standing across the way in their uniform dresses. Molly was there. Mrs. Gaines stood in her apron, a large painting propped against her thigh. A section of the third-floor wall tumbled into the flames. The Mockingbird was no more.

"Oh!" Lenore said again, reeling. Ady caught Lenore before she fell to the ground. A plume of thick smoke erupted into the sky. Ady held Lenore's waist firmly.

"I'm so sorry," Ady said.

Lenore shook her head and righted her body. After a moment, Lenore sniffed and laughed breathlessly. "I'm so sad. I can't do anything but laugh at this."

"I suppose we got to see a show after all," Ady said.

"Yes," Lenore said. "But next time leave the selection to me." And now Ady chuckled breathlessly. Lenore tried to smile again but faltered, as she watched chunks of the building fall.

The fire brigade arrived with their carriage and pump. More people had gathered on the dirt road, making the night seem festive, as in the aftermath of a sacrifice. It was then that Ady noticed figures watching the scene.

Three men waited at the street corner. Two wore the military uniforms of his guard. The third man was Johnny.

"Molly," Ady said. "Please take care of our friend."

"Right," Molly said.

Ady walked toward the men.

"It seems your compatriots are having an unpleasant evening," Johnny said as she approached. The soldiers scoffed. She recognized one of the soldiers next to Johnny as the bearded man who had been eavesdropping on Lenore and

Tremaine's conversation. The same man who had been following Tremaine.

Ady strode past them in the direction of the townhouse.
And she continued walking without looking back to see if she
was being followed.

The townhouse grounds were lousy with men in uniform,
cronies of his. The men stood along the banquette and clogged
the carriageway. She shouldered past them into the courtyard.
It was a Thursday, a day he was rarely in town. But clearly he
was present. And clearly in communication with his son.

It didn't hurt as much as she would have thought when he
backhanded her at the bottom of the steps. She hardly felt it as
he dragged her up to the balcony and pressed her against the
railing. He was a beast and there were actions she feared. But
they were in public, and she knew well enough that his intent
was to embarrass and subdue her. He gripped her by the hair
at the back of her head.

"You think I didn't know what you were up to?" he said.
"Young Johnny told me all about your employment. He's a
good boy underneath. Even offered me your funds out of fe-
alty. I declined. However, your receiving pay from another
without my blessing or remitting the same to me is theft of my
property by my property. Colonel! Convene the men."

Ady struggled to free herself from his clutches, but she
could hardly budge. It occurred to her presently that all his
ravings pertained to her work at the Mockingbird. He knew
nothing of her spying. Nothing of the Daughters. The fool.
Ady laughed.

"You cretin." He grabbed her shoulder and spun her
around. She was facing the courtyard as the men began to
gather. He spoke into her ear.

"Do you think I care about your comings and goings! Or whatever pitiful amount of money you collected! The days of those such as your fine Creole friend are over! Do you understand? This town deserves a purer class of gentry."

He let go of her, and Ady fell to her knees, breathing heavily. For once, she wished him to feel what she felt in his presence. The fear of darkness. The torture of what might come. Of endings. She looked up and was possessed by the spirit to leap and push him over the railing, even if she crashed to the ground with him, even if it meant both their deaths.

"What's that look?" he asked. He pulled her along by the arm to her quarters and tossed her onto her pallet.

"Bring up the manacle," he said to someone outside of her view. Shortly thereafter, two militiamen appeared hauling a ball and chain, each carrying their own end of the device.

"Careful not to damage my floor," he said as they laid it in the corner. It was the kind with manacles for each leg. She had seen them at the slave labor camps.

"You know very well what this is," he said to her. "I've used this on many an obstinate cur at Ascension. Few things get one back into line as quick." He picked up one of the manacles and clapped the end together like the bill of a duck. The clanking of the metal made Ady flinch despite herself. He reached for Ady's foot, but she moved back toward the wall. The bricks pressed through the cloth of her dress into her back. She couldn't allow him to place that on her body.

He cackled. "I could put this on you." He dropped the manacle. "But I know I don't have to. I've got you where it counts." He pointed at his head, then he turned and walked onto the balcony. He began speaking to soldiers from above.

"I say, hear me, men! Yesterday has passed and today is

ours. If we have to burn all their businesses to the ground we shall. If we have to place shackles on them all, we shall. A new day is arising and our way of life shall persevere." He raised his hand above his head, and the assemblage cheered. Ady smelled the charred remnants of the Mockingbird on her clothing. *I could push him over that rail, but then I'd never see her again.*

19.

DAYS PASSED. THEN WEEKS. The townhouse remained a hub of activity. Ady was not physically shackled, but she was not allowed to leave the premises. Each day she cleaned and did her best to avoid the militiamen on the grounds. Constantly, she thought of Lenore and the Mockingbird. Would she ever see her friend again? *Friend,* she thought as she washed a dish. An ant of a word. Too small.

One morning, the courtyard was mostly cleared of men. She hadn't slept a moment overnight, hearing their movements, their conversations through the broken slats of her quarters, their laughter in the low morning hours. Several more establishments owned by free people of color had burned, which accounted for their merry carousing through the night.

A man banged on her door. "The vice mayor wants you at the gate."

At the gate, he waited, already in the seat of his covered carriage.

"Don't contemplate too strenuously," he said. "Climb inside." He leaned out the window. "Take the Market route, driver. I'm in no rush this morning."

"Yessuh," the driver said.

Once inside, he presented a small envelope to her.

"Go on then," he said. "Open it."

Ady read the card. Her face fell.

To the Vice Mayor of New Orleans, an invitation for a business proposition regarding one in your possession named Antoinette. An audience one likely morning at the addressed residence requested. Adrien Pasquel, Esq.

It was signed by Lenore's father. But Ady recognized the handwriting, which told the true story. The correspondence was written by Lenore herself.

An offer appearing to come from Lenore's father made a certain sense. Neither du Marche nor Mr. Pasquel would ever conduct important affairs with a woman. But Lenore must have known this was a risky gambit. What did she think she was doing?

"Do you recollect? When I purchased you, you couldn't read a lick. Your mammy never learned." He placed a hand on Ady's leg. "Some of these planters fancy themselves royalty. The new dukes and earls. They cavort with mulattoes and octoroons at social events. They prefer the ones with refinement. The ones who carry on as though they're worthy women. I've never understood that."

Ady sat at his side. Her cheek was bruised, although she didn't recall being struck recently. There was a tightness from swelling beneath her skin. The night of the fire came back to her, though unrelated to the injury. Normally, she would brush aside the memory of thrashing against his grip on the balcony before his militia. But here she allowed the remembrance to fill her mind. She recalled her savage self. The part of her who cared not a whit if she shoved him over the railing and followed him to the stones below. She regretted missing her opportunity to strike.

She placed her hand on his knee. She stifled a retch in her throat and held her fingers firm. She had never touched him of her own accord. He lowered his gaze to her hand. She saw the small terror of the unexpected in his eyes.

"Why did you hire Mrs. Orsone if you wished me ignorant?" she asked. "Why have her instruct me in anything at all?" He sniffed and moved to detach her hand, but stopped.

"To see the look on your face when you read that note." He stared at her. "I jest. When your mammy died, I fancied selling you to one of those men, but you were so scrawny I wouldn't have gotten much of a price for you. I've preferred having you at my disposal for my purposes. And better to have you at my disposal as less of a buffoon than you might otherwise have been."

She left her hand on his thin knee, felt the warmth of the skin under his trouser fabric. She wished to withdraw her hand. The tightness at the back of her throat demanded no less. But she saw him continue to watch her hand. She did not move her hand.

Ady knew the street they turned onto. The carriage was moving at a clip. Startlingly quickly, they came to rest in front of Pasquel Manor.

"There are many men in my circles who believe your kind to lack any intellect whatsoever. Those men are dullards. It's obvious that the black is imbued with some of the same material of the soul as men like me. President Jefferson understood that. So did Washington and some contingent of the others of the revolutionary generation. My own daddy met Jefferson when he was old. Over in Virginia. But that's beside the matter." He placed a hand on her leg again. "Go into that residence and await my entrance."

"What do you intend to do?"

"I'm not armed," he said. "And not accompanied by the men. I have manners. The father of your acquaintance contacted me and invited us here, but such overtures shall be put to rest today. Tell them goodbye. I must run a brief errand."

Ady climbed down from the carriage without the assistance of the driver, who sat whistling. His job was to help ladies.

Edmonton, the butler, answered the door. He seemed reluctant to let her beyond the foyer. Lenore's house was as regal as before. The air smelled of wood polish, and a sweet scent from the kitchen hung in the air. Ady found it hard to be in the presence of a home. Ady had never had a home, she understood this now. Or rather, she realized as her feet carried her into the warm interior, the Mockingbird was the closest to a home she'd ever been blessed to know. Which meant she understood the vulnerability of Pasquel Manor. The manor, constructed of wood and masonry just like the Mockingbird, could burn as quick as kindling.

He knew as well the value of Ady's friendship with Lenore. Justice would not be done for any of the owners of the destroyed places. Standing in the hallway as Ady did meant further endangering Lenore, her family, and the others. Why did Lenore send the invitation? Why tempt the Devil? This infuriated Ady. Ady would use that fury to protect her love.

Ady went past Edmonton into the side hall off the foyer. From the card room, Lenore waved. Ady closed the door after she entered. Lenore flew from her seat and embraced Ady.

Lenore noticed the bruise on Ady's face and caressed the spot. "My dear, what has happened? I was so fearful about you." Lenore's eyes had circles around them. But more than that was Lenore's expression, that of deep-seated worry.

"I'm not hurt," Ady said. Lenore continued to touch Ady's cheek.

"We don't have time," Ady said.

"No. I don't imagine that we do at this juncture," Lenore said. "What does he know about the Daughters?"

"I don't know. He might have a hunch."

Lenore's lip trembled. Ady wasn't used to seeing Lenore in this condition. She felt a hollow in her own chest.

"I— I have to confess. I'm afraid," Lenore said.

"I know," Ady said. "I won't let them destroy anything else of yours."

"That's kind of you, but that's not what I'm referring to."

"Then what are you—"

"Ahem," said Edmonton. "Miss Lenore, your father inquires about your return to the breakfast table."

"Yes," Lenore said. "Of course. We should join the others. He just arrived."

"He who?" Ady asked.

Lenore pulled Ady into the dining room, where several sat. Mr. Pasquel took note of Ady's face but didn't hesitate before he gently kissed her on both cheeks.

"My dear," he said. "Please make yourself comfortable." Ady was obliged to sit at the end of the table beside Lenore. Lenore's father sat at the far end. And in between were Lenore's younger brother, Darrow, and a young woman named Cecilia who leaned into him genially. Another man sat on the other side of Lenore. He was tall and square-jawed. Handsome. Boring.

"I tell you that even in trying times there are few things as comforting as a happy home," Mr. Pasquel said. "Having Dr. Chevalier, the son of a dear old friend, down from Philadelphia is additional proof that our fortunes are indeed happy."

Dr. Chevalier sat with ramrod posture, his eyes striking and possessed of intelligence. Ady had never heard his name, but she knew then that he was the one to whom Lenore had been betrothed, and the thought sickened her.

"That's him?" Ady whispered. Lenore pinched her knee.

"Thank you for inviting me into your beautiful home, sir," Dr. Chevalier said.

"Of course," Lenore's father said.

"And it is a special pleasure to finally meet you in person, Lenore." Dr. Chevalier reached out. Lenore offered her hand and Dr. Chevalier took it in his and leaned forward to kiss it.

"You better watch your hand, doc," Darrow said. "Lesser men have lost theirs." Cecilia tapped Darrow's arm.

"Oh, stop it, brother," Lenore said. There was a hitch in her voice as though she were unable to speak above half her usual volume.

"And who here do I have the pleasure of meeting?"

"This is Ady, my very good friend," Lenore said. "She works—worked at the inn."

"Yes," Dr. Chevalier said. "I was sorry to hear about what befell your business. These conspirators in the South are a barbarous lot. I've heard that similar forces are massing in cities from Texas to North Carolina."

Darrow leaned forward. "They'll need to be opposed, to say the least."

"That's hardly your concern, friend," Dr. Chevalier said.

"You've still got schooling to do here in the city." Darrow frowned.

"It is indeed terrible," Mr. Pasquel said, "what they've done in the city of late, but I'm old enough to know these events come and go like the tides. It is important not to become too emotional at momentary circumstances. Lenore's little inn was destroyed, but she is safe. We don't need you taking up arms to counteract those forces, son."

"Father, it falls upon men like myself for that very reason. They have a force of men. We should have our own!"

"Dar," Cecilia whispered. "Please don't be rude."

Mr. Pasquel cleared his throat. "We will speak of this later, son. Our immediate concern is for Eleanor and Dr. Chevalier's move to Pennsylvania. Her defunct enterprise becomes a moot point."

"Move?" Ady asked.

"You sound surprised, young lady," Mr. Pasquel said. "Surely you knew of Lenore's engagement. Of their impending marriage."

"I'm not surprised, sir." Ady looked to Lenore. "Just disappointed," she said under her breath.

Lenore's eyes glanced down. "I wanted to tell you of Dr. Chevalier's telegram, which came in late. I was beginning to fear he might renege."

"My arrival was intended to be a surprise."

"A surprise," Ady said.

"I was surprised," Mr. Pasquel said. "We've been expecting the good doctor for weeks."

"Weeks!" Ady tried to whisper, but her voice squealed.

"Ady, please," Lenore said.

Edmonton stepped into view.

"Presenting the Honorable Mr. John du Marche, Vice Mayor of the City of New Orleans, Army General of the—."

Du Marche pushed into the room. "Pshaw! No need for all that pomp in this place," he said.

Ady stopped short. If she could have turned and run through the wall, she would have. Of course she knew he was coming, but she thought she'd meet him outside. Seeing him in this home, one of the few places she had ever felt a modicum of safety, disturbed Ady greatly.

Lenore grabbed Ady's hand.

"Our guest has arrived," Lenore's father said. Du Marche crossed into the room and placed his hands on his hips. *Our guest,* Ady thought, but she assumed Lenore had written the invitation, that it was all a ruse to get Ady there.

Mr. Pasquel stood and offered du Marche a seat. "I hadn't realized you had taken a military post with the federal government."

"Because I haven't. My confederate's business doesn't concern the likes of you, Adrien." He stared at Mr. Pasquel. "What is this all about? You know I don't frequent this part of town much. And what are you doing with my slave gal?"

"John, have a seat and some tea."

"Father, you know this man?" Darrow asked.

"Shush, boy!" du Marche said. "You should know better than to refer to me so disrespectfully." He placed a boot on one of the free chairs. "Know me? Who do you imagine ships a quarter of my produce per annum? I'm the reason you and your darkie sister are able to live in this finery."

Darrow moved to stand, but Cecilia caught his arm.

Ady found it difficult to catch her breath. She tried to meet Lenore's eyes, but Lenore refused to look at her.

"Mr. Vice Mayor—General du Marche," Mr. Pasquel said, "my daughter explained everything to me. I called you here to set affairs aright."

He pointed at Mr. Pasquel. "You mean to say that my property has been working at your inn without my explicit mandate for weeks?"

"John, please. Human relations are complicated until we get down to money. Then it's just ledgers and exchanges for value. I understand you're raising funds for an endeavor. I'm willing to offer double the girl's value."

"You'd help him fund his army!" Darrow said.

"Quiet, son," Mr. Pasquel said.

"What are you on about?" du Marche said.

"To be clear, I've purchased manumission for many a Colored in my day. You can imagine a man in my position likes to give back where he can. To whom much is given, you know?"

"Pfft. The legislature has outlawed the freeing of slaves anyhow."

"That may be the case, but it's still a legitimate offer, as are my funds."

"About that," du Marche said. "I've only just come from the savings and loan. I purchased several bank notes that you're indebted for, which means I can call in your debt and put you under with the stroke of a pen."

Mr. Pasquel's face closed.

"Now you have more important matters to attend to than this girl," du Marche said. "It's a terrible thing that men in this city have been doing. Razing establishments as if this were Rome at its end. I was saddened to hear about the inn. I've enjoyed its hospitality once or twice myself. But I am glad that this fine manor still stands." Du Marche glanced around the room. "It is a fine shanty, isn't it?" He squeezed Ady's shoulder.

"Yes, sir," Ady said.

"What none of you people can fathom is that this one was raised in my townhouse and has enjoyed a fine life there."

He removed a match and produced a flame that wobbled for a moment. He lit a cigarette, inhaled and exhaled.

"She doesn't want to leave the safety that I created for her, does she?"

Ady looked around the room, from face to face. Alabama was already free somewhere north of the Mason and Dixon line. Soon Lenore would be free of her father's purview.

It would take nothing for him to direct his men to burn down Pasquel Manor with Lenore and her family inside. This would be the last time she saw Lenore, Ady was sure. That would be for the best.

"No, Father. I'd never want to leave you."

He clutched Ady's hand and pulled her out of the dining room, through the foyer, down the steps, and all the way back to the townhouse.

For better or worse, it had been the work of her life there maintaining the premises from top to bottom. But now he was present more consistently. He brought on additional staff to suit his ambitions. Suddenly she had fewer duties. An Irish cook was employed to make stews and porridges. The cook also ran many of the errands that Sanite used to. The driver, the same free Colored man who had occasionally served him in the past, now waited outside the gate atop a new carriage daily. And a third was hired, or rather purchased: a cruel enslaved woman called Nary, who upon seeing Ady's freshly bruised face laughed from the depths of her belly. Yes, he had laid hands on her during those weeks since she was last at Pasquel Manor.

It was on a day when the cook was out to market and the driver away with du Marche that Ady leaned against the gate at the end of the carriageway. She held the bars and pressed her face between them. How odd it was that she had had the ability to leave with few restrictions in the past, but now she was as much a prisoner as a bird in a cage on a desert island.

The street beyond the townhouse was bustling as it had been for all the weeks since her reconfinement. Her section of the city seemed more populated, the people more animated. She had the sensation that the city was on the precipice of a change, a pot of water just before boiling. A pair of men carrying banners trotted by the gate, but she was unable to read them from her angle.

"Ady," a voice said. Ady wasn't sure of what she heard until the claim repeated. "Ady!" a woman said.

"Who's there?"

Lenore stepped into view. She wore a lush purple cowl, which she pulled back from her hair. Lenore reached through the gate and placed a hand against Ady's cheek.

"What did he do to you?"

Ady, of course, had developed a technique long ago. It dated back to those first dry days in the townhouse after Sanite died. Back then, Ady felt a sensation of having been poured out. Her tears were a manifestation of this. But the real sensation lay within her mind. When Mrs. Orsone began tutoring her in grammar, Ady recognized that she placed her true self in a cart and rode far away. Such was the case in most of her encounters with him. He wanted her to be present and to witness him in his acts. Her freedom was that she denied him this attention. What hadn't he done to her? He had done everything, but nothing that she could describe to her friend.

Yet Ady's weakness was that she had no such defenses with respect to Eleanor Marianne Pasquel. Every moment, every exchange, every touch was inscribed in flame upon the wall of Ady's psyche. The sense of betrayal that Ady felt toward Lenore's capitulation to her father's plan was jagged and glowing. She always imagined—believed!—that Lenore would never comply with the scheme. What a fool she had been. What a fool she remained.

"How are the Daughters?" Ady asked.

"Two others were captured. We've ceased all activities for now."

"Now isn't the time to quit!"

"Don't shout," Lenore said. "Their safety is most important. These men have become relentless in their pursuit. We have to be more careful than ever before."

"Of course you'd say that."

Lenore grabbed the wrought-iron bars of the gate. Ady felt Lenore's hands just below her own.

"What is that supposed to mean?" Lenore asked. Ady glanced back to see if Nary was nearby. Ady unlatched the gate and stepped onto the sidewalk.

"You understand," Lenore said, "that I have no other choice."

"All that talk about your grandmother's courage, your mother's genius. How your mother built on the wealth she was given without need of a man. They fought for their freedom."

Lenore shook her head and glared at Ady. "Do not speak of that which you cannot comprehend. This city was different for them. Not a paradise, but somewhat kinder. You can't tell me you don't feel it. The whole world is collapsing around us. The opportunities of my mother's lifetime are evaporating before our very eyes."

Ady raised her chin. "You came here to gloat," she said.

"What? No."

"I see a spoiled, sad woman of privilege." Ady picked lint from Lenore's shoulder and evened her cowl. "You were never ready to risk anything. You've always been so high and haughty. You've always seen me as your charity case. You've never understood anything about me!"

"Are we so different? My business is burned to cinders! I have no savings! No prospects! The sparrows have a brighter future."

"How sad!" Ady said. "I don't even have myself! You chose to run off with that man because you're afraid!"

"Why do you hate him so?"

"You don't even know him!" Ady said.

"Is that so unusual?"

Lenore lowered her face, then gazed into Ady's eyes. "The truth of the matter is that I do love you. I love how indomitable you are, how brave. I should have told you that night outside the theater, but I was a coward."

Ady shook her head. Lenore touched Ady's hand. "Now you're not afraid, n'est-ce pas?"

Lenore smiled her crooked smile in recognition. "No. I don't believe I am."

Ady clasped Lenore's fingers. "Then why won't you show it?"

"I'm just so tired of this war I've lived in since the day I was born. My mother and grandmother were Daughters also. I was brought into the fold as a child. That's why I was wearing tatters the first time we met. Mother had sent me to retrieve a message lost in the refuse. I've seen so much darkness. Do you know what that does to a person? I can't stand another day of it. You're so ready to overturn the order, but you understand so little. Unlike your mother."

"My mother?"

"She was a Daughter."

"That's impossible."

"When she was in the rural areas, she was a legend among us. Fairly shut down that slave labor camp called Constancia by performing root work on several generations of the planter's family, grandparents and children too. A number of them died. Although they never knew the full extent of her actions." Lenore smiled. "Suspicion of your mother's activities is how you both came to be sold down to New Orleans."

"I don't believe you."

Lenore stepped closer to the gate. "I think she even communicated with my mother, and Tremaine's mother certainly knew her as well. That pair is the reason the St. Thomas Hotel burned in '55. Those men held many meetings there. The destruction placed several of the owners into bankruptcy."

Ady remembered that night, first as the smell of cinders carried on the wind, then as the glow of fire in the night sky. While Ady had watched from the balcony outside their quarters, Sanite had come next to her and laid an arm around her shoulders.

Ady fell back against the iron gate. "But . . . why wouldn't she tell me?"

"I don't know. Perhaps she was trying to protect you, to provide you with some feeling of safety."

They were both crying.

Ady spoke in a whisper. "Marrying that man won't make you safe."

"Why do you care so much about who I marry? Isn't that what people do? They marry! Even the enslaved marry. You could if you wanted to!"

"Just leave me alone," Ady said.

"Ady."

"You have a life in Philadelphia all set out like a banquet. You'll have a mansion and a driver and beautiful children. I hate this, but I ain't jealous of you. I'm just sad. I hope you have a good life where you're going." Ady wheeled around and reentered the carriageway. The gate slammed in a way that she found satisfying. She knew that she was being cruel. She should have given Lenore a proper goodbye, but she couldn't bear it.

"Ady," Lenore yelled, her voice tear-cracked. "Please!"

Ady neither slowed her pace nor glanced back to see Lenore in the splendor of her purple cowl.

Ady wiped the wet from her own cheek. "I love you, too," Ady whispered once she was far out of earshot.

Nary stood on the balcony in her drab brown dress.

"Girl, now you know massa say you can't be going out there."

"I know," Ady said.

"I'm gonna tell on you," Nary said.

"Fine," Ady said.

20.

du Marche (TV Series)

Canceled Home Theater Network TV series

Du Marche (styled as *du Marche*) was a planned premium historical drama developed for Home Theater Network by Martin Sales and Charles Easter. The series was based on the book of the same name and would follow the efforts of a wealthy Louisiana Confederate and the enslaved woman who fell in forbidden love with him. The announcement of *du Marche* was met with derision on social media following a viral PromPost video by activist Melonie "Mel" Lovejoy, who claimed the series distorted the lived experience of her great (x4) grandmother, Antoinette du Marche. In addition, Lovejoy claimed that the rights to the source material had been stolen from her grandmother, Dorothy Heller, by a publisher in the 1950s and that she planned to pursue legal recourse to reclaim those rights, so that she could produce the story herself. Though development of the series continued after the criticism, cancellation of plans for the series was confirmed in May 2028.

The *Eastern Chronicle* reported "widespread anger on social media," but noted Lovejoy would have trouble winning her claims without the lost journal she believed supported her case and version of events.

21.

NARY HAD COME to take Ady's place. She took pride in her new position. She bowed and scraped with an earnestness that Ady had never before witnessed. Nary seemed to relish tracking Ady's movement around the compound. She went so far as to comment on Ady's perambulations. *Going down to wash those linens, huh? Good thing, since your sitting and staring ain't doing me no good.* Or *You been pacing a hole in those yard stones. Bet he wouldn't like that none, if'n he knew.*

Nary handled his morning rituals of shaving and grooming, his occasional bath in the metal tub at the near corner of the courtyard. She brought on his teas and meals. She greeted and served guests. Ady was happy to be untroubled by those tasks, at least. But Ady heard little of his planning.

In accordance with whatever duties du Marche owed to the state government as the newly installed lieutenant governor— Ady was uncertain when this promotion had occurred, but it was a fact—he greeted an endless array of guests, including businessmen, military officers, other politicians, and occasionally men whom he had known long ago who wished to view him in his elevated status and procure a higher order of favor from his position. There was planning afoot. The marshaling of troops, the raising of money, the appearance of scrolled maps that lay like large wood shavings around the main rooms and parlors.

Nary also took over running his errands. Du Marche didn't want Ady leaving the premises at all. Although, eventually

Nary stopped. Not because he was afraid she might run off. To the contrary, she herself refused to travel beyond the court-yard without him. *No, mass, I ain't one for being out amongst all them people, somebody might slap my head.*

For a time, Mrs. Beryl, the Irish chef, handled grocery pro-curement and other errands. But while she was competent at the former, she was disastrous at the latter. She came back to the townhouse with every shank of meat or seasoning she might need for a week, but failed to buy the proper strap for sharpening his shaver or the quill variety he favored. She was illiterate and had a terrible memory.

Ady found that during those initial months after her last encounter with Lenore, he relegated her to only those duties Nary was too overwhelmed to handle, such as bringing food to a guest of the property. The only activity that hadn't changed was his predilection for her body. The circumstance brought on odd new night terrors. More than once, she dreamed of being trapped in a chest of drawers. She grew larger in size until she emerged, only to realize that she had split his body in two in the manner of a sprouting seed.

This is what had grown inside her: darkness, a void be-neath the ocean, a place with no air or light. She could no longer contain the loneliness. It was devouring her.

One day Ady stood in his bedroom. He sat at the rolltop desk, writing a list.

"Why are you standing there?"

"I will procure your items," she said, looking past him.

"Do you demand that I allow you to leave this place?" He stood.

"I simply want to provide what you need, and the others seem incapable. Isn't that what you want?"

He laughed at her but snatched his list from the desk. "Don't be long. You know my men are everywhere at once, and if they catch any unattended slave beyond the city limits, not even my name will save you."

The trips Ady took beyond the townhouse that day and subsequently were not substantially different from those she had taken on many occasions in the past. The push and pull of errands, of entering the markets and certain establishments, of placing orders, carrying back goods. She felt like an automaton. There was little new in these transactions save for two points.

New Orleans had shifted once again. Militiamen—she learned that they called themselves Confederates—were to be found on the streets milling about in their gray uniforms. War had been declared with the North. Somewhere, battles with horses and cannons were being fought. But these men simply waited. Most of them were young, Ady's age or younger in some cases. They gathered on street corners or near food vendors. Many of the soldiers were not well provisioned, but occasionally she witnessed men she presumed to be officers with an ornamental sword dangling from their belt. These men she knew not by name, but from their position in the strata of the city. They were from the same class as he: owners, traders, political animals. Months ago, they would have walked with cigar, umbrella, and satchel.

Ady dared not dally in the old Third Municipality long, for the Confederates massed in a greater concentration there. However, skirting the edges of the area, she saw that some of the establishments of the free Creoles had been shuttered and others taken over by new proprietors. The world seemed to spin faster, dervish-like. And this part of town felt especially alien. The park, the ashen remains of the Mockingbird, even the jewelry store outside which Ady had first glimpsed Lenore in her not-disguised form: It was all within view as if laid in the center of her palm.

She hurriedly walked to the river and saw the brownish waters churning beyond the pier. How useless the brown monster was. Some of that substance could have put out the fire that night.

The second point was the Mockingbird. It was where she became more than who she had once been. She had been a kind of half self before her time there. Now, for better or ill, she was something more. She hoped. She desired. She was of a mind to procure what she needed.

She often wound up near the remains of the inn. Walking past the pile of debris. Or stopping to gaze upon it. The pass was crumpled in Ady's hand as she waited for the Good Children Street omnibus to move out of her way.

She walked across the cobblestones. Her boots, the ones she had worn for many years, had given out. Now she wore the delicate heels that he had provided in the past. They were not made for these streets or any streets, they were caked with dirt. This made her smile.

Although the front of the Mockingbird had been burned away, Ady saw that a good portion of the building was still intact.

Ady picked her way across the singed landscape and found several men scavenging through the rubble. One white man stooped down to collect something from the ground.

"Give that back," Ady said.

"What the blazes?" the man said. He was grizzled and gray-haired, but his clothes fitted well. He put his hand behind his back. "Who are you?"

"I worked here," Ady said. "This is my friend's establishment, and she wouldn't appreciate you taking her hard-earned supplies." Ady saw that the other men had stopped raiding the ruins to watch her.

"Well, if you used to work here, that's the past. This place is finished, that much is sure."

"It's not finished until I say it is. Now leave this place!" Ady poked the man's chest. His hands fell to his sides; she took the opportunity to snatch the item from his hand. He looked down on her with astonishment. She now held Lenore's fine writing pen. The metal-cased fountain pen she had kept by the ledger book at the front desk.

"How dare you! I'll—"

"Will you strike me down?" she said. "Will you call the authorities? Do what you want, but be ready for the consequences." Her heart was pounding against her ribs, and Ady realized that she didn't care what retribution the man enacted.

The man sniffed and glanced around at the others. "It's rubbish anyhow." He walked through the portal that led to what had been the main hall. Some of the dividing walls had burned away. While the other men followed the one she had conversed with, she watched with great satisfaction their exit.

She sat in the courtyard, speaking softly to herself.

Her hand was shaking. Ady spun the fountain pen in her fingers. She had done that for Lenore without thinking; the man could have harmed her, even killed her. She gazed around the ruins and saw in her mind's eye the Mockingbird as it had once stood. Ady saw herself standing at the door in amazement the day Lenore invited her in from the heat of that summer's day. Ady saw Lenore standing at the portal watching Ady on the night he had come to dance with that woman. Ady's eyes had been fixed on Lenore despite the merrymakers twirling between them. Ady saw herself walking about the halls with broom, with mop, with flowers, with herself. Possessed of herself. But something more because of the presence of Lenore.

Ady dusted off her dress and, stepping over a fallen beam, returned to the street. She walked until she rounded the corner and saw Pasquel Manor. She wasn't thinking, just moving.

One of the first-story windows was shattered and covered with crossed boards. Still, as she slowly approached, she felt, in spite of herself, a smile spread across her face. Despite everything, at the core of her experiences here was a sentiment of happiness. She grabbed the lion-faced knocker and tapped it against the base. Shortly thereafter, the door slipped open. Edmonton, even as he tried to suppress his feeling, smirked.

"The lady has returned."

"I'll have none of that from you," Ady said.

"Is that so?"

"Who's bothering the house?" a male voice said from the hall.

"I'm welcome, ain't I?"

"Oh. It's only you," Darrow said.

Ady stepped into the foyer and felt the coolness of the room on her face.

Darrow smiled. "I'll take it from here, my man."

"Very well, sir."

"And I'll make sure she stays off the furniture."

"You're in high spirits," Ady said.

"She said you would never return."

"She said that?"

"Yes. And I bet that girl the sum of three dollars. She hates to lose, you know. I can't wait to see her—"

"She's present?" Ady interrupted.

"Ha." He tapped the wooden finial at the end of the staircase. "You wouldn't know."

"Know what, Darrow?"

He beckoned her to follow him upstairs.

"Tell me!"

Darrow held his finger to his lips.

"Don't shush me," Ady hissed. Darrow laughed and turned the knob to Lenore's bedroom. As the door opened, and before Darrow spoke, Ady smelled Lenore's scent—earthy and fresh like the stem of a flower at daybreak.

"I hope you are gathered, sister," he called into the room. He motioned with his head for Ady to enter.

"Privacy, please, Darrow!" Lenore said.

"It'll do her good to see you," he said to Ady as he closed the door behind him.

"What on earth?" Lenore gathered her bedsheets about her body. Her light brown cheeks had a reddish tint to them. However, on the whole, Ady thought she looked ghostly, as if she hadn't been out of doors in some time. "Oh," Lenore said, dropping her covers. She wore night clothes. "It's you. I suppose you're here to wag your finger at me again, n'est-ce pas?"

"I don't even know what's happened. Why is Darrow so happy? And why are you here? Shouldn't you be in Philadelphia with your beau? I imagined you would be with child by now. Maybe knitting or at a ladies' club—"

"Don't mock me, Ady!" Lenore threw her pillow at Ady, who caught it. A few feathers fluttered out of the case.

"I'm sorry."

Lenore turned her legs out of the bed and sat with her feet on the step stool beneath. "Well, you may mock me a little." Lenore covered her face with her hands.

Ady sat next to her and placed an arm around her. "You never left. You've been here in the city all this time."

"No. I traveled with Chevalier to Philadelphia. Then I bade him farewell at the station and caught the next train back. I've been here in this room. Father isn't speaking to me. He sends messages through Edmonton."

"And you didn't tell me any of this."

"You practically spat on me last time we spoke! And . . . I was afraid that I'd put you in further danger. Of what that man would do to you. You were right. I'm a coward. In every form and fashion. I never know what to do about what matters most."

"That's not true." Ady moved closer to Lenore on the bed. "You're the bravest person I know. I'm sorry. I said things I shouldn't have that day."

"I'm sorry, too. We both said inappropriate things." Lenore grabbed Ady's hand and held it tightly between her own. "Don't you dare take back anything of what you said! You spoke the truth. I was so scared to make the choices I knew were right. I always acted as though I was so well put together, but it was only an act. I thought it was for the benefit of those who saw me as respectable. I'm a woman, but I'm also a girl, Ady. A frightened girl who couldn't even tell her father that she didn't wish to marry until she was practically at the altar.

I've just been so confused." Ady encircled Lenore and they hugged for an extended period. At such closeness, Lenore's garden scent was more detailed: magnolias, gardenias, roses, jasmine.

"But you chose yourself," Ady said when they released each other. "You took control."

Lenore stood up from the bed. "I suppose I did."

Ady stood up too, and they held hands facing each other. "Yes, you did."

"What's this in your hair?" Ady touched Lenore's hair as if to perform a magic trick. She held the pen.

"My Esterbrook!" Lenore smiled her crooked smile, her eyes gleaming. "What are you doing with it?"

"I was at the Mockingbird."

"You mean at its cinders."

"You know how many people you helped with that inn? Lives you changed? Alabama, Molly, Mrs. Gaines. Me!"

"No, I don't want to think about that place." Lenore sat down. Ady sat on her leg. Lenore laughed.

"I don't know about the money part of it," Ady said. "But if anyone could return it to its glory, Lenore Pasquel can."

"Eleanor Marianne Pasquel." Lenore put down her fountain pen and stood. She offered her hand.

"Come," she said. "I want you to see something."

They turned out of the bedroom and passed the other rooms of the second floor to a narrow stairwell in the back corner. Another, wider flight led to the third floor, but the narrow stairwell seemed to climb into a darkness far above the height of the second floor.

"Watch your footing," Lenore said, letting go of Ady's

hand. "There's nothing to hold on to going up. It's a defect of the house I find charming, but dangerous. Like you."

The attic was a broad expanse of sandy wood flooring. Sheets, easels, and canvases were spread around the edges of the room.

"This looks like your room behind the Mockingbird."

"I've been coming up here since I was a child. No one else in the family ever paid it much mind, and I was forbidden to spend time in this aerie. It was unseemly for a young lady to skulk around an attic, you understand. When Father agreed to have me trained as a painter—despite his belief that women lack the temperament to become masters of the art—little did he expect my canvases to take up residence in most of the rooms of the house. Eventually, he banished them and me to these confines." Lenore spun around and threw both hands outward. "Much to my delight." Ady and Lenore laughed.

Lenore walked to the far end of the room, past stacks of canvases leaned against the wall.

"These are mostly earlier pieces. But this is what I've wanted you to see." She went to an easel and carefully pulled away the sheet that covered it. "I'm grateful to Molly. The night of the fire she ran into the shed and rescued this." It was a painting. Of course Ady, in her time, had been in countless houses and stood before countless paintings as she polished the wood of an end table. She'd seen the banshee-like faces of family progenitors or replicas of masterworks copied by American apprentices. The works all had the shaky unreality of a story told by a child; they weren't quite right—they were in fact wrong. But the subjects had been painted out of a sense of worth. They were white and wealthy, so their faces deserved to be cast in amber for passersby to pull their eyes along the surfaces. But here in the attic of Lenore's family home was a painting of a woman in a dress of green with gold lace about the forearms and bosom standing before a shimmering gold background. It was a painting that Lenore had created from her own mind. The woman in the painting was Colored. Her dark skin glowed from the canvas. She exuded freedom. Ady had never seen anyone like her depicted in the immortalizing hues of the brushstroke. But the painting was well done, and it was of Ady.

"I have to qualify, it's not my best work." Lenore approached the canvas and pointed toward the left shoulder, which seemed to disappear as if into fog. "I haven't finished it, to be honest. But we can thank Molly for rescuing it from the Mockingbird shed."

Ady noticed—there on the bottom corner—the char of flame.

Lenore touched the burned area. "I've made some advances since then."

"I don't understand," Ady said, her face hot. She had seen herself in mirrors and windows, but not like this. The her of the painting seemed as real as her substantial self. Indeed, it felt as though Lenore had somehow placed a portion of her soul on that canvas.

"What is that?"

"How did you do this?" Her words tumbled out, quickly and unevenly. "I only sat for you the one time. You made a rough sketch."

"That was all I needed. I see you when I close my eyes, ma chère."

Ady brought her hands to her face. Lenore placed her hands on Ady's.

"Oh, dear," Lenore said. "I know it's not very good, but you needn't cry over it."

"It's wonderful. I don't deserve to be . . ." Ady pointed at the canvas. "There!"

"Nonsense. Ever since I met you when we were children, I knew that I'd do this. Then all I had was chalk." Lenore wiped a tear from Ady's cheek.

"I've always known you," Ady said.

"Say again," Lenore said. Ady took Lenore's hands in her own. She stepped close enough to feel Lenore's breathing against her face.

"You say we first met then in that back alley." Ady caressed Lenore's cheek. "But I feel we knew each other before that. Before our ancestors were born. Maybe before there was a world to speak of. We might have been two stars in the night sky."

"Are you reciting a poem? I know that old governess was fond—"

Ady threw her arms around Lenore, and again they kissed.

"Careful not to take my life," Lenore said.

That night, back in her quarters, she dreamed of Lenore, floating in the leaves of a treetop as if she were a flower. The sun made the leaves glow gold.

22.

Workhouse Interrogation Transcription of Dissident #342 following capture, in-process for digital behavior modification protocol pink/subtype12/with monitoring [y/n: y]

My name is Simone. I am a field commander and my affiliation is with the Daughters. Our purpose? We will overthrow your regime and restore autonomy to the women who nurtured this nation. No, I am not afraid of you. [sounds of struggle; then unintelligible sounds] You can do what you want to me. I won't tell you anything other than my name, rank, affiliation, and purpose.

My name is Sim— is . . . That old book? Is it true? [laughter] Is the Bible true? People like you went into the text and altered it. Then you pushed it out to children to make them think that they're helpless and at your mercy. So yes, I revised it. There are so many of us and we need stories to lift our spirits the same as any movement. The Daughters always have been and always will be. I'm doing what our mothers did before me. Fighting you.

My name? Is. I . . . As long as there are any of us left . . . we'll do everything in our power . . . to protect. That's not terrorism. That's . . .

[unintelligible] Not my name. Why can't I remember my name? I saw Venus pass in front of the sun. It was beautiful. Oridea? Are you here, my love?

23.

ADY WAS AWOKEN by the sound of commotion downstairs. She rose from her pallet and went to the broken slats. Through the gaps she saw some of the Confederates holding an ordinary-looking man by the arms. They punched him in the stomach.

"He's a Yank spy!"

"Give him another!"

Across the courtyard, Ady saw Mrs. Beryl moving about the kitchen. She went out onto the balcony and dumped garbage into the refuse area below.

Mrs. Beryl pulled a mallet from her apron. "I've got a tenderizer if you need it, boys!" she called. And the men laughed. Nary carried a bowl of water over to the main townhouse and pushed the door open with her narrow backside.

Courtland the driver was in the carriageway, top hat in hand.

"Why are they beating that man?" Ady asked.

Courtland looked around the courtyard. Apparently assured that no one was paying them any mind, he stepped back under the carriageway arch.

"It's bad, Miss Ady. Seems he was taking messages from a group of Colored women."

"Messages?"

"I don't know all of it, but I heard a bit driving them over here. Some kind of spy ring like back in the revolutionary war. Playing trickery with the white mens."

So Tremaine and the others were still out there. They hadn't given up.

"That doesn't seem possible."

"It ain't no fantasy, miss. Be glad you're not mixed into the business. You ain't heard my voice tell it, but they trying to catch them womens. They got one this morning. A little lady. Said she had a mouth on her." As Courtland spoke, she felt him place something in her hand.

"She dropped this in my carriage," Courtland whispered.

Ady left the courtyard as soon as she could. She made her way to the Third Municipality and Pasquel Manor, but Edmonton redirected her to the Mockingbird. Ady was amazed to find Lenore, Darrow, and a crew of men working to rebuild the establishment. Planks were set up in a corner. Men were erecting posts. Most surprising of all, Lenore was in knickers!

"What has happened to you?" Ady said. "Your daddy will disown you!"

"I could hardly do work in a hoop skirt. You don't like my style?"

"I think you look wonderful."

"Good," Lenore said, "and what Father doesn't know won't hurt him."

"You're building."

"Rebuilding. On the advice of a very intelligent someone I once conversed with."

Ady smiled, but then took Lenore's hand and pulled her to the side. "Come on," Ady said in a hushed tone, "you should see this." Ady brought Lenore into the draught hall. The flooring had been replaced. As had the stairs. Ady gave Lenore the slip of paper. It was a note from Tremaine.

"This means they're hard at work," Lenore said.

"You didn't know?" Ady asked.

Lenore shook her head. "After all this time. Why didn't they contact me?"

"I bet it's because you're being watched more than the rest," Ady said.

Darrow entered the hall.

"Don't be a busybody," Lenore said.

"Your business is my business," he said.

"Hardly," Ady said.

"Your master will be expecting you back."

"Don't ever call him that." Ady pushed Darrow.

Darrow frowned. "That's what you called him."

"Will you two settle down?" Lenore said.

"I am settled," Ady said. "I've never said his name aloud, and I've never called him my master, not a once."

Lenore smiled and looked up, as if remembering. "You honestly never have. Extraordinary."

"What are we going to do to help the others?"

"I can't believe the two of you are spies."

"You told him?" Ady asked.

"I've played my part in the past."

"You asked the other day what Darrow was so happy about," Lenore said. "I'll preface his scheme by saying I don't agree with his proposal."

"Proposal?" Ady asked.

"The war is upon us," Darrow said. "The Union is marching on the whole South. It's only a matter of time before they're knocking on New Orleans's door."

"And?"

"Your ma— That man is a central part of the defense."

"I'm not a fool. I know what he's involved in. But what does that have to do with me?"

"There's no delicate way to say this." Darrow shoved his hands into his pockets. "I mean to kill him."

Lenore gasped. "This wasn't what you told me."

"I wasn't sure then," Darrow said.

"They'll capture and execute you!"

Darrow placed a hand on the buffet. "What does my life matter when weighed against that of our people?" he asked. He stared at Ady. "You know as well as anyone that he's investing all of his money in support of their cause. Weapons, uniforms, war wages. He's gathering funds to pay for it all."

"He and his cronies," Lenore said.

"But he's the keystone," Darrow said. "Remove him and the structure collapses. This isn't about any of us in this room. If his defense efforts fail, then the Union can enter unopposed. Everything changes once they arrive. Every enslaved person in this city immediately becomes a freedman."

"You don't know that!" Lenore said.

"What do you intend?" Ady asked.

"I have possession of two guns. You get me passage into that courtyard. I'll do the rest to old du Marche and his associates."

Ady pressed her lips together. Though he was taller than both she and Lenore now, he was still a relative child; men always lag behind. But Ady knew he was serious. That made his offer all the more disturbing.

"No," Ady said. "I'm not helping you kill him in cold blood."

"After all he's done to you?"

"You don't know what he's done to me." Ady stepped toward him. Darrow stepped backward. She continued. "Spying on him was one thing, but murder?"

"So now you're afraid to kill?" Darrow said.

Ady pushed Darrow. "Don't you dare," Ady said. "What we— What I did to Alabama's attacker was an accident."

"No one is calling you a murderer," Lenore said.

"I don't know about that," Darrow said. "I was the one who hauled that body from this very building. You worked him over but good. Like you were in a rapture."

"Darrow!"

Ady walked out of the draught hall. She thought she saw them follow her, but she was too fast. Soon she was several blocks away.

The night she bludgeoned the man at the Mockingbird she had felt shame, hysteria, upheaval. But in the moment his convulsing body stopped moving, she also felt—perhaps for the first time in her life—power. She recognized this then. But she also believed that holding on to that feeling was a path to madness. If she could do that to Alabama's assailant, why hadn't she done the same to him? How many times had he been asleep off a flagon of ale and she awake, seated on the hard chair by his bedroom window? The thought of such an attack made her feel sick. She was a believer in some God. Even the thought was immoral. And yet she kept thinking, *Was it wrong?*

At the townhouse, he gave her orders for an event he was planning for the end of that very week. Five guests. No, seven. Put out the best table settings and order ingredients for a feast.

His guests were several men traveling by carriage. The

journey had begun in Virginia, where the first planter was collected. Then the carriages passed through the Carolinas, Georgia, Alabama, and Mississippi, gathering men of similar pedigree along the way. They had important business to attend to, and he wanted everything in perfect order. These were his peers, each man a substantial property owner in his own right.

But despite hearing all the commands and jotting down notations on a slip of paper, her mind remained back with Lenore in view of the unfinished painting of her likeness, a face that she finally felt she owned through and through.

"Get a rack of dresses," he said.

"Dresses?" Ady asked.

"Do I whisper?" he asked.

"No," she said.

Two days later, while scrubbing his floors, Ady heard the carriageway gate open. She went to the tall window and peered down. A group of women in chains were surrounded by several slavers and Confederates. The large woman at the front was Tremaine! And Ady recognized several of the others from about the city. And one was a child. No older than Ady when she was first brought to the townhouse. Yes. Ady recognized the child. She was the same one who had kicked the shin of the officer and saved Ady that day. These were Daughters. All of them.

That explained his request for dresses the other day. Under most circumstances, the women would have remained in the plain cotton in which they arrived. But he wanted them in finery. For the gathering. To sell them off.

"They some common-looking chickens if I ever seen them," Nary said, looking down to the street. She giggled. She seemed cheerful over the past several days, but that morning she had been chuckling and smiling even as she carried his chamber pot. Nary was an ass, but she wasn't a simpleton.

"Why are you so cheer-filled?"

"It's nothin'," she said.

"Come on now. You're acting like a cat with a dish of milk."

"I ain't supposed to tell." The manner in which she said the words is what caught Ady's attention. The shifting features of her face. She was in possession of a secret, one that gave her a feeling of proprietorship even while imbuing her with a sense of cruel pleasure. Ady grabbed her wrist.

"Ow. Let go," Nary said. "Or I'll call mass on you, you green-eyed dog!"

Nary wasn't in pain. She was faking pain for effect. But then Nary's face changed from manufactured fear to malevolent joy.

"He gone sell you." Nary laughed. "He gone sell you to a mass from Virginie. Gone sell the rest. Mass say they some hard plantations where y'all going. You're all gonna get yours. They prolly chop one of your feets off."

Ady released Nary's arm. Could this be the case? It wasn't as if he hadn't threatened to sell her before. He used to threaten her and Sanite often with sale. He had sold her brother, baby Emmanuel. But what would it mean now? She'd never had any control over the placement of her life and body. The languid nature of the previous years was an illusion. It was a fault of her for thinking that she was planted there in the community of New Orleans. But he could sell her east. Ady watched the slaver below tighten the bond around the girl's wrist. Ady had no intention of allowing him to sell them.

"We won't have to worry none 'bout your ugly behind," Nary giggled.

Ady raised a hand, and Nary shrank back. But Ady turned and walked out onto the balcony. He was in the courtyard, pacing from one corner to the next, an old-fashioned tricorn hat in his hand, his sleeping shirt half unbuttoned. She hadn't noticed. She rarely saw him when she looked. His chest hairs had gone completely white.

"What do you want?" he said when she approached.

"You intend to sell those women."

"The disposition of my property is none of your business. But yes. Those uppity negresses were causing enough trouble. We provided them a fine city to live in and they spat in the faces of their betters. My old friend Ebenezer is in need of breeding stock. There was a sickness in Lynchburg, so replenishment is the goal, I understand. Their value will add well to my work here. As will your sale." He squinted at her. "You don't seem surprised. That Nary's been running her mouth, is it? She leaks like a sieve."

He turned to look directly at her. "Why couldn't you be like the others?"

"What?"

"I've owned over two hundred of your kind. I can count on one hand the ones that have put wrinkles on my face. You and your ma'am most especially. All you had to do was my bidding, which is what you were put on this earth for. That is the Lord's way, and you've subverted it from the day I purchased you. I suppose you're going to flee again. And I'll have to have you rounded up again."

Ady saw her mother's feet traversing the courtyard from the bottom of the stairs to the laundry lines. Sanite had walked the grounds of the townhouse for those years, but in retrospect, it was clear that Sanite never believed the townhouse to be her prison. She said she would escape. She did temporarily. Then, in a way, permanently.

"There is nowhere that I would rather be than at your service," Ady said. "If sending me away helps you, then so be it." He tilted his head in confusion. Ady moved away and continued walking out of the gate and onto the street. She reckoned that he took her to be heading out for errands. She didn't care. Not a whit. She only cared about finding Lenore and Darrow. She finally understood what she should have long ago. Her fate was in her hands. She couldn't let Lenore's brother or anyone else do what had been placed at her feet.

She found them sitting on a wrought-iron bench just across from the Mockingbird. The front of the establishment had been reframed, but the siding was yet to be installed. She grabbed their hands and pulled them to their feet.

"What dragon has possessed you?" Lenore asked.

"We have to do it," Ady said.

"You're on the caper now," Darrow said.

"I want to be at the wheel. Bring me your guns."

Lenore's face opened in shock. "You know nothing of arms."

"Alabama taught me the fundamentals when you were doing your bookkeeping. How to load and aim. 'The rest is praying,' she said."

"I'll get them to you middle morning tomorrow," Darrow said.

"I won't allow it."

Ady scoffed. "He means to sell me, Lenore. And the others. Will you allow that?

"The market," Ady said to Darrow, "at the entrance arch."
Ady studied Lenore, looking into her eyes for just a moment,
then left.

That evening, the first of the guests arrived at the townhouse.
Ady, Nary, Mrs. Beryl, Courtland, and a trio of soldiers were
made to stand in line to greet the guests along with several
militiamen. Courtland collected the man's belongings as du
Marche chattered about what a pleasure it was to be in the
man's presence. He was by all accounts the most successful
planter in the state of Virginia, the descendant of early colonists, who turned against the Crown at the most lucrative moment. But Ady cared nothing of that. It occurred to her, as he
ascended the stairs to his quarters—the biggest of the guest
quarters—that she would have to shoot him in the face, too, at
the allotted time. She was in a continuous rage, which she
struggled not to show.

"That's him," Nary said into Ady's ear. "Your new massa.
Ain't he something special?" Mrs. Beryl laughed. Ady wondered if she would have enough bullets.

More guests arrived as the night wore on. There were
seven arrivals. By midnight, each had taken his place in their
lodgings.

In the morning, Ady left the townhouse grounds. He had
forbidden her to attend to the captured Daughters. Nary had
prepared their second-story quarters and ensured that they
were cleaned. Ady didn't want to leave them in Nary's clutches.
But time was short. Ady was to meet Darrow on the west side
of the city at Poydras Market. She would bring the gun into the
townhouse for later use. The gates having been left open, Dar-

row would make his way to the parlor. As the men responded
to his assault, she would make use of what she'd been given.

But first—feverishly—to the market. She trotted along the
street toward the American Sector, not concerned in the least
for the final additions she was meant to purchase for the gathering. Darrow was on her mind, or rather his weaponry. It was
a busy afternoon in the French Quarter. She supposed that
several large ships had arrived. There was an unusual number
of sailors in flatcaps and wide-legged pants, some of whom
called to her as she passed. But she paid them no mind. She
stepped around carriages and delinquent children. She was
short of breath from having moved so briskly once she came
to the market. She didn't see Darrow at the archway, so she
navigated around the edge of the bazaar past the vendors and
their tables. She heard her name being called from afar.

"Ady," the voice said. It was Lenore, standing across the
street.

"Why are you here? You said you wanted no part of this."

"I know what I said. I reconsidered, but I have news. Darrow has been arrested."

Ady stood gaping.

"I may have reported him to the municipality's security patrol," Lenore said. "He's not in captivity for this scheme. The
guardsman is an old friend of my father's. I told him Darrow
was in danger over a gambling debt. He'll be held overnight."

"I don't understand, Lenore!"

"Because I don't want you to die."

"This is my choice."

"Let me finish, ma chère. You know that unleashing a vol-
ley of gunfire against some of the most prominent citizens of
the South would only have led to you and Darrow being

swarmed by every soldier in the area. And that was if du Marche and his cronies didn't overcome you with their own weapons."

"You have no right to stop me."

"I have said nothing about stopping you." Lenore reached into her hip pouch. She produced a small vial with an X on the label.

She smiled. "We'll put this in their stew and beverages."

"We?"

"This scheme is just as likely to lead to your death, but if you are to leave the earth tonight, I shall leave with you."

"You can't come." Ady's lip trembled. "I won't let you."

"Pishposh. We should get back to the house before the festivities begin. We've got a long night ahead of us."

Ady glanced in the direction of the townhouse. "But they have a short one."

Lenore brought Ady's hand to her lips and kissed Ady's fingers.

Dusk was arriving, and above the townhouse, the clear blue sky darkened to aubergine. He questioned the presence of Lenore as she hung a banner that read WELCOME PLANTERS. Perhaps he was irked that he couldn't sell her too, but his ire was short-lived when Ady explained that Lenore's presence was for the guests' benefit. His planning had focused on dining and papers for any contracts they might at some point draft. But he had neglected to provide for entertainment. Du Marche's face had gone white at the realization.

"You're correct, it would seem. I didn't so much as charter a fiddle player. What do you suggest?"

"We can sing, and Lenore plays the piano as well," Ady said.

Lenore did a curtsy. "We'll make a charming duet." He didn't seem entirely convinced, but he nodded absent-mindedly. Ady knew him well but had never seen him as nervous as he appeared that night. The other men were already gathered in the dining room. Mrs. Beryl was completing the meal with Nary's assistance. The food would be brought in before long. Ady's concern was how to best pour the contents of Lenore's vial into the men's bodies. They had discussed it on the way over, pausing intermittently. Poisons were unpredictable, Lenore said. Pour it in the stew, they questioned, or in the ale? They might not consume enough stew, but every man present would likely drink himself under the table.

"The flagon," Ady said under her breath while watching the men from the adjacent room.

"What did you say?" Lenore asked.

"We've got to go down to the kitchen," Ady said.

"Let's." Lenore turned to walk, but Ady caught her hand. Lenore stared in confusion.

"Marry me," Ady whispered.

"What are you asking?"

Ady fell to one knee and took Lenore's hands in hers.

"Please say yes," Ady said.

"Not like that," Lenore said. ".Get up, please."

Ady stood and turned away.

"Call me Lenore Adebimpe," Lenore said.

Ady turned back to Lenore and smiled. "Then call me Ady Marianne Mocking—" But Lenore threw her arms about Ady and kissed her with such firmness that Ady would have fallen if not for Lenore's clutch.

"Can we do that?" Lenore asked as they held hands.

"We just did."

"Antoinette!" he called from the dining room. Ady inhaled.

"Wait here," she said.

Lenore squeezed her hand. "One moment, wife." Lenore removed the cross from her neck and fastened it around Ady's neck. "Now go."

Ady entered the room where the men were seated around the table.

"We don't have time to dally with black wenches," one man said. "We've got business to attend to."

"Black wenches are our business, Blake, or have you forgotten." The enslavers laughed.

"Run down, would you, and fetch the ones my men captured." There was a fabricated sweetness to his voice as though he was trying to convey that he was made of honey instead of mold. So Ady did the same.

"Yes, Master du Marche," she said. She felt a prickle at the back of her throat as she reached out. She almost touched his arm, but couldn't bring herself to do so. "I will surely bring them up at once."

"Oh, she's a smart one there," one of the men said. "Not like that other ninny of yours."

"That she is," du Marche said. "I've had her for the better part of her life now. Took a period of time to break her in, but she's been a good hand since."

"And you'd part with one so dear?" the Virginian said.

"I said she's pliable. I didn't say she was dear."

"Fair, that," the Virginian chuckled.

"Will that be all, Master du Marche?"

"Yes. Hurry along. Let's have the gents see their wares."

Ady exited the parlor into the hallway, where Lenore waited wide-eyed.

"What the devil was that?" Lenore asked.

"You're not the only one capable of putting on airs."

Lenore pinched Ady's side. They went outside and descended the stairs.

"What are we doing?"

"Just follow me." Ady went to the mostly vacant quarters that were used for storage. The Daughters were in there, ten in all, sitting on the odds and ends contained therein. She recognized a few of them, like Tremaine and the woman with bright eyes, but not most.

"I asked Jesus for a hammer and he sent a nail file and a spoon," Tremaine said.

"It's good to see you too," Ady said.

"We're going to coordinate our efforts if we stand a chance of surviving this," Lenore said.

"What you talking about, Sweetness?" Tremaine said.

"She's saying that it's time for us to go to war," Ady said.

"Tre, you know this skinny tree-branch-looking girl?" a large-cheeked woman said.

"Quiet down now, Mildred," Tremaine said. "Me and Ady go way back. She don't play around."

Ady took Tremaine's hand and sat on the pallet next to her. "They want to sell you all east. To North Carolina, Georgia, Virginia. They'll use the money from your sale to bar the Northern troops from coming here."

"What troops?" Helen, the young girl said.

"Child, they some kind of warring going on. Ain't you heard?" Tremaine said.

"They'd really sell us away in the middle of a war?" Bright Eyes asked.

"Wouldn't be my first time sold off," Mildred said.

"Ladies," Lenore said, "they know who you are. You know what they did to our sisters. Nothing but pain awaits at the end of that journey."

"What we gone do, though?" Mildred said. "We here now. And you prisses here ain't about to help."

Ady nudged Lenore. "I propose some root work."

Lenore pinched her vial between thumb and forefinger.

"You 'bout to get us kilt with that shit there."

"Oh, shut up, Mil," Tremaine said. "Why you gotta pooh-pooh everything?"

"Well, damn then," the thin woman in the corner who hadn't spoken said. "If we trying to lay these mens down, tell me what to do." The women laughed.

"Yeah, gal," Tremaine said. "You know I'm with you." The women nodded.

"There are two other women we need to bring down here and keep quiet. Lenore and I will deal with the men upstairs."

As Ady and Lenore crossed the courtyard to the stairs that led to the kitchen, Lenore tugged at Ady's sleeve. "Are you certain you know what you're doing?"

Ady faced Lenore on the middle of the stairs. "I don't know what I just did or what I'm going to do next. But I feel like I'm being guided by my mama. I'm walking in her footsteps now."

"Carry on then."

They turned into the kitchen. "He wants you to feed the women in the supply room first," Ady said.

"Feed the chattel before the masters," Mrs. Beryl said. "That's a queer way to go."

"I'm giving you his message. He's in a hurry."

"Who you?" Nary asked, looking at Lenore.

"She's from a cabaret hired for entertainment purposes," Ady said.

"Bullshit," Nary said. "You always take me for stupid." She pointed at Lenore. "I know this uppity bitch from across town. From when I used to work by the river."

"How dare you!" Lenore said.

"I'll get to the heart of this," Mrs. Beryl said. "The lord of the manor is in the parlor, I reckon."

"He is, but you're not going to talk to him, Mrs. Beryl."

Mrs. Beryl's cheeks reddened. "You're not the master of me."

"No, but we is," Tremaine said.

The women grabbed Nary and Mrs. Beryl. There was a struggle of sorts. Mrs. Beryl in particular thrashed against the pairs of hands that clutched at her wrists and body, whereas Nary became still. From several feet away, Ady watched Nary turn sullen. She did not fight as two of the women took her out of the kitchen into the courtyard. Mrs. Beryl had been rendered unconscious. The other three women dragged her behind the group holding Nary. It wasn't until Nary had almost reached the storage quarters that she twisted around and opened her mouth as though to scream. And she did make a noise like a squeak before Tremaine shoved a rag into her mouth and tied it in place with linen. The women marched the cook and the enslaved scullery maid into the storage quarters. Tremaine, standing at the door, met Ady's gaze and nodded before turning away and joining the others.

Ady found Lenore in the kitchen, the surfaces of which were crowded with large silver platters of steaming food.

"What are you doing? You don't know how to cook," Ady said.

"That is true. But I do know how to flavor." Lenore wiggled the vial, now emptied of its contents.

"How'd you know how much to pour?"

"You think I've never in all my time as a proprietress of an inn had cause to use an elixir or two?"

Ady saw the bottle of sherry perched at the end of a table and picked the bottle up by the neck.

"Don't drink from that unless you want to join du Marche and the rest of those ruffians in St. Louis Cemetery."

"You think we'll be invited to the funeral?"

"Come," Lenore said.

It was a laborious process, carrying forth the many platters, dishes, tureens, and serving spoons to the parlor. He cast curious glances at her as she placed the largest dish, roast beef, at the center of the table.

"Where is little Nary?"

Ady leaned close to him and whispered. "Did you want that scullery maid bringing food to your distinguished guests when you have me and elegant Lenore?" He grunted.

"And where are the chattel?" said the Virginian.

"Blame me for their tardiness, honorable suh," Ady said. "One of them had an accident, possibly dysentery. I didn't think you'd appreciate the smell. But Nary is cleaning them up. They'll be along before dessert."

"Aren't you agreeable tonight?" du Marche said. "If I didn't know, I'd imagine you were happy to be on your way to Virginia."

"Pardon my forwardness. I'm only following your wishes.

I thank you for the life you've given me here. I know that you'll succeed just fine without me."

"Well." He smiled. He half-stood, leaning forward over the table. "We have done well conducting our business tonight even as there's more work to do in defense of our holdings. But it's time for an interlude. The negresses will provide light entertainment while we dine."

A couple of the men groaned.

"Music?" one of the men said. "I'd rather see them unclothed." The enslavers giggled.

Lenore was standing near one of the men at the edge of the dining table. As she poured ale into his goblet, his hand touched her backside. Lenore showed surprise and turned away from his grasp. She came to Ady and took her hand.

"Yes, gentlemen," Lenore said. "You're in for a delight. We have prepared several songs, including a chanty, that we believe you shall enjoy."

"You're a comely darky," the Virginian said. "But less talk. Get along with it then." The man next to him slammed his mug against the wood in agreement.

"Hear, hear!" The others joined in, banging their mugs on the table. Ady saw that some of the ale was spilling over the lips of the mugs. She squeezed Lenore's hand.

"What shall we perform?"

"I don't think I know that fussy music you play," Ady said.

"Sing a spiritual."

Lenore sat on the bench and began pressing the keys of the clavichord. Ady didn't know that Lenore could play with such emotion. She was far from the French and English songs she had demonstrated before. Ady realized she had underestimated Lenore. What else of Lenore was unknown to her? What would she never know?

Ady sang. The pace was slow and Ady reached into her lowest register to convey the emotion that she felt. If the situation went well, all the men in the room would soon be dead. She recognized the sin of it. But she also felt something else.

Was she having reservations? Could that be?

No. She relished the justice of what she and Lenore were doing. Du Marche had committed countless acts of cruelty against everyone she'd loved. The same was true for the other men who had gathered around the table. They were the owners of innumerable enslaved people. They had collared countless lives and through rape and maiming and cruelty extracted from those people the raw value that propelled them, as enslavers, to greater heights of acclaim and power. There was no authority on earth who would ever make them suffer, even for a moment, the rippling consequences of their sin. Ady knew that men like them had been in power for generations, back to the time of her own unknown great-grandmothers. And she was positive that the children of the enslaved, even those yet unborn, would continue to suffer from the taint that men like these had cast upon them. If she were not the one to deliver justice unto them, justice would never come. It would sit offshore forever like a ship denied port.

Her true reticence was for the woman pressing the piano keys with her delicate fingers, her back perfectly straight, her chin lifted, her comely brown skin lightly glowing in the warmth of the room. It was likely that Ady would die. She had known that from the moment she woke up that morning. But it pained her to accept that this would also be Lenore's fate. Lenore, who by all rights should never have met Ady. Lenore,

who had a stable, improving life with her family and the workers at the soon-to-be-rebuilt Mockingbird Inn. Ady wanted to
take Lenore by the hand out of the compound. She wanted to
push her through the gate and tell her never to look back. But
it was too late. Lenore was playing the piano and Ady was singing from the depths of her belly. Lenore's eyes were now
closed. She played from memory and feeling. And Ady could
not hear her own voice, did not know what words she was
singing. She was in a place between her mind and the reality of
what was to come. In the place where she walked in stride with
Sanite.

The men, however, were not entirely impressed. One of
them, nearest, seemed delighted. But the rough fellow from
Mississippi was shaking his head.

"Enough of this nigger music," he said. "I don't let 'em
sing it on my fields, why should I hear it now?" He drank from
his mug.

"Fine, Curtis," du Marche said. "You two play something
else. She said you had a chanty up your dresses. Let's hear it."

Ady didn't know what to do. She didn't know any chanties.
But Lenore began playing in triple time, and suddenly Ady recalled walking along the piers when she was small. The sailors
on the decks of their ships. She only recalled a single verse, but
when she started into it the men cheered. Lenore sang and
embellished the melody. The men joined in, bellowing so
loudly that Ady was almost drowned out.

The change happened midsong. The Mississippian was
first affected. He had taken more than his share of ale during
the meal. His face darkened, he undid the flap of his high-
collared jacket. Two of the other men fanned their faces and
drank more ale to cool themselves. The Virginian stared into

his mug, and then placed his forearms atop the table—and lowered his head atop his forearms—for a nap from which he would not rise. Gradually, du Marche saw what was happening. He asked his cohort what the matter was. But they didn't respond. The men around the table were in various states of stupor. He stood up, struggling for balance, as though on a ship caught in a storm. He placed his rump against the table for support.

Ady and Lenore, curiously to Ady's mind, were still singing. Lenore had slowed the pace of the chanty and almost imperceptibly moved into a milder melody unfamiliar to Ady. It rose and fell, and Ady had no words to draw upon, so she sang wordlessly, humming and sighing.

He was still propped against the table, his eyes open, breathing heavily.

Ady reached down to the keyboard and stilled Lenore's hand. Lenore tilted her head upward to where Ady stood.

Ady went to him and stood above his flagging form, his reddened eyes, his drooling lips.

"You," he said.

"Yes," Ady said, "me." She turned away. "Sleep well, *Father.*"

Ady cupped Lenore's fingers and led her out onto the balcony. Ady imagined him speaking from his position at the table. She imagined that he wished to yell at her or call his men for assistance. But Lenore had given the soldiers in the courtyard mugs of frothy beer.

Ady squeezed Lenore's hand, and, for a moment they stood silently. Lenore looked back over her shoulder into the parlor. But Ady did not. She took Lenore's chin and gently directed her gaze to her face.

"I think all the time of a place called the Colonnade. I was born there."

"Is it one of the plantations?" Lenore asked.

"No. It's land I want to show you." They held each other's arms.

"I'd like that."

Ady pressed her lips against Lenore's and they kissed. Again Ady saw the path out of the city to the place that was her true home, the home of her bloodline, of her mother. The catfish cut water along the banks. Wind blew through the Spanish moss that comprised the Zombie Wig Forest. She saw herself hiking up the gentle slope of the Endless Path. She passed the Black Veil and came to the straight-lined trees that seemed to stretch back through time. Near the end of the walk, Ady saw scattered along the earth jewels of red, gold, and green.

Below, an omnibus pulled to a stop. The horses snorted mist into the air. A woman sat in the driver's box, a small woman who was unmistakable even in the evening lamplight.

"Alabama?" said Ady. "You're back?"

"Well, it ain't Mary Todd Lincoln!" said Alabama. "Get down here. We don't have much time."

"We should gather the others."

And so they did precisely that. As it turned out, Alabama had been in hiding within the city limits for some time. Word had reached runaways like herself that the Union was on its way. The enslaved would be freed should the battle be won. But those in danger needed to be rescued lest they be the last to die under the heel of slavery.

They hid in the home of a white friend of the Daughters. There, in the American Sector, they learned that the Confederates had expected a ground assault from the north. But the Confederates were surprised by the Union Navy attacking from downriver. The city's Confederates had concocted a last-ditch plan of defense. They had strung heavy iron chains across the Mississippi to bar the Union warships. But Ady herself had changed his purchase order for chains some time ago. Whereas a dozen such chains were needed, only two were shipped. When the first Union vessel hit the chains, the ship breached the barrier without pause. The Confederates at the downriver forts hastily abandoned their posts. The Union raised the Stars and Stripes over the city mere days later.

Ady, Lenore, and the other Daughters walked onto the streets as free women. They had cared well for each other in their short time at the American house: bathing, feeding, loving.

When they reached Jackson Square, they saw federal troops standing guard over the heart of the city. The formerly enslaved were out and about. The Confederates and militiamen who had watched every moment of Ady's life vanished, having burned their uniforms in their fireplaces.

Ady squeezed Lenore's hand.

"What do we do now?" asked Lenore.

"Anything we please," said Ady.

Federal troops had been authorized to assist in the reopening of the city as a free place. The combination of preexisting workers and soldiers made short work of the task. Soon the Mockingbird, too, reopened.

Lenore made over to Ady half of the business. Together, through all the ups and downs of the life of the city, the women ran the Mockingbird Inn for many years thereafter.

EPILOGUE

[Audio excerpt from Keynote Academic Presentation of Genly Senshaw-Homx, PhD (Literary Physics) called *Embracing the Unknowable Heterotopia: Methods of Ontological Shielding in Fictional Texts*

At the 73rd Human Materials Studies Conference that year held via astralpsync in Lagos, Nigeria, on March 26, 2172.

This section occurs after opening formalities, a discussion of life on the North American continent in the 19th through 21st centuries moderated by Asada Eubril, and presentation of theories about who or what produced the work known as *The American Daughters*.]

. . . But let's take a moment to consider the lead character of the novel, Adebimpe, also called Antoinette Marianne du Marche, also called Ady Mockingbird after the boardinghouse where she found a sense of community and self. Of course, the novel is such a part of our lived experience that we sometimes forget to consider its origin. Most significantly, some believe that she was purely mythological and deny that Ady was a historical figure.

I am here today to put those denials to rest and make three assertions.

First: Ady was a real person. She existed. She lived. She loved.

Second: The journal she wrote while in the captivity of slavery, known today by scholars as the *Crisis Notebook* but sometimes called *Ady, or the Confession of a Freedwoman*, was also real.

Third: As you know, authorship of the novel *The American Daughters*, which is based upon Ady's journal, has been disputed since its rediscovery many decades ago. I am here to settle the question of who wrote the book.

So who was Ady? Some details of Ady's life are unknowable due to incomplete or contradictory evidence. What was her birth date? How tall was she really? Where precisely was she before being taken to the city? Yet there are some facts that we can confirm with the technological resources at our disposal at my institute in Cloud City.

Ady lived in what was then called the United States of America during the tumultuous Antebellum Era. For comparison to other turbulent eras, see also the Chinese Warring States Period, the Roman Republic, the Italian Wars, and the Post–Internet Age Collapse. Ady's journal, the so-called *Crisis Notebook,* which has itself reached near-mythological status among many scholars, journeyed from the City of New Orleans to the former State of Alabama and back to New Orleans between 1870 and 1920.

You may ask how I've come to know these dates. At risk of sounding melodramatic, I've spent the greater part of my professional life searching for the truth about Ady, her work, and the origins of the novel based on her exploits. You see, Ady was my ancestor. My great, to the power of eight, grandmother.

[audience sounds]

As some of you, my colleagues, may know, I was born in a displaced persons camp in a disputed territory on the North American Continent. Orphaned.

After the establishment of the World Community under the auspices of the Matriarchal Communal Alliance, I completed my education and sought to learn more about the history of my foremothers. I studied archives and followed genetic trails by testing items that belonged to people in my lineage. Hair combs. Clothing. Bones. I didn't get as far as I would have liked. That is, until one day I met Oridea Colx.

Yes, *that* Oridea Colx. Leader of the Uprising that led to our present civilization. She was quite aged by then, and used a mobility carapace to walk, but her mind was as lucid as ever. She explained that she had been trying to find me for many, many moons. Mother Colx provided me with clues regarding the whereabouts of several items I was aching to locate. Following a very brief conversation, she said "Good luck," and she walked out straightaway. Doesn't that sound just like her from the holoviews? When you're speaking of the goddess in the machine, you're speaking of Mother Colx, n'est-ce pas? [laughter of audience]

With my team of investigators, we made use of the information provided by Mother Colx. I won't bore you with all the details of the subsequent search. You'll have my paper at the conclusion of this presentation. Suffice it to say, we traversed much of the Unspoiled World and parts of the Irradiated World and, yes, even the inhabited moons of our solar system. Our journeys turned out to be quite exciting and fruitful, and I want to give credit to my colleagues, some of whom did not live to see this day, and all of whose names you are observing on the main viewer as I speak.

I imagine that some of you are wondering where the *Crisis Notebook* is? The one that some believe is a mythical artifact?

This is the notebook. [audience sounds]

As you can see, there is evidence of significant wear. Water stains, rips, and spots that appear soiled with the leavings of a kind of stone fruit that was processed into a liquid and consumed in the past. Here you see there are even scorch marks. That this remarkable record has survived its travails is a miracle. [extended audience sounds]

. . . turning to my third assertion and the problem of the fictional work, *The American Daughters*. It is the same problem we encounter in studying the ancient notebook, which, of course, is very much the source of the novel. Both are full of lies. Both are rife with omissions. They raise questions about the very nature of truth itself.

The novel is full of historical figures who are also named in the *Notebook*. Based on my research, nearly all the major named characters were real people, with the exception of the characters called Alabama, Nary, and Johnny, who all appear to be composites or at least intentionally distorted in their depictions. There are also a pair of outlier characters. We'll return to them shortly.

The novel, in its final form, has been read by generations of our community. It has been said that the provenance of the novel is undetermined and that the name of the author is lost to history. I am here to assert that nothing could be further from the truth. In fact, the opposite is true. We now know the novel is not the work of one person. It is the work of a *community* over *time*. Indeed, the novel had no less than six authors and perhaps as many as two dozen. Does this sound far-fetched to you? Or does it sound like the Bible or perhaps the Nordic *Heimskringla* or even the works of Shakespeare, Marlowe, and Hawthorne, which we now understand were produced by a number of mostly women over decades as a means of outsmarting the patriarchy of their times?

As in those earlier works, we know many of the names and backgrounds of the individuals who contributed to the final work. Yes, I am well aware of the dubious theory that holds the author of the novel to have been an AI, but I unequivocally reject that hypothesis.

To say it plainly as possible: *The American Daughters* was primarily co-authored over time by Ady, her great-granddaughter, a corrupt male publisher, the great-granddaughter's grandson, and a final author whose name I will reveal shortly.

How can we know? Because the stylistic fingerprints of the various authors permeate the novel manuscript. Even as much of the direct identifying information seems to have been erased from our observation, we can see shadows and shadows of shadows that reveal the complex origins of this mysterious work. My team compared the writings of these individuals and found matches time and time again in cadence, word selection, and even comma placement. In addition, we well know that even the cleverest AI leaves a distinct trail of metadata. But a complete analysis of all possible programs revealed no conclusive matches.

One category of shadow observations relates to factual discrepancies that infect both the *Crisis Notebook* source material, which was recovered in a sweep of New Orleans before sea level rise subsumed the city, and the novel, which has come down to us through various means. I am here to tell you an AI would have handled those discrepancies less clumsily.

For example, Ady appears to have had at least one child, a son, in the time we read about. Both the *Crisis Notebook* and the novel log only one birth in their narratives, a boy named Emmanuel who is born to Ady's mother in the early 1850s. My best estimate, again based on research, is that Emmanuel is actually Ady's offspring. [audience sounds] In this way, the novel copies the mistake of the notebook. Mistake, or intentional misdirection by Ady herself?

Another example of these complications would be the mysterious woman called Mrs. Orsone, the ambivalently depicted governess who teaches Ady to read. I believe she is Ady's invention. No such person as Mrs. Orsone ever existed. I would note that like none of the other characters in the text, Mrs. Orsone rarely appears in proper person, but more as a presence whispering to Ady. She has scant dialogue despite the frequency of her name's appearance in the text. This is because she wasn't real.

Who then taught Ady to read? Who taught her to play the piano or write in elegant handwriting? I don't know. My suspicion is that Ady herself was working to protect the identity of her teacher or teachers. At that time, in her city-state, it was verboten to instruct enslaved persons to read. Ady likely believed that identifying the person would have placed them in danger.

At the other extreme is Sanite, the mother of Ady. The records regarding her life are surprisingly detailed. For our purposes, I'll simply note that she did not die from yellow fever at a slave labor camp during the decade before the onset of the First American Civil War. To the contrary, we know with great certainty that she somehow made it to Canada, and that she lived a long life and was survived by a number of later children, all born free. I even have reason to suspect that Ady *chose* not to flee with her mother.

So why the lies? Why the fabrications? Why the distortions? Did Ady, for example, merely wish to protect the people she knew? I propose that there is more to the matter. We all know that people of the past were obsessed with fictional stories. This obsession feels quite alien to us today. As alien as making sacrifices to the gods. But people of bygone eras created tales to make sense of their fractured world. To comfort themselves in an epoch of unbearable anxiety.

My thesis is that the woman called Ady was trying to protect the people she knew, herself, and perhaps us, the infinite later generations.

This is a well-educated gathering. I know that you're aware of the work of my partner, Ganymida Senshaw-Homx. Pardon the shameless attempt to bestow sparkle on their work, but it is relevant to our discourse. In their most recent book, *The Transfer of the Void: Epigenetic Implications of Generational Injustice*, they make the case that some events are so horrible that they should not be spoken of—that in some instances, memory is *itself* harm.

I see in Ady an attempt to rewrite her own history. Or rather, to take charge of it. By killing her mother and shipping her supposed brother away, she was likely considering the very real possibility that the *Crisis Notebook* would be discovered. Instead of giving antagonists the clues to recapture her loved ones, she alters their stories. And instead of revealing details, such as vicious physical attacks, that could cause psychic damage to her descendants, she remakes those instances to suit her purposes. In other words, the *Crisis Notebook*, written by Ady herself, is an act of love.

But what of the novel based on the *Notebook*? That is a more complex issue. You see, numerous versions of *The American Daughters* have existed. Much like variants of the Bible, later editions have added scenes and chapters that didn't appear in the earlier texts. Also, later editions omit certain problematic or puzzling episodes.

Still, the present text is full of such dubious flights of invention that were almost certainly inserted by later members of the community. We know, for example, that Ady's descendant, the great-granddaughter, was the author of the original novel in the 1950s. That book included memoir-like chapters from her own life. For reasons we have not yet determined, that manuscript was not published. Yet I believe that it was this descendant who wrote the memorable introductory scene, because the *Crisis Notebook* starts later on the timeline, with Ady and Sanite's arrival in New Orleans at auction. The great-granddaughter appears to have been influenced by the styles of many writers who preceded her, from Ann Petry to Virginia Woolf.

A third and as yet unknown author owned a small publishing house in the City of New Orleans. His name is lost to us, but we know that he sold the first publicly available version of the book. This man was not above, as the old saying goes, gilding the lily of the 1950s text. Many of the questionable plot turns appear to have been inserted by this writer. I call this author the Hand Waver for his heedless attitude toward fact and realism. His influences come largely from the defunct genre known as pulp, which shared his eye for the lurid and sensational.

Many textural challenges remain. Admittedly, we haven't confirmed that anything that happened after Lenore revealed the near-completed portrait to Ady is factual. This is because the *Crisis Notebook* version of the tale ends there. Many pages were ripped out of the *Notebook*. Our spectrometry indicates that some of the pages, especially near the ending, were ripped out *contemporaneously*. This means the great-granddaughter never saw them. This in turn means that the heroic events of the ending—the formulation of a plan against the townhouse owner, his banquet on behalf of others of his class, and his poisoning may not have happened as stated.

Have you read that ending? You'll admit, it seems a little far-fetched. Yes? [audience sounds] I attribute some of this ending to the Hand Waver, but not all of it. To be clear, it's likely that Ady and her associates did kill her owner. I also believe the removed pages of the *Notebook* possibly gave the true details of the killing and of Ady's later movements. My theory is that she was not accused of the crime nor punished for it because such an act, even during that hectic time, would have been the talk of the town and [unintelligible]

Let's return to what we have shown to be true. It does appear that both Lenore and Ady were part of a continent-wide, multigenerational insurgent group composed mostly of women, girls, and gender-queer individuals called the Daughters. It even seems that they were substantively responsible for the Confederacy's failure to mount a defense of their positions in the City of New Orleans, which led to the Union's taking the municipality without a battle. Daughters played a role in undermining pro-slavery forces in other locations such as Harper's Ferry and in the rescue of a family whose matriarch was called Jane Johnson. The Daughters were spies, insurgents, heroines.

Did I mention that the *Crisis Notebook* is written primarily in French? [audience sounds] Ady was bilingual, fluent in both English and French. In Ady's notebook, she repeatedly avoids using the owner's fictional name, du Marche, meaning "of the sales or market." This is clearly a placeholder name. But she also never calls him by his real name. This being her desire, though I have identified this distasteful figure, I won't name him here. However, I will note that his native tongue was English, and it seems that Ady wrote in French as an additional means of avoiding detection. Had he understood the true nature of Ady's intelligence, he [unintelligible]

Admittedly, I was even suspicious about that minor subplot involving the portrait of our Ady, but I couldn't help but devote time to that question because as my fond-ones know, I am something of a romantic. Some reference to the portrait appears in the *Crisis Notebook*, but there is quite a bit of embellishment attributable to that male descendant of Ady's writing in the 1990s. He recovered the great-granddaughter's 1950s manuscript and attempted to revise it in keeping with her intentions. To put it kindly, the male was quite young, not a professional writer, and, frankly, in a bit over his head. Without going too deeply into those aspects of the novel, and for the sake of allowing him to retain some dignity, I call that author the Lesser Hand Waver.

The section of the book that inexplicably gives the reported speech of Nary? That's Lesser Hand Waver. The discrepancies regarding Lenore's age or the vague details about the owner's family? Lesser Hand Waver. He even misnames Ady in the first line of the text! Purple prose and factual clumsiness aside, he was right about this . . .

[unintelligible and audience sounds]

As you can see, my grad assistant has just pulled the cover off the easel to reveal the original portrait of Ady.

[extended audience sounds and applause]

The painting isn't quite finished, non? But she has a certain presence, n'est-ce pas? Composite dating places the last brushstroke of this painting on or around April 18, 1862, which coincides with the torching of the Mockingbird Inn.

I told you after last night's plenary session that you would not be disappointed if you attended today's talk. [extended audience sounds and applause]

Shall we close? As for my final point of discussion, I am aware that in some of my statements I may have sounded as though I was belittling some of the authors of the novel, including the Final Author. What's that you say? I didn't mention the Final Author? Actually, I did. You see, the Final Author is Oridea Colx *herself.* She revised the book substantially to add certain political content and distributed her version in serial pamphlet form to her adherents. I believe she is the true author of the novel's fantastic happily-ever-after ending. She's also the persona responsible for the character called Alabama, who appears to be an aspect of Mother Colx herself.

I don't blame any of the authors for their faithlessness toward the original text of the *Crisis Notebook*'s version of events. Well, perhaps I blame the first Hand Waver, but he wouldn't care. [audience laughter] Yet I do have some sympathy for the authors' plights and real admiration, of course, for Ady herself, who was obviously a remarkable young woman. History has done its best to erase people like her since, well, the start of recorded history. I applaud anyone who attempts to resurrect their legacies.

. . . [unintelligible]

A note was tucked into the back of the original great-granddaughter's manuscript. That manuscript was produced at a time when humans used a petroleum-based substance called ink to print on processed sheaves of cellulose from trees. Primitive, yes? Can you imagine? [audience laughter] We don't have the original note. But our spectrometry was able to detect the faint residue of that ink even if many of the words were not legible. As we understand, the note was pressed inside the book for well over 100 years before being removed by someone.

On your viewers you will see the note in as much completeness as we could manage to glean:

See there were all these things I couldn't know about my ancestor [that] kept me from even taking a shot at trying to put her story down . . . one morning, I woke up in a cold sweat recalling this dream of her telling me to just do it . . . sometimes it's not what you know but what you feel.

ACKNOWLEDGMENTS

WRITING THIS BOOK was not the plan. I was on a residency in northern Mississippi, intent on writing a book about a New Orleans mother displaced to a small town with her kids. But sometimes a story isn't ready to be written, so I sat that one aside. After a break of several weeks, I returned to my writing desk at Christmas in desperation and this book came out—much to my surprise—almost all at once. But it wasn't really all at once. You see, the pump had been primed a long time ago. The book you hold in your hands was inspired by the remarkable lives of my women ancestors. Through years of research, visions of their world unfolded to me. I'm thankful for those ancestors and for the research that led me to them. My life is better for having met them. I'm also thankful to the following people and organizations.

Before my Mississippi residency, I put out a call on social media for any books about historical New Orleans. One of my friends shipped a box of seventeen nonfiction books, at her own expense. Several of those books formed the fertilizer of the soil that made the book you hold in your hands. So a special thanks to Veronica Brooks.

Of course, the John and Renée Grisham Writer-in-Residence program at the University of Mississippi provided time and space that allowed me to think, plan, and write. As such, thank you to the University of Mississippi, the English department therein, and to John and Renée Grisham for making the residency possible in the first place.

Thanks to my colleagues and students at Louisiana State University for their support and largesse. Knowing you believed in this project made the book possible. Speaking of Louisiana, a huge note of gratitude is due to the Board of Governors who awarded this project an ATLAS grant, which freed up critical time to write, revise, and rethink this work. Time is the greatest asset.

Thanks to all the archival spaces that shone light upon the vibrant past of my city, including the Williams Research Center, the Historic New Orleans Collection, Free People of Color Museum, the George & Leah McKenna Museum of African American Art, the New Orleans Pharmacy Museum, the Cabildo and Presbytère, the 1850 House, Gallier House, the Old Ursuline Convent Museum, NOMA, the Ogden Museum of Southern Art, the Beauregard-Keyes House, and the New Orleans Mint.

Thanks to everyone associated with the Randolph College MFA (Low Res) for allowing me to participate in one of the most positive spaces in the whole writing world. It meant a lot to me to share early versions of this book at our joyous readings.

Much love to some of the audacious writers I consider mentors, like Robert Jones, Jr., Kiese Laymon, Deesha Philyaw, Sarah Broom, Roxane Gay, Percival Everett, Victor Lavalle, Mat Johnson, Luis Alberto Urrea, Alex Chee, Margaret Wilkerson Sexton, Phillip Williams, Jami Attenberg, Chris Claremont, and Colum McCann. It's not only your writing that inspires me and countless others.

To the early readers of this text, thank you for your time,

attention, and direction: Emilie Staat Strong, Dr. Ben Morris, Jamila Minnicks, and John Vercher.

Thank you to the *American Daughters* team for your phenomenal support through every step of this process: Nicole Counts (editor), PJ Mark (lit agent), Will Watkins (film/TV agent), Chris Jackson (publisher), Avideh Bashirrad (deputy publisher), Oma Beharry (assistant editor), and the whole One World–Random House/Penguin Random House team.

Finally, thank you to all the mothers, grandmothers, aunties, and likewise in my life: Tanzanika Ruffin, Cassandra Ruffin, Louise Hearns, Claudia Washington, Cleopatra Washington, Nicole Bartlett, Danielle Pellegrin, Brittany Williams, Penelope Lincoln, Rhonda Alexander, Ciara Alexander Ilenrey, and to those beloveds who have transitioned to the next plane.

And thank you, New Orleans.

ABOUT THE AUTHOR

MAURICE CARLOS RUFFIN is the author of *The Ones Who Don't Say They Love You,* which was longlisted for the Story Prize and was a finalist for the Ernest J. Gaines Award for Literary Excellence, and *We Cast a Shadow,* which was a finalist for the PEN/Faulkner Award, the PEN Open Book Award, and the Dayton Literary Peace Prize and was longlisted for the Center for Fiction First Novel Prize and International Dublin Literary Award. A recipient of an Iowa Review Award in fiction, he has been published in the *Virginia Quarterly Review, AGNI,* the *Kenyon Review, The Massachusetts Review,* and *Unfathomable City: A New Orleans Atlas.* A native of New Orleans, he is a graduate of the University of New Orleans Creative Writing Workshop and a professor of creative writing at Louisiana State University.

mauricecarlosruffin.com
Instagram: @mauriceruffin
Twitter: @MauriceRuffin

ABOUT THE TYPE

This book was set in Garamond, a typeface originally designed by the Parisian type cutter Claude Garamond (c. 1500–61). This version of Garamond was modeled on a 1592 specimen sheet from the Egenolff-Berner foundry, which was produced from types assumed to have been brought to Frankfurt by the punch cutter Jacques Sabon (c. 1520–80).

Claude Garamond's distinguished romans and italics first appeared in *Opera Ciceronis* in 1543–44. The Garamond types are clear, open, and elegant.